FALTOFAR

MORRI STEWART

PALIMPSEST PRESS

Printed in the United States of America

First Printing, 2020

Paperback ISBN: 978-1-7347927-0-6

Ebook ISBN: 978-1-7347927-1-3

Palimpsest Press

PO Box 2282

Bend, Oregon 97709

www.morristewart.com

Cover Photo, courtesy of Unsplash, Xuan Nguyen

Author photo, courtesy of Brad Bailey Photography

For Jack. The best big brother ever.

CONTENTS

It shall come to pass that the Six will rise.
The Watchers will not judge but gather their power
from those below
and the Two will become One again.
What has been undone will be done.
So shall it be.

Prophecy, Faltofar circa 2948

PROLOGUE

His strength surprised her, the force of his weight propelling them both back toward the edge of the cliff. Still, she couldn't help herself and the laughter bubbled up from deep inside. Her hands on his chest, their faces inches apart, she whispered to him, her mocking gaze never wavering from his clear, blue eyes. Eyes bordered by lashes encrusted in icy particles.

"Don't do it." She pushed away from him, just enough to reach for the weapon. "You would miss me too much."

The dark blade in his hand shifted, light catching the deep grooves in its surface as the man hesitated. His world tilted with each gust of wind that blasted up from below. She laughed again, a rippling, triumphant sound cut short as the blade sliced upward through cloth and skin. She grabbed for him, her footing suddenly without foundation, her arms windmilling, her blood mixing with the tears he brushed from his face. Her dark strands of hair, the last visible part of her, wafted above her as she spun off the trampled snow, spiraling down through the cold, limitless air.

WINDS OF CHANGE

Lilianna leaned against the tree trunk, brushing dirt from her shirt. Her chest rose and fell, each exhale an angry puff. Pulling a twig from her hair, she narrowed her eyes, trying to navigate a way through the dense forest. Thom was nowhere in sight.

"Fiddlefut." The word slipped through her clenched teeth. A banned word, escaping. She moved another branch aside, filling her lungs.

"Just because your legs are longer than mine and you can see a way through doesn't mean you get to ditch me," she grumbled.

Lilianna pushed forward until a branch she landed on snapped backward, connecting with her shin. A red welt, about an inch long, began to form. Looking down at her leg, she gave a low growl, then jumped over another mossy log.

"Thom, wait!" she yelled, flinching at her loudness.

The sounds of the forest almost seemed to mock her efforts. Birds chirped softly, and the breeze in the higher branches peacefully patterned shadows across the girl's whole body. A chorus of frogs joined the birds' chatter, their croaking becoming louder as Lili pressed deeper into the woods. She leveraged herself onto an old stump, circling slowly.

"Where the heck did he go?" A soft chirrup at her foot startled her into a one-legged stance. Anyone watching the girl would have thought she played a game of stork. Carefully she bent and picked up the tree frog.

"I almost made a skittle cake out of you, my friend." Her eyes crossed as she held the tiny amphibian up to her face. The frog blinked slowly then puffed its cheeks out.

"Nope. Doesn't make you seem bigger." She laughed as its cheeks deflated. "That definitely would not have helped you."

Stretching out her arm, she placed the frog on a branch, glancing around once again.

"What the…"

Her words trailed off. As far as she could see, tree frogs covered the branches, their brilliant, tiny bodies sparkling like gems against the green backdrop. She could count twelve summers of exploring these woods, her rememories starting somewhere in the second year of her life, as a toddler. There had never been so many of the frogs gathered together. Her scalp tingled with nervous energy. A gathering of this size of any creature had to be an omen. Thom would know. She scanned the forest floor and, seeing a bare spot, jumped down, her landing cushioned by the quiet bed of needles. With one last glance above, Lilianna found a gap and wriggled through the bushes. She could feel a thousand eyes following her.

———

The impact sent the Sepherii spiraling through the air. Stars, clouds, and earth spun dizzily out of place as his body twisted and rolled over and over, downward into the canopy. Long branches slowed his descent, but the impact still winded the injured creature. In the darkness of deep night, he limped slowly to the rocky outcropping. The overhang would protect him for the time being. His wounded leg glowed an eerie red, lighting the forest floor with the color of blood. He swished his tail in irritated pain. Crossing his arms over his chest, he bowed his head to wait. Morauth's demon cats swirled in the darkness above, yowling in frustration.

Hours later, when the morning sun began to lighten the foliage around him, the Sepherii roused from his painful rest. The creature's immobile features, resembling the rocks he leaned against, morphed and softened as his eyes momentarily glowed a deeper blue. His head slowly turned, drawn to the sound of a human child's voice.

————

Parting yet another bush, Lili almost fell over her brother who was crouched low against a rotting log.

"Thom, you wouldn't believe the…"

Thom's hand shot up, wrapping tightly around his sister's wrist, yanking her down next to him. With his other hand, he covered her mouth. Shaking his head at her in warning, he jutted his chin forward, motioning Lili toward a thinning in the trees. She stuck her tongue out, and her brother jerked his hand away, wiping it on his pant leg in disgust. They glared at each other for a moment before Thom again nodded toward the distant something. Narrowing her eyes, Lili tried to see what her brother was focused on so intently, but, as usual, her vision was not nearly as keen.

"What's up, Eagle Hawk?" Her mock whisper, poking fun at his childhood nickname, was, obviously, not quiet enough for him.

"Shush, Lili. Hush." Biting his lip in concentration, he tilted his head to one side, muttering, "Something's there. Something big."

All Lili could see was a distant rocky hillside and lots and lots of greenery. She sighed and tried again.

"Thom, there's a bunch of . . ." This time her words were cut off as a tree frog landed in her hair.

"Frogs. They're everywhere, Thom."

Her brother looked at her more closely. The small green-orange frog, attached to the side of his sister's bright red pigtail, blinked slowly at him. His face softened, momentarily distracted.

"Maybe it thinks you're some crazy, exotic flower," he whispered, cautiously standing and stretching his back.

His eyes moved back to the overhang. Lili jumped up, cupping her hand gently over the frog. She felt Thom flinch slightly and realized she had shifted her weight from one foot to the other, stepping on her brother's boot. She offered a sheepish, apologetic smile, and he gently tugged at her pigtail. They could never stay mad at each other for long. Nodding his head toward the distant rocks, Thom mouthed the word, "Sepherii." He didn't sound convinced, even to himself.

Lili gave her brother a disbelieving smirk, then squinted into the dim forest light, her hand unconsciously stroking the frog. The only Sepherii she had ever seen was in the old picture book her father kept under the small couch in the main room. Sepheriis were the stuff of legend. The good gods, or maybe it was that they were created by the gods. She wasn't sure. The artist, commissioned to create the illustrations in the book, had depicted their forms as a perfect combination of human head and torso, coupled with the body of a horse. She had studied the drawings over many cold nights huddled next to the fire. She was never quite sure if the human in the picture was looking up at the mystical being with awe or terror. The brilliant color the illustrator had used for the Sepherii's eyes had magnified them. She could never forget those eyes.

According to that author, these mystical beings had last been seen in Faltofar during the Dark Days. She shuddered, remembering another graphic illustration in the same book. The sorceress Morauth, bolts of light streaming from her fingertips, her hair a dark mass around her pale, angry face, standing on a hillside, gazing down on her followers. Morauth, who was the source of the evil that had spread like a contagious disease across the lands of Faltofar. Morauth was the reason so many had died fighting for the One in a battle that had taken place hundreds of years ago.

"Sepheriis and sorceresses." She stifled a laugh. Thom nudged her quiet.

The children had explored these woods their whole lives. They knew every creek bed and cave, which trees were the best to climb and what parts of the forest were off-limits, forbidden lands belonging to the Old Ones. Not that they let that stop them. Today was the start of their summer holiday. It had been a season since they had been able to devote a full day to exploring. Their dad had told them that a fresh avalanche along the north side of the ridge had cascaded down into the forest, and they had spent the morning working their way there, convinced the freshly exposed earth would deliver up extraordinary treasures.

Lili chewed on the inside of her cheek, quiet now, waiting for Thom to suggest their next move, not quite sure if he was teasing her. The tree frog squirmed under her fingertips, working its way slowly down her pigtail to hang next to her ear.

"Torr," it garbled.

She tipped her head back and looked up at the tall cottonwoods, noting that not even a whisper of breeze shifted the green canopy. She shrugged, leaning her head closer to the small frog and rubbed it against her cheek. Torr was a word used for a special kind of wind that took place just before a storm. And tree frogs weren't known for small talk, but the bright little amphibian clinging to her braid seemed intent on expressing itself to her. Climbing closer to her ear, it stretched out and peeked around her cheekbone to make eye contact. Its bright yellow tongue darted out and flicked a freckle at the tip of her nose. Lili stifled a laugh, ignoring Thom's quick reproving glance. The tree frog blinked its big green eyes at Lili, obviously disappointed that its tongue had come back with nothing.

"Torr," it croaked again, as it launched itself onto her shoulder and blinked in the same direction as Thom.

Lili leaned toward the thicket, understanding and excitement blooming across her features. Its name. The frog was naming it. Excitedly, she began to step forward, but Thom's arm shot out to stop her.

"Lili, let's be careful, shall we?" Thom's voice had an edge to it.

"But Thom. The tree frog gave him a name!" she whispered excitedly. "The Sepherii or . . . whatever it is."

Thom's eyes faded to a softer shade of purple, his face crinkling into a broad grin. Everyone understood the power of naming. One of the first rhymes the children learned in their lessons was: "*Given once, it's for free. Naming twice, there's a fee. But thrice in the naming, 'they and you' become 'we.'*" He hesitated, lost in recalling the rhyme, his smile waning slightly. He gave Lili a supportive, if somewhat hesitant, nod of his head. When he nudged her forward, his smile was gone entirely, replaced once again by caution. Together, they inched their way toward the rocky hillside. The tiny weight of the tree frog on her shoulder and the quiet support of her brother behind her gave Lili courage.

She wound her way carefully over rocks and around low bushes, keeping her eyes on the large, dark silhouette beginning to take shape as she purposefully ignored the memory of her father's warning words.

"Always pay attention to your gut instincts, child," he had said. "If a situation feels dangerous, it probably is."

With no more than twenty feet between them, Lili and Thom felt, more than saw, the shadow shift. Both children froze. Another image from the picture book flashed across Lili's mind — a large Sepherii with glaring eyes, muscular arms raised in fists, hooves pounding, and wild hair whipping in the wind as it rushed at his enemy. Her hand, made sweaty from nerves, whitened in a grip around the last tree limb separating them from whatever stood in the shadows beyond. With her heart racing, she tentatively pulled the thick branch aside.

"You're hurt?" Her words choked out, more a statement than a question, as both children gawked at the most unusual being they had ever seen. He transferred his weight, taking pressure off the injured leg.

Lili looked over her shoulder at Thom. He slowly nodded again to her, and they hesitantly took another step forward. She could see the flanks of his horse-like body now, the strong muscles of his hindquarters quivering tensely. All that separated them from him was a low-hanging vine which she pulled aside, almost impatiently.

Her instincts told her the being was in pain. He raised his head, and, for the first time, Lili looked into the eyes of a real Sepherii. She understood that, without a doubt, the artist from her father's book had not merely created the illustrations from imagination. He had drawn them from memory, rendering perfect replicas of the same eyes, even though the vertical irises were now dilated, and the brilliant deep blue orbs were fogged with pain.

The Sepherii's human-like face remained expressionless, and Lili hesitated, her arm extended as she held the vine, not sure how to proceed. Abruptly, the tree frog pushed against her shoulder, skillfully arcing through the air, landing in the palm of the Sepherii's suddenly outstretched hand. Wiggling around to face the children, it repositioned itself and billowed out its chest in preparation to chirp again. Quickly, with a finger to her lips, Lili frowned sternly at it and shook her head.

"My turn," she whispered. Taking a deep breath, she stood as tall as her short frame would stretch and addressed the Sepherii.

"Torr."

2

THE NAMING

The Sepherii gently placed the frog onto the rock ledge above him. His bloodshot eyes never wavered from the small human. In an unspoken acknowledgment of solidarity, Thom moved closer to Lili's side, his arm grazing her shoulder. The Spell of Naming resided in threes, and she had only uttered the creature's name once. She took a deep breath.

"Torr."

The word seemed to ricochet against the overhanging cliff, echoing around them. Bits of gravel tinkled down the ochre-colored wall. The tiny frog hopped sideways to avoid one of the larger falling pieces and, finding a crevice in the rock's surface, backed itself into the cool opening. The Sepherii tipped his chin down, his eyes narrowing.

Thom placed his hand on Lili's arm in warning, his other hand hovered closely over the small dagger at his belt. Once a name was uttered a third time, the deep magic would be done. There would be an unbreakable bond, and with that bond, as with any genuine relationship, there would come responsibility. Lili calmly placed her hand over her brother's. The frog's yellow tongue darted out, catching an unwary fly, then relaxed into a small bump. Its tiny, sparkling eyes seemed to crinkle in anticipation of a stupendous show.

"Torr."

Dust began to drift around their feet, and tree branches swayed. The air bucked and twisted through the children's hair, and particles of dirt seeped into their eyes, making it hard to see through lashes thick with dust. Thom pulled Lili closer to him and reached into his shirt, fumbling for the engraved piece of metal that hung from a cord at his neck.

Thom's mother had made it clear that the children should always wear their talismans around their necks as protection. She had not said protection from what. Embedded in the coin was the sign of their clan, the Finn. Surrounding the crest along the edges were the markings of a language long forgotten. The metal began to glow, and he fought the urge to let go. Lili leaned into her brother, once again, every bit the younger sister. Weeks ago, she had lost her own talisman, during one of their short excursions on the way home from their lessons. She had not dared to tell her mother.

As suddenly as the whirling wind had started, it stopped. Silence descended throughout the forest. Rubbing the dirt from their eyes, the children warily and quietly pivoted, scanning the understory. Their father had warned them of stillness in the forest. Silence came hand in hand with either true danger or immense power. Thom gripped the talisman tightly, replacing his arm around Lili as the air sparkled with the last of the settling dust. The girl gave in to the sudden urge to reach out and part it. When her hand met the glittering mass, the particles separated like a golden curtain, filtering through her fingertips and falling quickly to the leafy floor. The sounds of the forest began again.

A pool of light now illuminated the overhang where the Sepherii had taken shelter. His brilliant coat shimmered in strands of red, his hair and tail resembled the color of early summer sunshine. The air above and just behind him rippled giving the illusion of cascading water. Or translucent wings. The pained eyes of the massive, glittering being now glowed an intense silver.

"You have named me, children of the Old Forest, but our bond is not complete until I know your proper names. Do not waste my time if you play games with the old laws. Speak and be final with the binding, or go, wordless, and leave me to heal."

The Sepherii's words reverberated inside Lili's head. The creature had not moved his mouth but had communicated his thoughts, rippling with absolute weariness, directly into her mind. From the tightened grip on her shoulder, she knew Thom had heard them too. Wiping a strand of red hair from her face and leaving a smudge of dirt across her forehead, Lili drew her shoulders back and took a deep breath.

"My name is Lili." She stopped. That wasn't right. She began again. "My name is Lilianna Rhianna Finnekin. I am second child to Olitus and Sarafina of the Finn."

She had never formally announced her name, and the words felt laced with authority and connection. The Finnekins had once been a prominent tribe in Faltofar, and the children had been raised to feel pride in their ancestry.

"Lilianna Rhianna Finnekin, it seems we are to be as one," said the Sepherii. "I am Torr."

The beautiful creature's eyes faded back to a bloodshot blue. Lili swallowed; the reality of talking to a real, live Sepherii felt slightly overwhelming.

"This is my brother Thom," she said. "Thomlin Rendisius Finnekin, first child to Olitus and Sarafina of the Finn," she corrected herself. The formality of the situation required manners. The Sepherii seemed not to notice her awkward introduction.

"Thomlin, son of Olitus and Sarafina, you are bound to me also." The Sepherii pawed the ground, giving himself a moment to reflect. "You stood at your sister's side in the Naming, and it will not be forgotten." His bloodshot eyes shifted again to Lili. "He has courage. Almost as much as you, little one."

Torr's chin dipped toward his chest, deflated with exhaustion. His wound oozed a bright red and yellow, and exposed bone glistened at the center of the cut. Lili could feel the Sepherii's pain like it was her own.

The low light through the branches marked a sun heading for the horizon. They had lost much of the day, and Lili's stomach gave a loud rumble. She curbed the urge to search for berries. It was too early in the season, and there were more important things to deal with than her hunger.

In the distance, a peal of thunder announced the inevitable afternoon showers. The noises of the forest increased in volume, competing with the impending storm. Bees wove through the bright foliage, their contented humming mingling with the sound of the clacking wings of the grassbobbers. Like a huge, slumbering green giant, the forest seemed to have awakened from some timeless place where dreams were filled with mythical characters who could come to life out of a picture book.

Lili's hunger, and her desire to help the injured Sepherii, made her think of her mother and home. Thom seemed to read her thoughts as he took his arm from her shoulder.

"Lili?"

Thom had always been the leader of their pack of two, but something had changed during this glittery, magical afternoon. For once, Lili felt almost his equal.

"Torr," Lili said and cautiously stepped forward. "We want to help you. My mother has the art of healing." She was close enough to touch the Sepherii's flank. "She can make something to help your leg get better."

Torr nodded his head in acceptance. Lili reached hesitantly toward him and, for the first time, placed her hand against his coat. Immense muscles jittered under her fingertips along with something else, an electric current of sorts. Tingling slid down her arm. She had felt the very same, somewhere in her past, but she couldn't name the memory and let it rest at the back of her mind for a quieter time in the future.

Another peal of thunder close by warned them the storm was moving in fast. The air began to feel charged not with the electrifying energy of "The Naming," as Lili was to think of it later, but with the crackling ripples that precede a summer downpour. The safety and warmth of home were much too far to protect them from the weighted clouds. The children and Torr shifted further under the overhang.

Above them, the little reptile wiggled deeper into his crevice, utterly content with the outcome of the afternoon. Its job done, the frog reveled in the promise of afternoon rainwater puddles. The thought was almost as satisfying as the fat fly it had just devoured. Lili heard the frog give a wet, rounded 'urp' and made a mental note to thank it for giving her the Sepherii's name. Quietly, she leaned against Torr's soft flank.

3

AFTER THE STORM

They watched the sky cloud over, draping the forest in the hues of twilight. Pattering raindrops fell in a slow staccato at first, then began to bang out a tempo on the carpet of leaves and needles. The steady beat of the droplets from the water-soaked limbs above them reminded Lili of the past summer's clan gathering. Unconsciously, she leaned in closer against the Sepherii, remembering that long summer night.

Lili and Thom, along with their parents, had traveled two days to join the clans of Faltofar in the Remembrance Days festival. Their first night was filled with laughter and drink, Ruba Punch for the children and Pago for the adults. The sounds of that night had been a cacophony to the senses - the crackling sound of the bonfires, the stomping feet of dancers lit in a brilliant, orange glow, and the heady beat of the drums. Well into the night, long after the children had tired of running through the surrounding meadows playing games of tag, Lili had sat at her father's feet, propped against his leg, blinking in wonder at the spectacle of men and women twirling around the fire. Her legs itched from the tall summer grass, but her distracted scratching quickly slowed as she began to pay attention to the dancers. Their mesmerizing steps, choreographed by ancestors long silent, sent them leaping and pirouetting round and round the fire and each other. Every individual's colorful dress denoted where they came from geographically in Faltofar: deep greens of the river valley clans; browns, ochres and red for the hill people; white and gold of the tribes from the highlands, where the snow rarely melted year-round; and the shimmering purple and blue of her clan, reflecting the coastal villages and the waters of the vast ocean adjacent to their fertile fields. The firelight and the swirling colors wove an intricately textured tapestry in the darkness, as the night sky glittered cold and distant overhead.

Coming back to the present, Lili realized she had experienced the same sense of power there that now emanated from Torr. That long-ago night filled with dance and starlight had created a feeling so life-affirming it was like a vibrant wave pressed against her very being. She had wanted to ask her parents about it, but weariness had taken a firm grip on her slight frame. The last thing she remembered of that first night was the brilliant canopy of stars and the warmth of her father's hand on her head as she drifted to sleep. Awakening the next morning inside her family's warm tent, nestled in her soft fur bedding, she had forgotten about the fire and the dance in the excitement of the busy following days of the gathering. Until now.

Of course, she understood that power was everywhere. Around her and inside all of them. Thom had his amazingly keen eyesight. She could speak with animals large and small. She smiled for a moment and glanced up at the ledge, looking for the tree frog. Not seeing him, her thoughts circled back. What Lili couldn't quite grasp was how some things seemed to radiate more than others. Like the Naming of this magnificent being. And the Dance.

What about the talisman she and her brother wore? She reached instinctively for the leather cord at her neck and flinched, feeling its loss once again. Each child was given a talisman at the time of their Naming. Naming took place when the child was deemed a young adult, earning the right to more independence and a voice in their family's and tribe's decisions. The timing of the Naming was different for each person. Lili's had been a year ago, and she had proudly shown her talisman to her friends at school for weeks. Thom had had his for several years, but he was older than Lili by three seasons.

The raindrops had slowed to a quiet patter as rivulets of water softly hissed down the rock wall next to the overhang where the trio had taken shelter. In no more than a quarter of an hour, the downpour had transformed the forest. Freshly washed leaves and flowers that had been bent under the weight of the heavy rain moments before began to raise their fragile heads back up toward the sun, deepening the color of the forest. The sun's heat morphed bare earth into steaming patches of warmth, giving the woods a misty, otherworldly feel. The children, along with the injured Sepherii, moved out from under the overhang. Torr shook his head, and droplets of rainwater that had found their way into his hair shimmered in all directions. Lili tentatively smiled up at her new friend and gave him an unspoken invitation to follow them. Wearily, the Sepherii nodded his head, bending forward to Lili's height, his uncanny eyes probing deeply into her own. The closeness of his piercing eyes startled the girl, and she took a small step backward before regaining her confidence. Whatever he saw seemed to satisfy Torr. He nodded again and raised himself to his full height.

"Good," she said and grasped Thom's hand.

Together they parted the thicket to allow the Sepherii to move through the thick brush.

————

The walking was slow. Torr's leg seemed to be getting worse. An eerie reddish glow now emanated from the wound, as if the raw skin had been exposed to some malignant force intent upon destroying the tissue. Thom did not ask the Sepherii to explain the injury, instinctively knowing that Torr was conserving all his energy for maneuvering through the dense and rocky forest. Besides, Lili had begun to limp too, lagging slightly.

They had been working their way through the woods for more

than an hour and had only just paused for a brief rest when Thom spotted movement behind them. He would not have seen it, had they not stopped. Neither the Sepherii nor Lili seemed aware of anything unusual. Had he been mistaken? He stepped away from the others with a mumbled excuse. Torr's unwavering gaze followed Thom, but the Sepherii remained where he stood. Just out of their eyesight, Thom quickly backtracked. He was an expert woodsman, having spent most of his young years learning to hunt and track with both his parents. His keen eyesight had been a blessing in assisting his parents to put food on their table.

Yes, there behind them, something, or someone, was following their route through the forest. Crouching lower, Thom relaxed and let the deep sight take over. Past trees and meadows, beyond a massive cluster of blackberry bushes not yet ripened by long summer days, he narrowed in on their pursuer.

"Unbelievable." He crouched even lower.

Emerging around the edge of the blackberry brambles, a short, stumpy, little man wriggled over a fallen log, righting himself to land on his feet. His stubby arms and legs, and the size of his head revealed the distinctive characteristics of a forest dwarf.

Thom had seen their kind only once. A woman had come to their cabin, a dwarf child bundled in her arms, asking his mother for assistance in healing the toddler. Thom was small enough at the time to hide behind his mother's leg and curiously study the small folk at the door. He could see that the little one she held had some sort of deformity or injury to its arm. Later, after the dwarf woman had left with a package of medicinals his mother had put together for her, he had asked about the creature.

"She is not a creature, Thom," his mother had said as she put away her healing supplies, her brow furrowed. "Forest dwarves have lived in this land far longer than we." She stopped, her task forgotten for a moment, knowing the importance of the lesson she wanted to impart to her son. "They deserve our respect and our distance."

"But," Thom said.

"No, Thom. The old ones of the forest are to be left alone. Do not try to find them. It is a fragile truce we hold with them."

Thom watched his mother closely. He could tell by the way she kept glancing at the receding dwarf woman carrying her child that she was not satisfied with the help she had tried to give them. The injured young dwarf saddened and disturbed Thom. His mother had always helped everyone in need. Hesitantly, he reached for her skirt, holding onto the material for comfort as he would his favorite blanket. She had been busying herself with placing her healing items on the high shelf in the kitchen but stopped. Dusting imaginary particles off her skirt, she bent down to her son's height.

"Sometimes, all we can do is lend comfort, child." Gently she tousled his hair. "Now, little Eagle Hawk, off you go to feed the cow."

Crouching behind the log, he assessed the dwarf's movements. Thom had no doubt the dwarf was tracking them. But why? He hesitated, wondering if he should stay and confront the little creature — little man, he corrected himself — or head back to Lili and Torr and keep moving. They would be wondering what was taking him so long, but the dwarf, even with his short legs, was gaining on them. Torr's voice, inside his head, decided for him.

"Thom, come. Three are stronger than one."

With a final glance at the dwarf, Thom quickly retraced his way back to the others. Lili blinked up at him from where she sat on a rock. In the time they had stopped to rest, his sister seemed to have almost diminished in size, curling into herself. Distractedly, she rubbed at her shin, her hand drifting listlessly back to her side after a moment. Whatever had caused her to slow down was affecting more than just her leg strength. Her ordinarily light skin was even paler. The sun reflected a soft glitter of sweat on her forehead, and her pigtails drooped on either side of her head. Torr stood behind her, his hand on her shoulder and his head close enough to her hair that each time he exhaled, little tendrils of red hair moved at the base of her neck. Thom momentarily forgot about their follower and knelt at Lili's feet.

"Lili, what is it?"

She lifted her head, but her eyes remained unfocused. When Thom placed his hand on her forehead, as he'd seen his mother do, he could feel the burning heat from her body.

"We have to get to Mother. She will know what to do," he said more to himself than to either of his companions as he stood.

And, that is what saved him.

The rock that came zinging through the air would have hit him in the temple had he not shifted his weight when he rose. Instead, the stone hit Thom at his knee. He buckled, falling to the ground at Lili's feet, and rolled just in time to avoid a sharp stick that came down near his shoulder. Laying on his back, Thom glared up into the angry eyes of the forest dwarf and froze. The dwarf, more a giant than a dwarf from this angle, hovered over the boy. He had tossed the stick aside, and now his beefy hand was wrapped around a large club. Thom didn't dare look away but hoped both Lili and Torr were unhurt. It had all happened so fast.

A scowl crossed the dwarf's face, and he waved his weapon from side to side, tempting Thom to make a move.

"My forest, human."

Thom felt Torr shift behind Lili, but he kept his attention on the dwarf's face. A little whimper escaped from Lili. It proved just enough to distract the dwarf. When he glanced her way, Thom saw his opportunity and rolled once, taking the dwarf's feet out from under him. They tumbled across the small clearing, grunting and hissing in their efforts for control of the club. The stunted man was strong, but Thom, with his longer limbs, was his equal. The Sepherii, standing silently, watched the two closely. When their struggles brought them close to the rock where Lili slumped, and Torr stood, he lifted his hoof and, with impeccable timing, brought it down on the club handle, missing both the boy and the dwarf's fingers by a fraction as he pinned the weapon to the ground. The two released their grip and scrambled to their feet, squaring off and glaring at each other.

"Enough!" declared Torr.

The dwarf jerked, momentarily startled at the Sepherii's voice in his head. Thom stood his ground, not sure what to expect from the small woodsman.

"We pass through your forest with no disrespect," said the Sepherii. "Why do you follow us?"

Lili, whose head had hung low even as the struggle between her brother and the dwarf took place, suddenly fell forward. The dwarf moved, faster than one would believe of such a short-limbed being, grabbing the back of the girl's jersey before she hit the ground. With his other hand, he reached into the pocket of the vest he wore. Thom, fearing for Lili, lunged forward, but was too far away to narrow the gap before the dwarf drew forth the object.

"Back away," he growled as he held up his hand.

4

A DEBT REPAID

The talisman dangled in the air, swinging like a magician's hypnotizing trick. The glow from the object radiated brighter than the dappled sunshine through the surrounding trees. With one gnarled hand, the weathered huntsman gently raised the unconscious child by her jersey, and gingerly placed the leather cord around her neck. Lili's head rolled limply to one side, but her breathing, for a moment, seemed more natural. Thom, ignoring the dwarf's command to back away, quickly knelt at his sister's other side. The two of them lowered her to the forest floor. Relieved of his burden, the dwarf gently placed his index finger on the girl's forehead, making two small circles with the dirt from his fingertip between her eyebrows. Thom could see a flicker of something like kindness flit across the dwarf's face as he touched the human child.

"A debt repaid," the dwarf grumbled in a deep, earthy voice, abruptly standing. Staring up at the Sepherii, the old dwarf bowed slightly, then pivoted on his heel, his beady eyes traveling over the girl to land with a glare at Thom before he stomped away.

"Wait," yelled Thom to the departing back of the compact woodsman. "I don't understand!"

The only response Thom got was a loud, incoherent grumble, and a dismissive hand gesture that would have sent Thom to his room had he done it in front of his mother. Holding tightly to his little sister, Thom watched the squat form of the man until he faded into the green of the forest.

His heartbeat finally began to slow. He bent and, with an uncharacteristic show of love, kissed Lilianna on the forehead, noticing for the first time the image the old one had drawn between her eyes glowed similarly to that of her talisman. He recognized the protective quality, but not the symbol. The dwarf's gesture was one of kindness. Thom looked to the woods again, shaking his head. The encounter made no sense to him. Gently, he tucked Lilianna's talisman inside the folds of her shirt and turned to his companion.

"Do you have enough strength to carry her, Torr?"

The Sepherii had removed his hoof from the club and stood with his head lowered. Thom didn't know what a healthy Sepherii was supposed to look like, but he was sure Torr's condition had worsened too. At Thom's question, however, Torr seemed to rally his strength, raising his head high and stepping forward. The Sepherii was tall, but Thom's strength was growing, and adrenaline still coursed through his body. He needed to get his faltering companions to the healing hands of his mother. Thom easily picked up his sister's sagging body, heaving her onto Torr's back. The Sepherii flinched slightly, and Thom watched him closely, ready to grab Lili if her weight was too much.

"She is not a burden, Thom."

Thom stepped back, wiping his nose with the sleeve of his shirt. It came away with dirt and snot.

"A far cry from the type of day I imagined I would have." His thoughts drifted to the buried treasures they had intended to find in the landslide. Scooping up the club from where it lay in the dirt, he gave a cynical laugh and shoved it into his belt next to the slingshot he always carried. Here was a treasure he could put to use. "The old grump. Serves him right."

With more ponderous steps, the trio headed west, following the long light of the sun through the trees.

―――――

Sarafina stood up from the porch bench when she saw them coming. Next to her, Sir Erathus Mosely, their temperamental house cat, who had kept watch also, swished his tail back and forth in obvious agitation, a low growl emanating from his puffed-out chest. Sarafina had been sitting at the door of the cabin for the past half hour, her hands busied in the preparation of thin strands of catgut for sutures. Her last batch had been thicker, backup for her bowstring. Something told her she might need both.

A pot of water simmered on the stove and her herbs were laid out on the bench next to her. She had been blessed with more than just the art of healing. She could pull knowledge from the currents of air that wafted around her, things she shouldn't be able to know. Some called it the Sense, but Sarafina sometimes thought of it as the Senselessness; it often only served to make her worry. This time, however, it had allowed her to prepare, at least in part.

She knew her children were bringing home a being in need of her skills - one too large to enter their home. However, what she saw across the pasture took her breath away. The sparkling Sepherii glowed in the late evening light, his beautiful coat shimmering, just as it had when the children had first seen him. They were still too far away for Sarafina to see the small, slumped figure across Torr's back, but, as they neared, she recognized the Sepherii's burden.

"Lili."

The realization propelled her off the porch into a full run, stopping inches away from Torr. Grasping the child around the waist, she slid the girl's limp body into her capable arms.

"Thank you." She held Lili to her chest, acknowledging the huge Sepherii. Torr bowed his head in response as Sarafina's eyes traveled down his leg to the glowing, red and oozing wound.

"Come," she said, adjusting the heavy weight of the child in her arms. There would be time enough later to ask questions of her son after she had tended to her daughter and the Sepherri who had carried her home.

———

Hours later and too tired to cook, Thom and his mother sat eating a small meal of bread and cheese by the crackling fire. Lili lay in a corner of the main room on a soft pallet of furs. Her breathing, which had been rough and burdened with soft moans, now came out in quiet little puffs, eased by the medicine her mother had forced her to swallow. The cat, Mosely, had coiled himself into a ball under one of Lili's outstretched arms, his head resting on his paws, eyes half-closed but still very alert.

They had left the silent Sepherii alone outside. His leg was freshly bound in clean gauze, a poultice of healing herbs plastered to the wound. He seemed to want, or need, nothing else, at least at the moment.

Thom shuddered, his body weary from assisting his mother. He settled deeper into his chair, recalling again what he and his mother had found when they had gotten Lili inside and onto the clean surface of the table. He had waited tensely, leaning against the kitchen counter, ready to assist his mother if she needed him. Her healing hands had hovered over the girl's small frame, beginning at the top of her head and moving slowly down her body, searching for the source of her affliction. She had paused when she saw the dwarf's markings on Lili's brow, giving Thom a quick, quizzical glance. The heat that emanated from Lili's forehead had dulled the glow left by the dwarf's touch, but seeing its dim shape only intensified Thom's recollection of everything that had happened to them since sunrise.

The kitchen had closed in on him. The cabin, the safe haven of his childhood, had never felt so small before. Sepheriis and dwarves in one day? He shook his head, studying the fire, replaying the afternoon for the umpteenth time.

"Her leg Thom," his mother had said with an intensity he had rarely heard in his mother's voice, her hand hovering just below Lilianna's knee. "Get me the scissors."

Reaching up on the shelf where her supplies of bandages and containers of herbs were stored, Thom found the scissors Sarafina reserved for healing purposes only. The blades gleamed softly, their edges sharp and sanitized. Her tools had always been off-limits to the children. She quickly began to cut away Lili's leggings. As the exposed skin came into view, both Sarafina and Thom gasped.

"Mother, it's like the Sepherii's wound. Almost exactly the same."

Lili's right shin glowed a brilliant, angry red, the skin pulling back and away from a cut several inches long and deep. Even more disturbing, streaks of red coursed up her shin and along her right thigh. Sarafina moved quickly to her jars of herbs and salves, waving a distracted hand at Thom, implying she needed a bowl.

"Place it in the boiling water first, Thom," she said. "Then give it to me."

Deftly Sarafina mixed a pungent combination in the bowl, efficiently crushing it into a paste. Meanwhile, Thom elevated his sister's leg with blankets from the other room and dabbed her dry, cracking lips with water as per his mother's muttered directions. He was surprised when Sarafina asked him to remove Lili's talisman, but did as he was told.

Moving to the edge of the table closest to Lili's leg, Sarafina began to dab the poultice along the laceration working quickly and whispering to herself. Thom could not hear what she said, but instinctively knew she was reciting the healing chants of her trade. With each application, Lili moaned, her head shifting from side to side.

"Give me her talisman, Thom," Sarafina said as she tied off the bandage.

Thom retrieved it from the corner of the table. Once in her hand, Sarafina lay it gently at the center of the bandage on Lili's leg, pressing it down. The coin began to glow, its light radiating through the healer's fingers, illuminating her anxious features. Lili began to thrash more violently.

"Hold her shoulders," she said to Thom, increasing her grip on Lili's leg.

He followed her directions, pressing down hard on his sister's fragile collar bone. His sister was stronger than he had imagined. He concentrated on keeping her centered on the table, hoping he was not bruising her.

"A bruise is far better than her falling," Sarafina said, having understood his concern. "You're doing fine, Thom. Keep holding her."

Sarafina kept her hand pressed on the talisman, pressing against the movement of Lili's leg. Thom could see a fine layer of sweat on his mother's brow, and upper lip as Lili's anguished moans cut through the dense air of the cabin. His head buzzed with the humming concern emanating from the Sepherii outside. Mosely had jumped onto the sideboard, his agitation evident in a soft hissing, punctuated by the fierce whipping of his tail.

And then, it was over.

Except for the rise and fall of her chest, her breath escaping her mouth in soft moans, Lili once again lay motionless. Whatever demons she fought were now trapped inside her fevered mind. Thom released his hold on her shoulders, guiltily noticing the red hand-prints he'd left on her skin.

Sarafina took her hands away from her daughter's bandage, coming to the top of the table where Thom stood.

"You did well, son." Lifting Lili's head, she placed the talisman back around her youngest child's neck.

They had gently finished their ministrations, wrapping the uncon-scious girl in furs and settling her on a pallet closer to the fire. With a final tuck of the blanket around Lili, Sarafina had given Thom a weary but encouraging smile.

"That is all we can do for her now, Thom. The battle is hers to fight from here forward."

The healer, distancing herself from her patient, understood the coming battle of fever - burning heat, followed by bone-rattling chills so violent the child's teeth would grind in her skull. The mother in her gave a silent prayer to the Poppy and its medicinal powers.

"Bring the deep sleep soon."

She moved an imaginary strand of hair away from her youngest child's forehead. "Now, we must have a care for the Sepherii."

Already weary from his efforts to get the wounded pair to his mother, Thom had poured himself a cup of water, and downed it, listening for any changes in his sister's breathing. Mosely padded back and forth near Lili's head, having determined he was the only one capable of guarding her safety. Thom watched the cat pace, then, setting the cup down, had hurried outside.

He looked up from the fire, but Sarafina seemed lost in her thoughts as well. Neither had any desire for small talk. Thom shifted lower in his chair, his thoughts drifting back to the earlier events of the evening.

———

Darkness had wrapped itself tightly around the cabin, but Thom's mother had lit several Wur lanterns. She and the Sepherii were illuminated in double pools of the bluish light. Torr stood silently, his coat bearing a sheen of sweat that gave it an eerie slickness. His eyes were bleary and now completely red-rimmed, his arms hanging limply at his sides. Without hesitation, Sarafina reached up and rested her hand on his forehead.

"Let me work the healing art on you, dear Sepherii." Her free hand gently rubbed his coat.

Torr nodded his head slowly, and Sarafina took the right hoof, gently placing it on the large chopping stump next to the woodpile.

"By the One, you share the same ill."

She hurried back inside to retrieve the poultice she had made for Lili, ignoring the supply of herbs and salves she had placed outside earlier. The Sepherii remained motionless, statuesque, with his injured leg perched on the stump.

Thom breathed in the night air. Outside the circle of Wur light, the sky shone with the clarity of early summer. Brilliant patterns of stars crisscrossed the jet blackness. One could almost be convinced that nothing had changed in the young boy's life. Simultaneously, the Sepherii and the boy snorted.

"You shouldn't read my mind." Thom's voice sounded petulant, even to himself. Any response from Torr was lost in the flurry of activity as Sarafina returned.

With the efficiency of one long used to the healing arts, she worked swiftly to spread the thick ingredients and wrap the Sepherii's leg. For the second time that night, she placed a talisman, hers this time, on the moist bandages and whispered the incantations of her trade. Those powerful words, handed down through centuries, healer to healer, that would boost the body's natural efforts to mend. The Sepherii's thoughts buzzed like the night insects attracted to the light of the Wur lantern, in a mixture of pain and confusion coupled with immense relief. With the diminished pain, the Sepherii could once again think.

"Ah, just so," the Sepherii mused. "You and she are true descendants of the One Healer. It makes more sense now, Thomlin, why you and your sister found me."

Sarafina's hand still rested on the Sepherii's leg. If she had heard Torr's thoughts, she had not acknowledged them.

"I am thirsty," the Sepherii said, tiredly.

Thom rose from where he sat on the porch steps and hurried to the well at the side of the cabin, returning with a sloshing bucket. Sarafina watched as he handed the dipper to Torr. Then taking an empty bowl, she dipped it into the water. Pulling a cloth from her waistband, she soaked it and ran the fresh material along the Sepherii's flanks. Her slow movements with the towel eased his discomfort. He had brought her afflicted child home, and she had worked the magic that would heal him. Tucking the cloth into the pan of cold water, Sarafina began to gather the rest of her supplies.

"Thom," she said, her smile conveying her thanks. "I'll be inside." The stairs of the cabin creaked as she climbed slowly, her arms full. The cabin door clicked shut, and Thom found himself alone with Torr.

"I am yet thirsty." Torr held out the dipper to the boy.

"Right." Thom frowned. "Okay."

Wondering if bending over was too much for his tall frame, Thom filled the dipper again, obligingly holding it out to the Sepherii. With lightning speed, Torr's marble-like hand wrapped tightly around Thom's wrist. The water in the dipper sloshed from side to side, spilling to the ground, but Thom refused to flinch. Instead, he stared up at the creature. His chiseled features softened for just a moment before Torr released his grip. His eyes shone kindly in a silent acknowledgment of Thom's help. Self-consciously, Thom smiled back, taking the extended dipper and dropping it back into the pail.

In the soft light cast by the Wur lanterns, he quietly gathered the last of his mother's supplies, then with a snap of his fingers extinguished the floating orbs. The glow from the cabin window beckoned him inside, and Thom realized just how tired he was from this most extraordinary day. He wearily navigated the stairs, not looking back. His mother was already seated by the fire. They would wait up for his father who was due back from the village at any time.

5

A REUNION OF SORTS

Olitus waited silently, blending into the darkness as he assessed the familiar scents and sounds of his home and those not so familiar. The grouse hens nestled quietly in their coop next to the barn. Their lack of concern contrasted with the very fibers of his body that warned him something was not right. With his back to the coop, he slowed his breathing to bring focus and hunched lower, cautiously moving forward to get a better view of the cabin. Light glowed encouragingly through the front window, but at the perimeter of the brilliant pool it cast on the ground, he could see the massive form of a creature. The gilded dagger he always carried at his belt now rested in his palm, the blade jutting down toward the dark earth. Holding it thus, Olitus could stab or punch. He inched ahead, freezing as the front door of the cabin opened. As Thom stepped down from the porch and turned toward the shadow, concern for his son almost strangled Olitus. He bolted out of the darkness.

"Thom, aware!" he yelled.

Thom's head whipped around, stunned at the sight of Olitus hurtling out of the darkness toward the Sepherii, dagger raised. Instinctively, he launched himself at his father, tackling Olitus and sending them both rolling in the dust of the side yard. He had only had time to get out the word "Father!" before they both hit the ground. Winded, he lay partially on top of Olitus, both of them coughing for breath.

"His name is Torr. He is a friend." His words were muffled, his face plastered against his father's pant legs.

Startled, more by what his son had said than finding himself on the ground, Olitus sat up and looked from the boy, wrapped around his legs, to the massive being emerging from the shadows. Thom released his hold and quickly stood, feeling guilty for having taken his father down but rather pleased with his newfound strength. Grasping his son's extended arm, Olitus rose from the dirt, sheathing his dagger and swiping at the dust on his clothes. Patting Thom on the arm, Olitus nodded and gently shoved him aside, his focus on the Sepherii.

No more than ten paces separated the two. As Olitus moved forward, so did the Sepherii, until they were both within feet of each other. To Thom's amazement, Torr extended one long leg and bent the other in what could only be defined as a Sepherii's equivalent of a bow. Olitus acknowledged the Sepherii's formal greeting with a nod of his head.

"These are strange times in Faltofar. No human would deny the blessings of your kind at his or her side," Olitus said, with the beginning of a smile. "I speak for my family in saying we are honored."

Torr stood to his full height, his head tilted proudly back. His eyes spiraled and a low hum emanated from him. The previously unconcerned grouse hens, disturbed by the activity in the yard, flapped and squawked in their pen. Olitus, displaying the sense of humor he was renowned for, began to laugh at the clamor of anxious bird noise that filled the air, and the formality of the moment dissipated in the fresh night air. His father's laughter was infectious, and Thom joined in, the tension he'd felt all day disappearing in the dusty yard. Olitus gathered his son to his side in a bear hug.

"The Sepherii is well taken care of, Thom?" he asked, waving a weary hand at the bandaged foreleg.

"Good!" he exclaimed at Thom's nod.

Olitus swiped his hand across eyes bleary with dust and travel, scratching at the growth of a beard. "Then let us leave him to the night for now." Before turning away, Olitus stepped even closer to the Sepherii and spoke softly. "Well met, Torr. I am glad for your company." He nodded a goodnight and moved toward the porch.

Thom hastily stepped closer to the Sepherii, awkwardly raising his hand, indecisive as to whether he should extend it in a handclasp or just wave. He opted for the wave.

"Good night Torr," he said, then hurriedly followed Olitus, almost bumping into him when his father stopped abruptly.

Olitus pivoted and was about to address Thom when his eyes alighted on the dwarf's club tucked into Thom's belt, all humor gone. The moment stretched out.

"I would gather you have a story to tell me, son, but I am in need of the comfort of our hearth and your mother's kindness, and words are better woven in the light."

6

LILI'S DREAMS

Mosely cautiously sniffed at the girl's damp curls. Lost in the depth of her foggy dream, Lilianna twitched reflexively, brushing the cat away.

The trees were shrouded in a dense fog. It gathered in Lili's hair, weighting it in damp strands across her face, tickling her. Water dripped from every leaf, dappling Lili's arms with droplets the color of a dull winter day. Her leather summer boots, covered in a thick, oozing mud the consistency of gruel, stuck with each movement she tried to take. The mud held to her as if desperate for company. Lili shivered, pulling her thin jacket tighter around her, and took another slow step.

"Thom!" she yelled again.

This time she thought she heard something. The sound of wind in feathers warned her, and she ducked just in time to avoid the claws of a mocking kay as it flapped over her head, landing on a soggy tree limb in front of her.

"Thommmmm," it cawed.

Lili sucked in her cheek and bit down on the soft inner skin. She had had this habit for as long as she could remember. The pain kept her centered, kept the tears from coming. The pain kept her from giving in to panic.

"Thom?" she said in a low, desperate voice.

"Thommmmm," gargled the big, blue-black bird. Lili took another soggy step and snapped up at the bird.

"If I could find a rock in this nasty slime, I would take you out bird."

"Alonnne, you'd bbeee, Liiiiiliiiiii of the Finnnnnn," it croaked.

"How do you know my name?" Lili demanded.

In response, the bird fluffed up its feathers and shook itself. Lili decided to ignore it and directed her attention again on her surroundings. Fog rippled around her in muted, damp waves. The dull outline of trees and shrubs defined the space close to her, but beyond that it was as if nothing existed, as if an artist, using only a palette of muted pigment to create the landscape, had stopped, almost at the edge of the canvas, having run out of paint. Or inspiration.

Lili's tongue played with the ridge of skin on the inside of her mouth. It hurt where she had bitten down. Where was she?

The bird hopped along the branch, moving closer to where Lili stood. She could feel its beady eyes following her and decided she had been better off alone. Taking a deep breath, she tried again to move forward without falling. The sucking of the muck kept throwing her off balance. After a few teetering steps, she managed to reach ground slightly more solid. Here the rotting brush was thicker. She could hear the bird cackling and cawing softly to itself behind her, but ignored it, focusing her attention on what was before her. Just past the line of brush, she could make out what seemed like some type of structure. A small building and a fence. Carefully, she parted the branches, trying to avoid the sharp thorns that grabbed at her shirt like greedy little hands trying to stop her. One branch snapped across her face, leaving a cut across her jaw deep enough to bleed. She rubbed at the wound with her palm. The ribbon of blood crisscrossed her light skin, its silky path a bright contrast to the gray and brown of her surroundings. She quickly wiped her hand on her pants, leaving another red smear, and stepped through the last of the brush.

She found herself at the edge of what at one time must have been a corral. The rotting wood of the fence lay almost buried in the limp grass at her feet. The smell of decay permeated the fog. Tasting the foul air around her, Lili fought the urge to spit.

Following the line of the old fence, she could see two posts still standing, sentries to nothing now. The building stood far enough into the thick fog that she still could not see it clearly. Her footing was better now, but Lili moved forward slowly. The framework of the building was solid enough, but dark brown moss covered all the boards, eating its way through the structure inch by inch.

Something about the building triggered a memory in Lili. Something about the fence and the building. She had seen them before.

"No, it's not possible," she whispered, swallowing the bubbling horror at the back of her throat.

Gritting her teeth, she turned away from the small building and what was left of a coop. The fog had thickened, dense clouds of moist air surrounding her. But she didn't need to be able to see. She knew the way between this building and the next, having walked the path her whole life. Nonetheless, she stumbled as she hurried across the wet grass, tripping over something and landing heavily on her hands and knees.

A small whimper escaped her mouth as she realized what she had fallen on. The stark, bleached bones punctuated the bleak world of the dream, the only contrast around her besides the smears of blood on cheek and pants. She stood quickly and stepped out of the clattering mass. In front of her, the second building loomed out of the fog. The rotting door hung from rusted metal. The roof had fallen in, imploding like the dark stars her father had told her stories about as a little girl. What had once been a haven and her home now stood before her, nothing more than a memory and a crippled, mossy shell. Tears rolled down Lili's face. Despair and loneliness trickled from her dry mouth in tiny whimpers.

From out of the swirling fog, the mocking kay flapped into the yard, landing on the brittle, hollow-eyed skull.

"Haaahahaaaaahaaaaaaaaaa." The bird's cackling cry drifted into the fog.

Lilianna moaned, unconsciously shifting her body on the pallet. Mosely, resting his head on his paws, studied the girl's face. His twitching whiskers and the swish of his tail were the only outward signs the cat was distressed by his mistress's disturbed dream state. Caught in her fever-induced nightmare, the girl moaned again, unaware of her protector.

———

Sarafina glanced up as the door opened, expecting to see Thom walking in. She gave a small gasp at the sight of Olitus, surprised her Senses had not given her the knowledge he was back.

"No matter, we are one again," she thought to herself and stood quickly, moving to her husband's embrace.

Thom waited near the door, giving his parents a private moment to reunite. He studied his sister laying on her pallet, a light quilt covering her small frame. Lili's eyelids fluttered but did not open. Her hair was matted in sweat, and her lips parted in a soft moan. Sarafina had left a cup of water near her head, with a soft rag next to it. Thom knelt, dipped the cloth in the water, and put it to his sister's lips. Mosely moved in closer to Thom and sniffed at the cup, surprised when he snorted in water. He stepped back, offended.

Thom could hear his parents conferring near the fire but kept his attention on his sister. Her already pale skin seemed to glow, her freckles standing out like a brilliant constellation across her nose. Olitus moved to Thom's side and knelt, gently placing his hand on Lili's chest. Thom could hardly bear to witness the raw emotions shift across his father's face as Olitus lowered his head toward his youngest. Both offered their soft prayers to the gods. The silence was broken by the cat's wet sneeze. Olitus reached over and patted

Mosely gently on the head, then softly touched Thom's shoulder, motioning him away from the sleeping girl. They moved to the hearth and the warmth of the fire and stood quietly, lost in their thoughts of Lili and the battle raging inside her. Sarafina, emerging from the kitchen with a tray of steaming mugs of Pago, broke the silence.

"We do little good, without knowing each other's stories," she said, placing the mugs on the side table. Thom and his mother had not spoken of the events of the day, choosing to wait for Olitus to return so that they could all be together in the telling. Thom and Olitus accepted the mugs Sarafina offered them.

"To the One," Olitus said, tapping his cup first against his wife's and then again, lightly, against his son's.

"To the One," Sarafina and Thom responded. They raised their mugs to their lips, and Thom grimaced slightly at the unfamiliar bitterness.

"Now, let us sit, and we can fill in the blanks of this day," Olitus said, glancing once again at the club on Thom's belt.

While the logs burned low and the warm light illuminated the dark corners of the cabin, Thom told of their experience in the woods. His words came slow and soft at first, but, as the Pago took effect, he became more animated. Sarafina watched the emotions skitter across her son's face, the worries and responsibilities of the day replaced by the novelty of all that had taken place. She had not given the boy enough Pago to muddle his mind, just enough to ease the tension under his skin. Olitus did not interject his questions, understanding there was much to be learned in a story uninterrupted. As Thom's last words dropped softly to the cabin floor, Olitus shifted in his chair.

"Did the dwarf give his name?"

"No," said Thom. "The only thing he said was something about a debt being repaid."

Thom recalled his mother's reaction when she saw the symbol smudged on Lili's forehead by the dwarf. Sarafina seemed lost in thought, staring into the dwindling fire and offering nothing. Olitus gave a small sigh and shifted his weight again. His hip was rather sore from hitting the ground.

"I suppose it is my turn," he said softly.

At the sound of his voice, Sarafina reached for Olitus. She knew her husband, and it did not take the Sense to hear the concern in his words. Squeezing her hand, Olitus began.

"As you know, the meeting of the heads of the clan took place two days ago. All were there with the exception of Liannan." He chose his next words carefully. "Her skills were needed elsewhere."

Thom had met Liannan, his grandmother, only once and once was enough. The only characteristic Sarafina had in common with her mother was her tall, thin frame. Liannan was a daughter of the north country, cold and distant, her white skin only a shade darker than her long, white hair. Her eyes, in contrast to Sarafina's green, were a blue the color of the deep ice of the northern lands she ruled over. Those eyes, once drawn to someone, could seep under their skin, distilling with frigid clarity a person's strengths and weaknesses. Thom gave a little shudder, remembering his introduction to Liannan and her piercing scrutiny of him. Thom had left that meeting feeling he had, somehow, let his grandmother down.

Sarafina, the youngest of Liannan's five children, was one of the dark children. With her long auburn hair and her olive complexion, Sarafina resembled more a member of one of the clans of the coastal regions than that of her birth clan. As was the custom of the clan of the north, those dark children were sent away, their coloring predetermining them to act as liaisons to the lower lands.

While her marriage with Olitus had not been a grand affair, their joining had been an important one. Both houses had a long history of natural leaders and competent healers. Their union had been no mistake, and Liannan had a hand in it, as she did most things.

The logs in the fire, finding a pocket of pitch, sparked and flared briefly. The radiant glow lit the room brightly, overtaking the shadows. Lili shifted on her pallet, one arm jerking the covers hard enough to expose her frail body. Mosely, nestled against Lili's hip, raised his head from his paws, then curled more tightly into a ball, tucking his tail around him. His eyes glowed in the dark. Olitus stood, his knees crackling almost as much as the logs in the fire, and crossed to the child, covering her again. When he sat back down, there was a heaviness to his appearance that weighted his words with the burden of worry.

"Everyone came with stories of change in their lands." Olitus gazed into the fire, recalling the meeting. He, himself, had brought news of the fruit withering on the vine and the barren crops of this season.

The light played across his features, etching lines deeply across his face. It startled Thom to see the weariness in his father. He had always seemed untouched and untouchable by time or anything else.

Olitus was the leader of their clan along the fertile coasts of Glennburrough. His father's father had sat at the Elder Table in the last of the Golden Days, before the disbursement of power, decades after the Great Battle. Thom was kind of vague on much of the history of Faltofar, but his ears always perked up when Master Blisk, their history professor, spoke of a time when the elder leaders maintained control and balance across the land. At recess time, Thom and the rest of the boys in his level would often play out the stories Master Blisk told in his lectures, creating teams of good and evil that battled passionately. They had all suffered their share of bruises as they re-enacted their land's history.

Before the Golden Days, the people of Faltofar lived in unease and uncertainty. Both sea and land were filled with dangerous predators and unimaginable curses. Thom's great-great- grandfather, Rendar, had fought for the good, those sworn to protect the well-being of Faltofar, and was said to have had powers strong enough to gather the ocean swells to sink a ship or smother beasts far inland. The jeweled dagger Olitus wore at his belt had belonged to Rendar, handed down from father to son. It would hang from Thom's belt one day. When the boys played out their history lessons, Thom always took the name of Rendar as his own. None of the other boys disputed his right.

Olitus took a deep breath. "There is a quaking in the Red Hills, and the capital of Purth has seen plumes of smoke rising across the drylands. Joleeth brought news of the river clan. Ill omens abound. Her people are seeing fish dying by the thousands and washing up along the shores of every major river. And," he paused, taking a sip of the Pago, eyeing Sarafina over the rim, "Liannan sent word of an avalanche that has buried one of the high villages. They did not know the losses yet."

Sarafina sat rigidly in her chair, taking in the news.

"I am sorry, Sara," Thom's father said, setting his drink down and reaching forward to grasp her hand.

Thom knew his mother missed the high country with its windswept beauty and snowy peaks. He had traveled there with her once, meeting Liannan on that trip. Lili and his father had not gone with them, and Thom had cherished spending time just with his mother. He had learned things about her, outside of her role as mother and healer. What Thom remembered most about the two weeks they traveled was how self-sufficient she had been. She had easily taken care of both of them in the wilderness, foraging for food, and killing only out of necessity. When they had encountered strangers, Sarafina was both kind and distant, clearly defining their independence, giving just enough information that others found her trustworthy, while, in turn, acknowledging her faith in their goodness. She had demonstrated to her son that there is a fine line with strangers. Perhaps especially for a woman traveling alone, save for a young boy.

Shifting out of his chair, Thom crossed to the far wall where his parents kept some of their most prized books on a shelf. Taking the club from his belt, he studied it a moment, then placed it reverently next to the stack. Something had been bothering Thom, and he broke the silent exchange between his parents with a question.

"What of Cleo, Father?"

Olitus squeezed Sarafina's hand and released it, settling back in his chair and rubbing his eyes. He was tired from the travel, the tussle with Thom in the yard, and the weight of his responsibilities.

Sarafina rose and gathered up the cups but paused long enough in the doorway of the kitchen to hear her husband's response.

"I sent her north, along the coast," he said, taking his hand away from his eyes. "There has been word of a purple tide moving down from Belethel."

The coastal town he referred to was the main port for the whole coastal region. Purple tides meant death for sea life and the birds who fed from the sea and shore.

"I expect her back within a fortnight with news."

Thom had never seen his father without the vibrant parrot Cleolina, his constant companion and confidant, at his side. She and Mosely had always had a subtle truce about their domain, avoiding sills or shelves, fence posts, or rooftop, where the other was perched. They were both attentive to the humans in a way Thom had always taken for granted. Not having Cleo fluttering around his father was unsettling for Thom, bringing back the nagging anxiousness he had felt since arriving home with Torr and Lili. Sarafina returned to the room and moved to the hearth. Picking up a piece of kindling, she snapped the wood, almost violently, in two and threw the pieces on the fire in a movement that revealed her troubled thoughts.

"We have had enough for one night," she said softly, but with finality. "There are things your father and I should talk about, but you need your rest, Thom."

She nodded at Olitus. "We all need some rest."

With that, Olitus rose, signaling his agreement. Father and son hugged briefly.

"I would like to make a pallet next to Lili's for tonight, Mother, if that is okay."

Sarafina smiled, nodding her agreement. She hesitated at the edge of the room, her concern for her children at odds with her desire to be with her mate and hear what he had not spoken in front of the boy.

"Call me if there is a change in her, Thom," she said.

He looked at Lili, nodding distractedly, as he watched his sister's face contort for a moment, lost in some bad dream. With his parent's departure from the room, Thom suddenly felt very much alone. The walls of the cabin clicked and popped like the joints of an old man. He listened to the familiar sounds, grasping at anything that might help him feel his world had not shifted on its edge. It didn't work. Moving to the shelves where the extra bedding was stored, he pulled down a pillow and thick quilt. By the last of the firelight, he worked in silence to make a bed near his sister. He resisted the urge to look at the club on the higher shelf.

———

Much later, Thom lay quietly on his pallet, listening to the sounds of the night. Sleep eluded him. Behind his closed lids, he revisited time and again the long, eventful day, trying to make sense of everything that had taken place. The Sepherii in the forest, the dwarf and his strange words, the worry for his new friend Torr, and fear for his ailing sister. He traveled the country in his mind, trying to visualize the dying fish, fissures erupting as they were said to have done in the old days across the desert lands, a purple tide oozing down the coast. Master Blisk had recounted a world like that in Faltofar's past. But that was the past, when . . . Thom stopped himself, sinking deeper into his bedding. His mind was finally falling into much-needed oblivion.

"I will think about the whys tomorrow," he promised himself.

The last thing Thom remembered as he drifted off to sleep was the feel of his mother's hand on his hair. The memory of her touch eased the last of his worries, if only for the night.

———

"The land is as bad off as the stories we have been hearing, Sara."

Olitus lay on their bed, his hands behind his head, staring up at the beams. Sarafina nestled in next to him, resting against his shoulder, her hand on his chest, feeling the reassuring beat of his heart.

"Each clan leader spoke of turmoil. Losses of crops, lack of wild game. Streams running dry. There is disease spreading across our lands."

Olitus brought his arm down around her. "There is more," he said finally. "When word came from Liannan, it was read to the clan leaders as a whole, but the Messenger handed me a private missive from her. She is requesting that the dark children gather."

Sarafina made no response in the darkness, but Olitus knew she had heard everything he had said.

7

BROKEN BRITCHES

"It amazes me you can take care of yourself from one day to the next, let alone be out in the forest by yourself," said the small dwarf without stopping the movement of her needle's mending. Her nimble fingers slid the metal through the soft leather of the pants. The thimble, made of hammered copper, glinted on the tip of her finger.

"You go pridin' yourself on being responsible and a mentor to the younguns, but here you come, stridin' into town, all rumpled, like you'd been dragged behind some ostrick bird." She tossed a curl back from her forehead and continued stitching. "If I knew better, I'd say . . ."

Her words were interrupted by the dwarf standing in his underwear in front of her.

"Enough, woman," Berold snapped. "It's enough that I'm standing here in me skivs having to listen to you go on."

She knew that was not what was bothering her husband. He'd been grumbling about the loss of his club since he'd come back. She hadn't asked where it had gone, and he hadn't offered to tell her. From the looks of his clothes, whoever had it would be sorry the next time they met.

Tilga stood, and with a smug smile, handed her husband his fully repaired pants. She watched him as he hopped from one foot to the other, awkwardly pulling the dusty pants up muscular legs that resembled the trunk of the old Holy Oak tree in the yard. Perhaps not quite as thick and strong as the tree gifted to him for his history in battle, but he was, after all, only one piece of Faltofar's history and not the oldest and most revered tree in the land.

"Not bad for an old guy," she thought to herself and resisted the temptation to nudge him over while he wobbled there, half-dressed.

Tilga had a wicked sense of humor about most things. Berold did too; he just had a hard time showing it, especially if it was about him.

With a final snap of his suspenders and a glance in the mirror at the door, Berold stomped down the front steps of their home. He blinked as he emerged into the daylight, taking inventory of the busy road in front of him. Deep in the folds of the forest, the dwarf village nestled against rock cliffs, each home skillfully camouflaged by rock and vine, simple in their construction. The love the dwarves felt for the ornate was reserved for their metalwork.

Tilga gathered her basket and shawl and followed swiftly behind. Not long after he'd come home, Berold had called for a meeting at the well. The shift of men and boys at the mine would not be there. But, those men not working underground, as well as the women, olders, and the children, gathered quietly. Tilga's basket swung from her arm. She planned to head for the community garden after Berold said what he had to say. Her store of dried herbs was running low, and the stew on the fire needed carrots.

A handful of children were chasing a small doggin at the edge of the crowd, but when Berold tapped the iron bell that hung near the well basket, the children's parents quickly ushered them to their sides. The doggin gave a few muffled barks before settling down, its tail slowly wagging in the dirt. Berold puffed up his chest and spoke.

"I saw a Sepherii in the forest today," he stated.

Several of the women cried out, and a small child clapped its tiny hands together before being quickly stopped by an older.

"There's more," he went on. "There's signs of the darkness comin'. The Sepherii wouldn't be here unless delivered by the oath, but we need to know what part of that oath is callin' those human hoofers here."

He panned the faces around him and received nods of encouragement. Several of the dwarf men snapped their suspenders in nervous energy, shuffling their feet and grumbling under their breath.

"It's an epidemic of mumbling fools," Tilga thought to herself.

Although she was impressed with Berold's news of the Sepherii, Tilga hadn't seen any signs of darkness. Of course, she hadn't been digging around for it either, and she hadn't left their village in a very long time. There didn't seem to be much need, what with all the idiotic humans taking over the land. She corrected herself. Not all humans were idiots, just most.

"I'm askin' five of our strongest to travel with me to the outskirts," Berold said, holding up one hand with five stubby fingers splayed for emphasis. "We need to find out what's comin'."

The villagers kept their eyes turned in any direction except toward each other, their rounded, bulbous faces masked, not wanting to make a choice that would take them away from their homes, the mine, and their precious metalwork. The doggin gave a small woof, and Tilga coughed into her hand to avoid acknowledging the storm cloud brewing on her husband's face.

"By the Gods of the Metal Earth, I am surrounded by weaklings and snivelers!" bellowed Berold. "You're all no good to be called dwarves." He reached for his club, ready to swing it in the air as emphasis, but grabbed at nothing. He gritted his teeth and slammed his fist down on the edge of the well. "Is it that I'm to stand alone?"

The crowd shuffled from side to side. Several of the young girls giggled in their nervousness, as the boys poked at each other to get one to step forward. No one seemed to take Berold seriously. Tilga understood more about the villager's reaction than her husband. They saw him as an old fool, lost without his son, forever mumbling that the "Ends of the Days" would gather about them. His pronouncement today just added to his image. He had been their leader, but those days were long gone. Without threat, who needed to tell any of them what to do? The metalwork was their nature. The village was organized and nicely maintained, the community garden efficient and producing, the children well behaved. Let the old man head back out on his own.

A movement at the back of the group created a ripple in the crowd. An older boy, larger than those around him, stepped forward, his gait ungainly, even for a dwarf. He slouched, masking his height in the burden of his mixed bloodline. The crowd moved aside, many of them looking away. Dundar was a half-blood, part dwarf and part human. And, Dundar was a mute. His mother lived on the outskirts of the village, her small home tucked deeply into the rocks bordering the old mine. She rarely ventured out, counting on Dundar to bring her roots and berries from the forest. There were those in the village who whispered that Dundar paid the price of silence for the actions of his parents. The gods of the dwarves were not known for their kindness.

Berold's face was unreadable as the younger dwarf moved through the crowd. Only after Dundar stood directly in front of him, leaning slightly on his long spear, did Berold clear his throat to speak.

"Um. Ah."

Rather than address Dundar, Berold's eyes swept the crowd for any other takers. His glare moved passed the yellow curls of his wife's head, then back. Tilga gave him a nod of encouragement. She had put her basket down and stood with her hands on her round hips. Berold stood taller, his lips puckering, his mouth a small volcano about to erupt over the crowd.

"Dundar has come forward, and Dundar will travel with me to the outskirts!" sputtered Berold. "Unless someone steps forward now. Well?"

The only sound from the crowd was the soft snuffling of one of the tiny children whose rheumy eyes and red nose advertised an uncomfortable summer cold.

"He is worth fifty of you snivelers." Berold jutted his chin forward, his eyes narrowing at the dwarf in front of him.

"We leave in two days, boy," he announced, addressing him for the first time. "Say your goodbyes to your ma and pack lightly. I will meet you here at the well, same time."

The boy didn't respond, and Berold wondered if he was deaf too. He leaned closer, looking up at the lad and yelled for emphasis. "Two days hence, this same time!"

Unfolding his long frame from its customary slouch, Dundar locked eyes with Berold. The intensity, and the intelligence he saw there, startled Berold.

"The halfling hides behind his shell," thought the old dwarf with grudging admiration.

Dundar blinked twice, the moment passing, his eyes sliding down to the ground once again. As he tipped his spear toward Berold in a sign of loyalty, the others stood by, and for the first time that afternoon, no one shuffled or made a sound. Then he moved off through the parted crowd, his gait slow, his eyes downcast, and his shoulders slumped over. Berold frowned at his departing back. With a final nod at Tilga, he cracked his knuckles and stomped off in the other direction toward their home, forgetting almost immediately the change he had briefly seen in the younger dwarf.

Tilga grabbed her basket in one hand, her skirts in the other and skittered after him, her shawl dragging in the dirt behind her. The herbs could wait. She needed to speak her mind to her husband.

8

ASLEEP OR AWAKE?

L ili lay back on her improvised bed, watching the dust motes shimmer in the light from the front window. Sensing an opportunity for attention, Mosely rubbed his face against her hand and idly she scratched behind his ear, her thoughts directed inward. She had woken at first light, shaking off the dream state that had left her bedding soaked with sweat. Thom lay on a pallet beside hers, sleeping peacefully. It comforted her that her brother had been by her side throughout the night. She could not remember much after the rainstorm from the day before. She desperately wanted to ask Thom but didn't wake him.

She shifted her weight on the pallet. Her leg ached, the bandage and the poultice heavy against her skin – her mother's handiwork healing an injury she couldn't recall sustaining. Did she fall in the woods? Her whole body was sore as if she had run a race that required hurdling immense obstacles.

Her hand drifted from the cat to the soft hairs at the nape of her neck, damp with sweat from her dreams. Impatiently, Mosely put a paw on her hip, and she obliged him again with a scratch under his chin as she settled back on her pillow, reliving the murky, dark world she'd traveled in her fevered mind during the night. In the soft half-light of early morning, she concentrated on the creaking of the house and the contented purring of her cat, using these familiar, comforting sounds to anchor her back into a world before her nightmare.

"Home."

The single word, uttered softly, held new meaning for her. Her mother's harvested herbs hung from the drying rack by the fire. In the corner was her father's favorite chair, where he sat most evenings with Cleo perched on one edge. Mosely and Thom liked to curl up on the couch along the far wall. She and Thom had entertained themselves many nights sitting there looking at her father's book with all the pictures of Faltofar's past.

Lili sat up so quickly, Mosely jumped away from her hand. Her heart hammered in her chest.

"Torr." Her friend. Was he real? Was any of it real?

She reached out with her mind, trying to feel his presence and was startled at how easily she could sense the Sepherii. Torr greeted her warmly.

"Little one. You are awake."

She could 'hear' happiness in his word thoughts. She knew a wall separated them, but reached up for the window, willing him to appear. Memories from the day before cascaded through her mind.

"Torr! Are you okay? Your leg, is it healed? Did you meet my mother?"

"Yes, yes, child." What felt like laughter filtered into her mind. "I am better, but not yet whole."

Excitedly, Lili propped herself up, forgetting her injury. The pain in her leg brought a cry to her lips and sent her quickly falling back against her pillows. Awakened by his sister's voice, Thom scrambled out of his blankets, fumbling for the slingshot at his waist.

"Oh, Thom." The ache of her injury could not stop Lili from laughing at her brother's awkward, half-awake effort to protect her. "I'm so sorry." Sheepishly, she nodded toward the window. "I just wanted a glimpse of him."

Thom stood there, blinking the sleep from his eyes, then knelt and hugged his sister in relief.

"Gads, Lili," he said, "it's good to hear you laugh. Even if I am the reason."

Lili hugged him back.

"Thom, help me up. I want to see Torr."

Despite the urgency in Lili's voice, Thom hesitated, noting her paleness and the dark circles under her eyes.

"Just to the window, please," she begged.

The Sepherii was nowhere in sight, but she could feel his presence, which eased her mind and her memory of the bleached bones in the dream yard. She held herself up to the sill and scanned the yard and close-in pasture. After a bit, even though she had yet to lay eyes on Torr, she allowed Thom to help her back to the pallet. Settling her into her bedding, Thom grabbed his coat, wrapping it tightly around himself against the brisk morning air, his worry over the Sepherii making his movements almost awkward.

"Promise we can talk when you get done, Thom?"

She lowered herself gingerly into her blankets. Her brother nodded at her and closed the front door. Lilianna swallowed a tiny bit of envy, alone again with her dark thoughts.

"Ah, Mosely," she said, laying back and idly scratching under the cat's chin, her forehead creased in worry. "I have to believe it was just a dream." The loud purring emanating from the cat soothed her, and the nightmare's dark, scary world began to fade.

Thom moved across the yard to the grouse coop, pulling his collar tighter under his chin. The day had broken cold and clear. Summer was not yet fully upon them, and the morning still carried over the chill of the night. The birds fluttered around their enclosure, cooing a welcome to Thom as he ran his hand through the sack of grain. Finding the cup, he scooped it to a brimful and scattered the seed through the woven reeds of the enclosure. With his other hand, he pulled a piece of toast from the pocket of his jacket, having saved it from the previous night's small meal. Nibbling on its edges and deep in thought, he barely heard the birds pecking away at their breakfast.

Glancing out to the field, Thom counted half-a-dozen head of cattle grazing contentedly. He was about to look away when he noticed what he saw resembled big stalks of grass swaying in the nonexistent breeze in the far pasture. He narrowed his eyes and brought the sight to himself. Then he began to laugh. A real laugh from the gut that carried away the worries of the past 24 hours. Torr was rolling, obviously enjoying a good back-scratching. Unaware of his audience, the Sepherii shifted to his side and gathered his legs under himself, standing in one muscular lunge and stretching his arms to the sky.

"He really is magnificent," Thom thought to himself.

Torr's head swung around. Anyone else would not have seen the Sepherii from such a distance and in such detail, but Thom's sight brought him within inches of the startling blue eyes of the colossal creature.

"Ah, Thom. Just the human I wanted to talk to." Torr's voice echoed inside Thom's head. He would have to get used to that.

Thom waited at the fence, watching the Sepherii make his way past the cows, which he disdainfully ignored. Torr walked with a slight limp, but his coat shown in the sun, and his eyes were clear. Stopping at the fence, the Sepherii tilted his head slightly, crossing his arms over his chest.

"I listened to your father speak of the ills of Faltofar last night," he said, swishing his tail. "I did not pay attention to who you were, Thomlin, son of Olitus, until we came to your home."

Torr stood quietly for a moment, and Thom was about to speak when the Sepherii continued.

"I have been like the cattle, there in the pasture," Torr said as he swept his arm wide, motioning toward the field. "Dumb animals. Without thought or direction. I have been asleep."

Thom waited, but the Sepherii seemed lost in his own thoughts. Thom studied the cows pulling up grass, their jaws moving incessantly. How was it that some of the animals of his home had intelligence and some meandered aimlessly through their lives? He thought of some of the boys he knew at school. His friends laughingly called them slouchies. Kids who didn't care much about anything, just wandering through their days, dull-eyed. Thom wanted to believe they were just 'asleep' as Torr had said of himself. Slouchie or no, the time had come for all of them to wake up. Torr's voice reverberated in his head bringing him back to the present.

"We have work to do, young Finn. I will stay here at the healer's home. I will stay here not because I must, but because powers move us together and apart. Together is better."

The Sepherii's cryptic speech was cut short by the voice of Thom's mother calling her son to breakfast. Thom ignored her, not out of disrespect, but out of his desire to understand his unique new friend. Impulsively, the boy reached across the fence, touching the Sepherii's side for just a moment. He needed to assure himself Torr was not merely a figment of his imagination. The Sepherii stood quietly. Sarafina's voice carried across the yard again, and Thom started toward the cabin. Halfway across the yard, the Sepherii's voice broke into his thoughts.

"When you come out again, Thomlin, bring your slingshot."

Sarafina had risen early and found her children sleeping soundly on their pallets, their shoulders touching. She had knelt, kissing them both on the forehead, but lingered over Lili to feel for a temperature. There had been none.

"Your fever is gone, child. Perhaps the worst of this wound is behind you." She had a habit of speaking softly to herself when diagnosing any of her patients. Sarafina combed her fingers through Lilianna's red hair. Wisps escaped from her pigtails, and there were still small bits of grass from the forest floor matted in the braids. "Let's get a good breakfast in us and see what this day has in store."

Sarafina moved off to her kitchen, determined to feed her family a meal that would sustain them through whatever the day would bring. She poked her head around the doorway a bit later when she heard the children, but saw that Thom was caring for his sister, helping her to the window. With a meal to cook, Sarafina decided to leave them alone, barely glancing up when she heard the slam of the front door a few minutes later.

With nothing to do but work on her patience, Lili shifted uncomfortably around on her pallet. Disgruntledly, Mosely eyed her, quite content to spend the day curled up on the blankets. Realizing that was not going to be an option, he stood and stretched, stepping delicately off the quilts and into a patch of sunshine. A fly buzzing past his head caught his attention, and he twisted, lightning-fast, to swat at the unaware insect. Lili smiled, amazed at the cat's speed. With the bug trapped helplessly under his pad, Mosely's tail, an indicator of his moods, swished happily back and forth in the air. Slowly he lifted his paw and let the fly buzz away.

"If I didn't know better, Mosely," she said with a laugh, "I'd say you were showing off."

Stretching again, Mosely yawned widely, showing rows of sharp yellow teeth. Then, tail high, his whiskered face a reflection of cat smugness, he sauntered off to his own breakfast just as Thom came bounding in the door.

"Lil, it's going to be a glorious day! We have to get you outside, if Mother agrees."

Thom's mood was contagious, and Lili shifted on her pallet, ready to rise.

"Not so fast, my girl," her father said, coming in from the back porch.

"Father!"

Lili hadn't realized her father was back, and she smiled up at him, happy to know her whole family was reunited. Olitus beamed down at his youngest child, noting the color returning to her cheeks. He knelt and hugged her small frame carefully, appreciating the scent of youth and summer.

"You seem far stronger than last night," he said, gently tousling her messy hair. "I expected a better greeting from you when I got home."

His eyes crinkled in kindness. Lili grinned at his attempt to tease her.

"Let your mother tend to you before you take on the world," her father said, rising. He and Thom headed into the kitchen, where smells of breakfast wafted out to Lili. Her stomach rumbled, reminding her she hadn't eaten since yesterday.

Soon enough, all three of her family returned to the living area, closely followed by Mosely, with plates of steaming food: grouse eggs and dumplings with gravy, one of Lili's favorite dishes. She was grateful they did not ask about her leg. It ached dully under the blanket, but she did her best to ignore it, focusing on her meal. It wouldn't do to complain. Sarafina would take that as a reason for her to stay indoors. That was the last thing Lili wanted to do.

Mosely wandered from plate to plate in the hopes that someone would spill a drop of gravy. Sarafina narrowed her eyes at him as she set her plate down, but he pointedly ignored her.

"Before you and Thom make any plans for today, I think we need to take a look at your leg. If it is healing, as I suspect by your coloring," she ran a finger along her daughter's flushed cheek, "you can spend some time outside. But with care, Lilianna." The edge in her voice made it clear this was not a suggestion.

Olitus had taken the plates to the kitchen, and Sarafina moved the chair he'd been sitting in toward the light from the window, helping Lili up and into it. Thom nudged Mosely off the stool nearby and carried it over so Lili could rest her injured leg on the cushion.

"You gave us a scare last night, daughter," Sarafina said, lifting Lili's foot to unwind the last of the blanket still wrapped snuggly around her.

Mosely had positioned himself under the stool, the breakfast plates forgotten. He began to growl softly. Sarafina eyed him quizzically, attuned to the cat's version of the Sense. She adjusted her attention back to her child, unwinding the bandage carefully. Even so, Lili winced slightly. Abruptly, Sarafina stopped.

"Lilianna, did you get up in the night?" she asked hesitantly.

The girl's face mirrored her mother's confusion. Tentatively,

Sarafina reached out her hand beneath the stool, a frown creasing her features. Readjusting her weight in the chair, Lili craned her neck to see what her mother and brother were so fixated on. Mosely had moved forward, his nose twitching, the fur on his back high. Olitus stood frozen in the kitchen doorway.

"That's not possible," Lili whispered, beginning to shake.

A thin, oozing layer of mud dripped from the underside of the blanket, and as they all gaped, several small, brittle bones fell from the folds of the blanket, landing with a hollow clatter in the dirty puddle beneath the stool. With a low hiss, Mosely inched forward, but Sarafina's hand stopped him. Gently she nudged the cat away, her other hand fumbling to open the pouch she always carried at her waist. One by one, she picked up the bones, dropping them into the soft leather container, then pulled the strings tightly, closing the mouth of the pouch. Studying her youngest, Sarafina watched as the girl seemed to curl tightly in a ball, her arms wrapping around her stomach tightly.

"Lilianna, please, can you explain these to me? To us?"

Lili closed her eyes, her stomach a knot of anxiety. Her words stayed tightly bundled in her throat. What could she say?

9

HERBS

T ilga was spitting mad.

"Well, and why did ya not tell me of the children?" she demanded, slamming another pot down on the counter. "And the Healer's children, at that!"

Berold, sitting by the hearth, glanced up at the pot of simmering stew Tilga had been stirring moments before. She'd stomped back to the kitchen without a sideways glance. He hunched his shoulders and continued sharpening the blade in his hand. He had a feeling he wouldn't be eating his dinner anytime soon. Tilga's anger was worse than a blizzard in the darkest months of winter.

"The Healer's children!" she said again, pointing her ladle at her husband's back for emphasis.

Berold opened his mouth to speak, but Tilga wasn't finished.

"I don't like it. Those children have been a wanderin' these woods far too long, closer and closer to us, and now, here you go, gettin' yourself into a fight with the boy-man."

Whipping the hand holding the ladle up to her forehead, she tucked a stray curl back, splattering soup onto her ample bosom. She was too distracted to notice.

Berold stood up from the fire, his jaw set, his mouth tightly closed, glaring at his bride. He knew he would not get a word in when she was this angry, but he was done listening. Reaching for his sharpening tools, he brushed past Tilga and stomped out the kitchen doorway. Moments later, she could hear the swing of the ax as it connected with wood.

"He's always choppin' at that wood when he's heated," she thought to herself, wiping down the counter in furious strokes. Abruptly she stopped, an idea forming in her mind. Leaving the towel on the counter, she quickly gathered her shawl and basket and headed for the front door.

"There's more than one way to skin a dogger," she said under her breath. Around the corner of the house, the sound of chopping had been replaced by the soft swish of the shaping tools Berold used for carving. And, for making weapons.

"That'll keep him busy a bit." She closed the door quietly behind her and scurried down the road.

An hour later, coming back inside, Berold found the stew burning on the fire and moved it aside. The house was quiet. If he had to choose between blackened stew and a little peace, he didn't care that his dinner was ruined. Setting the newly made club on the ground, he pulled his favorite chair closer to the fire, gently lowering himself and leaning back into the cushion. Putting his feet up on the stool, a sigh escaped his lips as he closed his eyes and settled into the solitude. Just before he slipped into a dreamless sleep, he wondered briefly where the she-devil had taken herself. Soon his soft snores drifted into the quiet room.

———

Tilga hurried through the village, waving off invitations from some of the women to come and sit. A ball crossed her path, and she kicked it back toward the boys playing in the late afternoon sunshine. Normally she would have stopped to visit with the children and speak to her friends, but she was preoccupied with her destination.

"Desperate times require determined action." She pulled her

shawl tighter around her as she passed the last of the main houses. It had been a long while since she had come this way.

The far side of the village was quiet, populated mostly by abandoned smaller cottages. The forest had even begun to take back some of the structures. Tilga stopped in front of a weathered gate. This house sat alone, distanced from the next nearest home by a thick collection of blackberry bushes and twining sweet peas that buzzed with honeybees. Summer in this corner of the village was in full bloom already. Lifting the latch, she entered the well-maintained yard, noting that while the wood appeared past its prime, the hinges made no complaint when she opened the gate. Stepping up to the porch, she took a deep breath, thumping her knuckles purposefully on the old wooden door. She waited. And she waited. She was about to turn away, almost relieved, when the door opened just wide enough for an eye to peer out at her. With pursed lips and a defiant wiggle of her nose, Tilga stifled the urge to step back, focusing on why she was there. Her words came out quickly, fueled by her resolve.

"I've come to talk."

The moment the words came out of her mouth, she wanted to kick herself. Obviously, she'd come to talk; it was just that this she-dwarf made her nervous, what with her reputation. The eye didn't move, and Tilga, taking another deep, bolstering breath, determined to try again.

"It's about your son. He's volunteered for somethin' he shouldn't of, and I think . . ." Her words trailed off as the door swung open to reveal a small dwarf in an apron and headscarf of vibrant colors. Tilga had not seen Dundalee for years, but she was astonished that the woman didn't seem a day older. "And here, all by herself," she thought.

Dundalee stepped back away from the door, nodding for Tilga to enter. The door swung wider, and as Tilga entered the small house, she found herself enthralled with the beauty with which the woman surrounded herself. Herbs hung in an orderly manner from a drying rack in her little kitchen. Two chairs, a colorful lap blanket hanging over the back of one, were pulled close to a cozy fire that crackled in the hearth. An intricate vase of hammered metal sat on a sideboard, overflowing with flowers from the garden outside. Beautiful hammered metal pieces hung from the walls, and the kitchen area gleamed with utensils made by what Tilga could only describe as a talented craftsman. Some of the best work she had ever seen.

Motioning Tilga to one of the chairs, Dundalee went to her kitchen at the far side of the room. Tilga tried not to stare around her, knowing to do so was rather rude. She busied herself instead with taking off her shawl, noticing the splatter of stew on her chest for the first time. Dundalee came from the kitchen with a tray filled with a teapot, cups and saucers, and a jar of what Tilga could only guess was honey. There was also a small, damp rag on the tray, and as Dundalee set the tray on the table between them, she handed it to Tilga, nodding at her chest. Embarrassed, but also appreciative, Tilga quickly wiped the spots away. Dundalee sat in the other chair, her hands folded delicately in her lap. Tilga looked up from her now semi-clean bosom and chided herself.

"There's nothing threatenin' to her at all." Tilga wiggled her bottom more comfortably in her chair, preparing for a good talk and warm cup of tea. "I've come here to speak o' your son," Tilga began again, more relaxed.

Dundalee leaned forward, taking the teapot and filling each cup with amber liquid. Tilga bit her lip, impressed by how delicately the other woman poured the tea. Small bits of tea leaves spun in each of the finely crafted, delicate clay cups, distracting Tilga, their move-ment mesmerizing. They swirled and sank and rose again. She forgot for a moment about why she had come, then shook her head to clear it. Damn the woman!

"Don't try your magic on me, Dundalee!" she bristled, throwing the rag to the floor, where it arched up, assuming the shape of a snap-ping mouth, and nipped at Tilga's ankles.

"I've got some of the ways in me, too," she blustered, jerking her feet away from the rag.

The rag was a parlor trick, and they both knew it. Tilga glared from Dundalee to the rag as it dropped limply to the floor. Dundalee's powers were renowned, and Tilga was insulted. Dundalee, who had still not uttered a word, blinked once at the now lifeless rag and returned to her task of pouring, smiling for the first time. When she spoke, her voice cracked slightly. She hadn't put voice to thought in a long time.

"Forgive me if I sound hoarse," she said softly, ignoring Tilga's outburst. "There is little use of words in this home."

She flicked her fingers toward the rag, which had begun to growl softly. It inched away across the floor in the direction of the kitchen.

Tilga pursed her lips, slightly irritated the woman had not apologized for the grumpy, dirty rag, but refrained from saying anything more. She had come here for a purpose, and it would serve her none if she annoyed her hostess, magic or no. Dundalee offered the jar of honey, and Tilga, who had a sweet tooth, consoled herself with a gooey daub of the thick liquid. The leaves settled to the bottom of her cup as she set down the spoon she'd used to stir the honey. With an effort, she looked away. They sipped in silence, both of them gazing into the fire. When Dundalee spoke again, her eyes drifted lazily with the sparks from the logs.

"I know why you have come." The tea had cleared the woman's throat. Her voice had a melodic lilt to it, but when she spoke, the words came out stilted. She continued. "Perhaps my son is unwise, taking up a fool's errand, but I think not."

Dundalee set her cup down and stood up. Tilga sat back quickly in her chair, afraid the woman would touch her, but Dundalee merely moved to the fire and placed a small log on the dwindling coals. Tilga only knew bits and pieces of Dundalee's story. Gossip in the village mostly. There were rumors of dark magic and travel to foreign places, and of course, Dundalee's half-breed boy.

She sipped her tea to calm her nerves. She had to think quickly. Tilga was determined to convince the woman there was no good in her son leaving the safety of their village, no good in muddling up the world of the humans. And certainly no good in dabbling in the magic. She wanted to kick Berold.

"Do not be angry with your husband for what he believes," Dundalee said. "He has seen firsthand the changes in our world."

Dundalee's voice had become stronger. Tilga wondered if the dwarf woman in front of her had read her mind. She took a deep breath to calm her suddenly racing heart, realizing her mission to change her husband's plans was not going to be as easy as she had thought. She could feel the heat in her face, her cheeks flushed, but her pulse slowed with her determination to make the woman understand. She set her cup down, pointedly avoiding the draw of the leaves floating in the bottom, and tried again.

"Your son, Dundar, has he ever left this village?" she asked, her new tack based on her belief that a protective mother would never place her child at risk. She, herself, had only left the village once, out of necessity. That had been for a son, too.

In response, Dundalee sat back down, picking up her cup and smiling over the rim. The smile grated on Tilga's nerves. Now she wanted to kick her. They both were quiet for a bit, Dundalee contentedly sipping while Tilga tried not to fidget, her hands clasped firmly together in her lap.

"It's like we's playing a game of Chookers, and no one's informed me of the rules," Tilga thought. She fought the urge to fuss a curl back, noting how peacefully Dundalee sat.

Dundalee took another sip from her tea then gently set her cup down next to Tilga's and gracefully stood. Tilga eyed her warily. Dundalee had moved to the drying herbs, plucking a sprig off one that Tilga did not recognize. She moved back to the fire and tossed the twig into the flames where it caught and briefly flared white-hot. A thin line of smoke drifted up from the pile of ash made by the burnt herb, curling up toward the ceiling. A sweet scent permeated the room as Dundalee sat back down, adjusting her chair to face Tilga and the small table set with the tea items. In the silence that followed, Tilga could hear chimes on the back porch of the house. Distractedly, she wondered why the woman had chimes. They were a human thing. Humans did not understand that to make noise in the forest was dangerous. Sound in the forest could draw unwanted attention to yourself.

"Just another thing not to trust about this woman," she thought, withstanding the urge to wave the smoke away from her face. Tilga couldn't remember what the other things were that she shouldn't trust, but she had heard things. Oh, had she heard things. The boy, for example. And where was he? Tilga pursed her lips in irritation, refusing to squirm in her seat. She narrowed her eyes at her hostess, not sure what to expect next.

Dundalee smiled at Tilga, leaned forward and motioned her guest to do the same. Tilga cautiously obliged the other woman, thinking she was about to hear something whispered privately. Instead, Dundalee's hand shot out with a pair of scissors. Before Tilga could do more than suck in her breath, Dundalee had snipped off one of Tilga's curls and thrown it into the fire, where it landed on top of the ashes of the herb. The acrid smell of burnt dwarf hair now wafted out of the fireplace.

"Piddle damn!" Tilga thought, grabbing her shawl and wrapping it around her angrily. She stood, ready to move to the door. Dundalee quietly stood also, reaching for Tilga, who jerked away.

"Forgive me Tilga, but it was a necessary . . . ingredient. Please, do sit back down." Her eyes radiated a sincerity that belied her actions. "Let us see what the wind brings in our futures."

As she spoke, a shuttered window by the back door banged open, and the sound of the chimes clattered into the room, drawn to the smoke, which coiled around their heads and in the exposed rafters.

Tilga, bolstered more by her anger now than any fear, pinched off a retort.

"I'll leave if I darn well want," she thought, even as she sat back down. The woman's audacity amazed her, but she couldn't stop herself from being cautiously curious. It had been a long time since she had been around true magic.

Dundalee nodded, sitting back down as well. They both leaned over the teacups where the tea leaves had settled to the bottom of each cup. She began to softly mumble as she swayed back and forth in her seat. Tilga found herself holding her breath, and not just from the smell from the fire. She forced herself to relax, trying to hear what the other woman said. Her words were neither dwarfish nor human, but some ancient language Tilga didn't recognize. She fought the growing urge to scurry for the door, knowing that to do so would break the magic, and make her seem like a sniveler.

Dundalee's headscarf shimmered in the smoky room as she rocked. The chimes grew louder to the point of distraction, and Tilga wondered briefly if a storm was coming. Abruptly, her hostess stopped moving and slumped back in her chair, her eyes shut. The chimes gave one last metallic clatter, then stilled, and the smoke drifted to the floor, disappearing as it touched the worn wood. Tilga leaned back, waiting. With the other woman's eyes closed, she was free to take in Dundalee's features and couldn't help but think she was quite a striking dwarf.

Dundalee opened her eyes, and Tilga felt a moment of embarrassment for being caught staring. "I'd be a sniveler to look away now though," she thought. When Dundalee spoke, her voice crackled from a deep weariness, a frown crossing her face for the first time, her words stilted.

"You will find your answer in the forest, Tilga, on the first day of the new moon, in the bones at the foot of the supreme Holy Oak. But it will be days from now and they will be gone. Your man and my child. Let them go." And with that, Dundalee closed her eyes, leaning back in her chair, her head resting against the blanket draped there.

Tilga waited a moment, expecting more. She wondered if Dundalee had fallen asleep but didn't dare touch the woman. Tilga was brave, but not that brave. She decided it was time to leave. Wrapping her shawl around her, she moved to the door. As she grasped the door handle, Dundalee's voice, once again, cracking with disuse or strain, stopped her.

"Do not forget your things," she said, not opening her eyes.

Tilga was halfway home before she glanced down at her basket. A cloth of brilliant colors lay in it, and when Tilga reached in to touch the beautifully woven material, she found beneath it the vegetables and herbs she had wanted earlier in the day. Grasping the basket tighter, she hiked her skirt up and hurried her step to the comfort of her hearth, the wind twining leaves around her feet. Thunder boomed in the distance. A storm was definitely brewing.

10

NEW SKILLS

Lilianna sat in the warm sunshine of the yard watching Thom and Torr work together in the field beyond the grouse coop. Their endless practicing over the last week had finally paid off, although her brother bore scratches and bruises from his efforts. She had seen him tumble in the dirt alongside the Sepherii so many times she couldn't tell if his darker skin was from the summer sunshine or layers of earth. Thom could now keep up, running next to Torr, in what seemed almost like a dance to Lili.

"Running at Torr's slowest," she corrected herself.

She admired Thom's grace as he pulled himself onto the Sepherii's back with such ease, but she couldn't help but yell teasingly at him.

"Show off!" Her words were laced with pride.

"Wahhhhhooooo!"

A flock of Yellow Warbils in the field adjacent to where they had been practicing took flight, startled by the boyish cry. Lili barely glanced at the birds, assessing Torr for any sign of a limp. His leg had healed more quickly than hers. The pair arced a circle in the field, bringing them a bit closer to her. Clumps of dirt and grass flew from beneath the Sepherii's hooves.

"They make it look so effortless." She chided herself for the little flame of jealousy she felt.

They circled once more toward the main yard, Torr's hooves pounding the earth. Close enough now, she saw Thom's jaw set in determination as he realized what Torr intended.

"The Sepherii has a sense of humor," Lili thought, hearing Torr's laughter in her mind. He was about to enjoy terrorizing her brother. Torr bunched his muscles and leaped over the fence, bounding to a halt several feet away from the girl. Thom's face relaxed in the relief of staying mounted.

"Ah! well done, Thom!" Lili looked up at Torr, turning her head just enough so her brother could not see her face. She winked at the Sepherii. Her leg may not have healed yet, but her sense of fun was untouched. She laughed when he, uncharacteristically, winked back.

Thom swung his leg over the broad back and landed by her chair, a grin on his face.

"Gads, Lil!" Thom said breathlessly. "That was about the most fun I've ever had!"

Lili, careful of her injured leg, stood slightly wobbly and smiled at both of them.

"Could I ride for a bit, Torr?" she asked as she walked to the Sepherii and laid her hand on his sweaty coat.

"Child, I would be honored," he said as he bowed to the young woman. Torr's attitude had drastically improved with her brother's success of moments before. "Since your brother can ride now, he will join you."

With a laugh, Thom mimicked the Sepherii's bow.

The children walked to the fence, where Thom helped his sister climb a rung. Standing on the fence waiting for Thom to mount the Sepherii first, Lili caught a glimpse of color on the blue horizon. After she had climbed onto the Sepherii's back, with her arms snugly wrapped around Thom's waist, she brought it to her brother's attention.

"Thom, in the distance there? Is that Cleo?"

Both Sepherii and boy turned to where Lili pointed, and Thom narrowed his eyes. His face broke into a smile, and he let out a long whistle that made Torr cross his arms and shake his head.

"Sorry," Thom said, patting the Sepherii's back. "It's Cleo, all right, Lili! Father will be glad."

Thom leaned down and opened the gate to the field, and Torr walked through, his arms still crossed over his chest. The children soon forgot the bird as they practiced balancing on the Sepherii together. Torr moved slowly at first, adding prancing steps forward and to the right and left when he felt the children were ready to move on in their lessons.

"Show off," Lili thought, with a laugh. The Sepherii's voice reverberated inside Lili's head with a seriousness that surprised her.

"There will come a time, Miss Lilianna, when you will be grateful for these games we play today," said the Sepherii, coming to a jarring stop that sent Lili's chin into Thom's back. Thom's shoulders bunched together, but he didn't complain. Lili felt reprimanded, but she couldn't remain downcast for too long. Not on a glorious summer day, playing with her brother and her newfound friend.

They continued around the field for another quarter of an hour until Torr asked Lili to get down. She used an old stump in the field as a step to dismount and then sit. Thom and Torr continued their practice. At Torr's suggestion, Thom had taken his slingshot and loaded it. They spent an hour moving athletically through the field, Thom hitting targets, one after the other.

While she watched, Lilianna entertained herself by picking small pieces of bark off the stump and tossing them at a rock several feet away. Three or four tosses into her game, a movement in the grass at her feet caught her eye, and, after a moment, a tiny titmouse poked its nose into view. The little scavenger stood on his hind legs, a miniature, live telescope focused on the rider and Sepherii, completely ignoring Lili. His whiskers wiggled like antennas in a breeze, and his tiny front paws ruffled in fretful motion. Lili laughed at the mouse's face but felt sorry for its concern.

"It's a Sepherii," she said as she reached out, tentatively, to the mouse.

It backed away from her offered hand, taking a running leap instead and landing on her pant leg, before scurrying up to her shoulder.

"SepheriiSepheriiSepherii Sepherii Sepherii," snuffled the titmouse, in what Lili could only describe as a worried tone.

"He's not going to harm you, little one."

The mouse allowed her to rub the top of its head for a moment while it studied the Sepherii. Nervously, it skittered over Lili's head and onto her other shoulder, balancing again on its hind legs to better see into the distance.

"Ohdearohdear, oh dear," the mouse whistled through its teeth.

Lili looked out to the field and tried to imagine Thom and Torr as this small animal would see them. Perhaps they were like a big monster to the mouse. She shifted her weight and reached in the pocket of her sweater for the cookie she'd been saving for a snack, breaking a bit off and offering it to the titmouse. Greedily it grabbed the whole mass, shoving it into its mouth.

"Mymymy mymy my."

Small pieces of cookie landed on Lili's shoulder like bits of dandruff. The mouse lowered itself from his hind legs and quickly cleaned up the crumbs. Then, in a flurry of soft brown fur, he was gone, scampering down Lili's back and out of sight. She searched for it in the grass at her feet, but the furry bundle of energy had disappeared as fast as it had shown up.

After the mouse's departure, Lili began to grow bored. Thom was far out in the field, repeating drills that would test his skill at mounting and dismounting the moving Sepherii. Her injury ached less each day, but the muscles had grown weak, so she decided to work on getting strength back while she waited for them. The stump was a perfect place on which to step up with her injured leg.

Olitus, working his way across the field where he had met up with Cleo, watched his daughter in the distance. He could see her determination and the pain it caused her as she stepped on and off the stump. Far beyond Lilianna, Thom and Torr practiced. Watching his children, he felt a surge of pride.

"They will need to be strong for what is coming, Cleo," he said to the brilliant bird on his shoulder.

Cleo fluffed her feathers in response, for once too tired to voice her opinion. Olitus reached up and patted his companion.

"My girl, you are rarely without words."

Cleo darted her beak forward and nipped at him. Laughing, Olitus pulled his hand quickly away.

Lili, hearing her father laugh, waved a greeting. "Cleo!" She stumble-walked to her father's side and reached up to pet the large bird. Cleo blinked and ducked her head at Lilianna, her beak decidedly closed. Hearing the sound of hooves pounding the earth, they turned to watch Thom and Torr gallop up. Olitus nodded with pride at how lightly Thom dismounted.

"You both do well in your training. The Sepherii knows what he is doing."

Olitus's eyes creased in a smile, acknowledging a greeting to Torr. Torr nodded and pawed the earth, bowing forward slightly toward Olitus. In his excitement, Thom did not notice the exchange between them.

"This is so much better than any of the games we play at school, Father!" Seeing the seriousness in his father's eyes, Thom took a breath and calmed himself, rethinking what he meant.

"I know there is more to this than the sport, Father," he said, haltingly. "Lili and I have been talking. We know things are not right in Faltofar. We," he stopped, unconsciously looking to his sister for support. " We think you and Mother should include us when you..." Thom trailed off.

Thom and Lilianna had overheard their parents' heated discussions over the last week after the two of them had gone to bed. The children had shared a loft bedroom their whole lives, where a small crack in the floor allowed them to peek down into the living area. Their parents often sat for a while after the children had said goodnight, discussing the day's events. Several times the adults' voices had been raised in disagreement, an unusual and disturbing occurrence. The children had never been able to hear the complete discussions, but they understood from the snippets that drifted up to them that Faltofar was morphing into a menacing place.

Sarafina had left the day before and had yet to come back. Their mother often took short trips into the forest alone to gather herbs to replenish her supplies. Their father had always supported their mother in her healer's work, but they had argued about this journey into the woods. It confused the children, who had whispered late into that night, guessing at the real reason their mother had gone.

Olitus glanced at Torr before he spoke. "Your mother has been summoned by Liannan to the high country." His boot ground a clump of dirt into the grass. "Thom, you've traveled with her there. You know it's not an easy journey." Gently he stroked the colorful bird perched on his shoulder. "She will prepare to leave for her homelands when she returns from her…gathering trip."

His hand drifted from Cleo to rest on the hilt of the dagger at his side. His eyes shifted toward the woods, knowing a glance could not conjure up his wife, but wanting her back so very much.

"If what the clan leaders say is true, and I have no reason to believe they weave falsehoods, she will travel in treacherous times." Olitus tried to soften his words, noting the concern that animated his children's faces. The Sepherii's features were chiseled in stone. "I have no doubt your mother can take care of herself; it is just that . . ." His voice trailed off.

Cleo leaned in close, rubbing her head against Olitus' ear, obviously saying something only he could hear. He nodded understanding, and the bird launched herself into the air with a powerful flap of her wings. She glided around the Sepherii, bringing a rare smile to his stoic face.

"I have yet to hear Cleo's report of the north coast and Belethel," Olitus said, watching the bird depart. "She has gone back to the house to eat, and I will join her there."

He looked from Thom to Lilianna and added, "I have misjudged you both. You have grown up, and I should treat you accordingly." Thom started to speak, but Olitus's raised hand stopped him. "No,

Thom, your mother can take care of herself. I have need of you here."

Already half departed himself, he glanced across the field toward the house as he addressed the children one last time. "We must all be prepared for what is to come." His hand moved again to the dagger at his belt. "I just don't know what that is yet."

The Sepherii slowly crossed his arms, silently acknowledging Olitus's words with a single nod, his features as frozen as the glacier lakes in the high country.

11

AND BONES

S arafina felt the sharp edge of the twig under her soft moccasin before it snapped. She flinched at the noise, knowing better. Blending in with the forest had its advantages, survival being one of them.

Squatting down near the creek, she splashed water on her hot face and scanned the area around her. Behind her, her overnight pack leaned against a tree where she had left it. The lightweight bow and quiver of arrows, wedding gifts from her husband, rested next to it. This two-day outing into the familiar woods around their home would serve as her warmup for the longer trip ahead to the high country.

She had departed from the cabin midday the day before and spent the night in the forest. She cherished the scents and sounds of the night around her and harbored no apprehensions of sleeping outside. Growing up in the harsher climate of the mountains, she and her siblings would spend days away from their home, hunting and fishing, at ease in the wild. Sarafina was a master archer but preferred her healing skills to killing. The hunt was always only out of necessity.

She had told the children she was headed into the forest to collect herbs, but the pouch dangling from her belt was a constant reminder of why she had actually taken this trip into the woods. The weight of its content bumped against her, demanding attention.

"Soon enough," she said under her breath, blinking at the brightness of the sparkling water as it cascaded over the mossy green rocks near her feet. Dipping her leather bladder into the creek, she filled it, bound the top tightly, and slung it over her shoulder. She stood and stretched. "I have grown a bit soft," she thought, feeling the soreness of muscles unused to sleeping on hard ground.

As she picked up her pack, her thoughts shifted to her upcoming journey. One did not decline a summons from Liannan. Not for any reason. "Unless you're dead," she thought with a cynical snort. "Even then, Liannan would expect you to make an effort." That brought another snort.

Deeper into the woods, the understory became more dense, forcing Sarafina to backtrack several times when she came to areas so thick with vegetation she could not see a way through. It had been a long time since she had been this far. The deep forest belonged to the dwarves. Their territory had been laid out as part of a truce made long ago.

The warbling of songbirds was the first sign that she neared her destination. She could just make out the meadow as she stepped past a mullbush, its thorns grabbing at her pack. Sunlight dappled the forest floor where she stopped at the edge of the clearing. While the dense foliage had been challenging to hike through, it served to hide anyone or anything in its shadows. The field would not. She scanned the area carefully.

Early summer flowers bloomed throughout the lush grass, their swaying color giving the clearing a festive touch. Near the center of the meadow, a single pile of rocks jutted up from the earth. The jumble of stone was no more than ten feet high and appeared even more stunted next to the ancient tree. Sarafina smiled at the sight of the gigantic Holy Oak, one of a handful that peppered the land. With a final scan of the open area, she stepped into the sunlight, moving swiftly to the base of the tree.

The Holy Oak. She bowed her head a moment, acknowledging the beauty and age of the first tree. Her family had carried its symbol on their talisman for generations, honoring its image of power and bond with all the lands. For as long as Sarafina could remember, it had been their crest, her family's rightful emblem in the history of Faltofar. She was proud of this and awed by the power that emanated from the tree.

"Well met, Grandfather." She reached forward, touching the rough bark, her eyes traveling upward into branches as thick as her body.

Mixed in with the dark leaves, tiny brilliant birds shimmered and called to each other. An acorn, perhaps loosened by one of the birds, clunked down on a lower branch, hitting Sarafina's shoulder before falling at her feet. She laughed at the gift, her pack shifting slightly on her back as she bent and picked it up. The acorn felt warm in her hand when she pocketed it, as if the tree was reassuring her that all would be well in the world. This small token from the majestic oak felt jarringly different than the content of the pouch.

She moved away from the massive trunk to the pile of rocks, setting her pack on the ground. Leaning against the warm rock face, Sarafina closed her eyes, enjoying, for a moment, the feel of the early summer day. Thorns from the mullbush she'd wrestled aside earlier had pulled strands of her long, dark hair loose and she began reworking her hair back into a braid, binding it tightly again and securing the end with the leather thong. This simple task cleared her mind and allowed her a moment to focus on how best to understand the contents of the pouch and explain her concern to the tree. Her water bladder still hung across her shoulder, and she took a long swallow before setting it down next to the quiver of arrows. Pulling her talisman from inside her shirt, she moved off the warm support of the rock and stepped forward into the shade beneath the magnificent branches. Without taking the necklace from around her neck, she placed the coin to her forehead, bowing slightly.

"Grandfather, I come to you as a child of the light. I am in need of your wisdom and your strength."

Her words quieted the birds. The loss of their song filled the clearing with an eerie silence.

"I know not what I bring to you today." In the silence of the meadow, her last words reverberated in the air. *You today, you today, you today*, then drifted into nothing.

Holding the pouch in her palm, she unbound the strings that tied its mouth closed. Its contents had stained the leather a dark, ugly green, and a sickly-sweet stench of decay wafted up to her nose. She tried not to flinch as she reached inside.

———

Tilga had stewed for days as Berold prepared to depart. Dundalee's mystical pronouncement banged about on her insides, making her jittery and anxious. She had kept her eye on the changing moon throughout the week but grudgingly, and to Berold's surprise, helped her husband prepare for his trip. They had not spoken again of the human children after the "night of burnt stew," as Berold thought of it. Tilga's actions confounded him, but he wasn't going to question her.

The morning Dundar met Berold at the well, his wife accompanied him there. Tilga seemed resigned to their departure and actually kissed her husband quite thoroughly and in public too. Dundar had politely batted at an imaginary fleck of dirt on his sleeve, but not before Berold had seen the glint of amusement in the younger dwarf's eye. Purposely ignoring the boy, he shouldered his pack and smacked Tilga on her plump behind. He just hoped she wouldn't pick up a rock and fling it at his departing back.

Tilga stood at the well, stoically watching the men march through the village and out into the forest. She'd bit at her lip so hard it had begun to bleed, but the blood was better than tears. She wanted to run after Berold and hold onto him to make him stay but instead had marched resolutely back for her home. She had sweeping to do and a decision to make. Housework had always helped her clear her mind and Dundalee's words weighed heavily on her.

That had been days ago. Early this morning, the new moon following her like a leaf blown on a disturbing wind, she had left from the village, making her way through the deep forest toward Father Holy Oak.

She had been in the meadow less than a quarter of an hour, waiting for some sign that Dundalee had cryptically predicted, when she heard a branch snap in the shadowy forest at the edge of the clearing. Moving as fast as her tiny legs would allow, she tucked behind the rocks adjacent to the mighty tree, looking around for a better way to conceal herself. Her stubby fingers found the cracks in the rock. Quickly and more nimbly than one would expect of her tiny, plump frame, she climbed up to a small ledge. Keeping her stocky body lowered to the rock, she peeked cautiously over the lip. There were those who swore the first dwarf had been hewn from stone. Stone was their element. Stone was their friend. Her thick, little hands dug deep into the grain to calm herself as she cursed Berold, Dundar, and Dundalee for her current situation. The sound of the songbirds covered her mumbled, angry words. Her grip tightened when she saw who came out of the forest.

"Well, I'll be," she thought. "If it isn't the healer woman."

Hidden on top of the pile of rocks, Tilga was close enough to hear Sarafina acknowledge the sacred tree. When the human moved toward the rock, Tilga's heart skittered in her chest, but she quickly realized Sarafina had not seen her and was merely leaning her pack against the base directly below her. The rustling of gear and the sloshing sound of a water bladder drifted up to her. Tilga licked her lips, her jittery nerves making her thirsty as well. She didn't dare move to drink from her flask, though.

After a moment, the healer walked to the tree, once again in Tilga's line of sight. She couldn't bear it any longer. Her tongue stuck to the roof of her mouth, and with the human's back to her, Tilga quickly took a sip from her hip flask. The healer's words stifled the song of the birds in the massive tree as they drifted up into the limbs. They rippled around Tilga, their echo sending chills up her spine. Mesmerized, she slowly bent to put the flask away and realized her mistake a split second too late. Sunlight glinted off the hammered metal.

Sarafina's hand froze inside the pouch, and her head snapped around to look at the top of the rock. Human and dwarf studied each other warily. Tilga swallowed, her mouth completely dry again. Sarafina slowly removed her hand from the pouch, her face emotionless except for her eyes, which darted briefly to the rock below Tilga. Instinctively the dwarf knew the woman searched out her bow. Tilga straightened and moved her hands wide, away from her body, showing the human she held no weapon.

"I. Um. I was, um, just ah, here relaxing and gathering flowers." She pointed at the rock she stood on, its porous surface showing little more than a mild growth of lichen clinging to the stone.

Tilga's weak smile looked utterly unbelievable. Sarafina cocked her head, narrowing her eyes up at the dwarf.

"You are . . ." Sarafina stepped away from the tree, the pouch momentarily forgotten in her hand, and squinted up at the dwarf. "You are the dwarf woman who came to my door years ago."

Tilga had no intention of coming down from the rock. The height gave her a sense of security. She knew the healer to be a kind human, but she was a human all the same, history or no history between the two of them. Tilga swallowed again and nodded in agreement. No use denying the truth.

Sarafina relaxed just a bit, consciously untensing her muscles. She had been prepared to fight. She stepped closer to the rock to bridge the gap of distrust between her and the dwarf woman. Belatedly, she realized her mistake when the dwarf crouched defensively. Sarafina stopped, her mind quickly searching for a way to ease the situation. She was impatient to finish her task here and be gone. The hand that held the pouch had begun to itch, and she desperately wanted to let go of the smelly thing. They both broke the stillness at the same time.

"I always meant to thank you for . . ." Tilga rose slowly. She wanted nothing more than to be gone from the meadow, the Holy Oak, and the healer.

"How is the boy now? His arm, did it heal?"

In other circumstances, Sarafina would have sincerely listened to the dwarf's response, but the pouch was bothering her more and more. Her hand had begun to tingle in a very unpleasant way.

"He's, um, fine."

"You had no need to thank me, the boy . . ."

They both stopped, embarrassed, their words jumbling together in nonsensical order. Sarafina's jerky movement startled them both. The pain in her hand had become intense. She swore she'd felt something oozing out of the pouch, something with stinging tentacles. She threw the pouch away from her, grimacing down at her hand. Red welts had begun to form on her palm.

At Tilga's gasp, Sarafina tore her eyes from her hand and looked up to the dwarf, who wordlessly gestured to where the pouch had landed at the base of the tree, its contents spilling out on the ground. She had not opened the pouch since the day she'd scooped the pieces up from where they had fallen under Lilianna's stool. The brittle white bones, coated in a sheath of slimy green mud, had clattered out onto the mossy earth beneath the tree, forming a distinct pattern both women recognized as menacing magic. The bones were just as vile as when Sarafina had first seen them, but now they seemed created for a purpose. She bared her teeth, turning back fully to face the dark magic beneath the sacred tree. From her perch on the rock, Tilga studied the pattern of bones and mud, a trickle of dread, like unwanted icy fingers, tickled down her spine. The human stood far too close to that kind of evil and, with sudden clarity, Tilga acknowledged her misjudgment. She scurried down the rock and hurried to the healer's side, mumbling to herself.

"Dwarf and human differences be damned. This is bad magic, and I know the healer is a good woman."

Sarafina did not take her eyes off the bones. Tilga's words were muffled, but Sarafina believed the dwarf woman came to her side as ally, not enemy. Cautiously they moved forward to better interpret the pattern, Tilga still mumbling under her breath until the taller woman laid a hand on her shoulder. Tilga drew courage from the healer's touch.

"Stay ready, dwarf woman. There is nothing good coming from these things."

She withdrew her good hand from Tilga's shoulder, reaching for the cord around her neck and slid her hand down its length to the talisman. Eyeing her sideways, Tilga wished, enviously, she had something that powerful with which to protect herself. Her squat little body moved closer to the tall woman. She squared her shoulders, pulling a small knife from its sheath at her belt.

"I can put up a good fight, at least." In a moment of doubt, she wondered if Dundalee had sent her here to destroy her.

Sarafina still held tightly to her talisman, her lips now closed over gritted teeth, her eyes narrowed in concentration.

The air at the center of the pattern had begun to swirl, the tree disappearing behind the smoldering cloud of billowing, thick smoke. At its center, a darkness began to form, slowly congealing. At first nothing more than a mass, it thickened ominously, rounding and stretching into the form of a human, floating just above the earth. The grass inside the circle of bones had begun to wither and die, and the soil shifted as if coming to life. And indeed in a sense, it had, as night-crawling earthworms wriggled up from the dead ground. The leaves directly above the shifting mass crinkled and folded into brown death, in contrast to the tree's vibrant green canopy. Tilga drew in a breath as the features in the smoke began to define themselves into that of a woman.

"It looks like . . ." Her words trailed off. The wraith had distinctive features. She felt Sarafina tense and knew she saw it, too. Tilga readjusted her grip on the knife. The smoky form hovered just off the writhing ground, a malevolent half-formed replica to the healer, its dark hair flying wildly.

Tilga waited for Sarafina to do something, anything, but the woman remained motionless, her face pale, obviously severely shaken. Nonetheless, the healer stood her ground.

"I'll be damned if I let a puff o' smoke scare me into bein' a sniveler," Tilga whispered.

Lifting her chin, she stood taller, brushing her shoulder against the human for reassurance and addressed the specter, which shimmered and shifted, its predatory eyes drifting thoughtfully around its surroundings.

"What do you want of us, you?" Tilga tried to sound as if she did this every day, addressing eerie, nasty wraiths in conversation. Hearing the quiver in her voice, she mentally pinched herself and determined to try again. "Be gone from here! This is a place of healing and goodness. You have no authority here!"

Tilga's words reached the morphing, smoky mass but did not have the effect she had hoped for.

"I don't think it got the message."

She glanced up at the human but had to look away. The healer had turned a greenish-yellow.

The apparition faced them fully for the first time. Dark hair writhed around a high forehead, and startling green eyes widened and then narrowed as the spirit saw them. Whoever or whatever she was, she tilted her head slightly to the side as an evil smile spread across her features. Sarafina's chest felt compressed, and she found she could not take a deep breath. She took a step backward, addressing the magic evilness.

"It's not possible. You were banned."

Tilga had remained where she was, her knife hand raised and ready. She had not noticed Sarafina drop back. The wraith, not taking her eyes off the two women, bent and, with fingers now more solid than smoke, picked up one of the bones that created the circle. Twirling the brittle white stick between its fingers, the dark mass of the woman rose back to her full height.

"Banned? Well then. I believe you have just done me a favor. One step closer to being . . . unbanned." She spit the last word out like broken teeth. Drifting to the edge of the circle, she addressed Tilga.

"You." The creature tilted its head to the other side, using the bone to delicately draw imaginary circles in the air around the dwarf. "It's Tilga, yes?"

At the sound of her name coming from the leering face, Tilga felt her legs go weak. She shifted her weight and held her small knife higher, clenching her teeth. The half-formed woman laughed.

"I should think you'd be hovering in your cave, dwarf woman. Unlike your son, perhaps you do not yet understand where you should place your allegiance." Her words drifted out of the magical circle in a malignant puff of smoke, and hovered above Tilga, settling into her hair like some unwanted dank cloud. Tilga blinked, her eyes suddenly heavy, her focus diminished to nothing. She felt herself falling. She clung to the memory of her son. His face was the only thing that kept her from losing consciousness as she toppled to the grass.

Like a serpent about to strike, the ghostly apparition pivoted in midair to face Sarafina, ignoring the limp, semi-conscious form of the dwarf. A smile oozed across her face. The rest of her features seemed dead.

"Ah, the dark daughter. We meet." Her wispy form shifted forward but was stopped at the circle's edge. "Dark child of the present. You have brought me forth into the last of the light as only you could have done."

Tilga lay in the grass, her head foggy and drugged. Slowly she opened her heavy lids and cautiously tipped her head up to study the floating woman. The fact that the ghoulish woman ignored her allowed Tilga time to process what she saw without drawing attention to herself. Blearily, she looked from the shifting mass to Sarafina. The woman of flesh and the woman of smoke were almost identical, and yet there was something very different about the one inside the circle. If decay and despair could take form, this creature would wrap both around her as a dank shawl. She could hear small incoherent sounds coming from Sarafina.

"Our time has come, child." It rolled the bone between its fingers, pointing it at Sarafina. "I have waited far too long." A smile spread across the wraith's face. "Join me or die. I will give you the choice. The others are nothing. Pawns."

With an effort, Tilga pulled herself up, and on wobbly legs staggered back to the human, not taking her eyes off the evil apparition. It had begun to twirl, laughter bubbling up from its smoky center. When it stopped its revolutions, its features settled into an even more solid form.

"How quaint. Human and dwarf, dwarf and human. What an unlikely match. And rather worthless. Unless you choose wisely."

Her words tapered off, a hissing sound emanating from her mouth. Her tongue slid out between her teeth like a serpent testing the air for the scent of her next kill. She began to laugh, at first low and soft, then louder and clearer. The air inside the circle became smokier, and Tilga realized, not without a great deal of relief, the thing was drifting back to nothing, its features becoming less distinctive, except for the startling green eyes. The vile, wispy woman addressed Sarafina again.

"Tell Liannan I am back, child." Laughter, oozing with hatred, bubbled forth from the smoke. "Better yet, give this to her as a gift from me."

Emerging from the last of the hazy mass, the bone which the wraith had been twirling in her fingertips arced through the air, landing at Sarafina's feet. Both women stared down at the thin, bleached stick where it lay in the dying grass, the length of it glistening with green slime. It began to undulate, a dead thing made living. Before Sarafina could react, it slithered up her boot and under her pant leg. She grabbed at the material quickly, lifting it, but the thing had already begun to coil itself around her skin in a viselike grip.

She dropped to her knee, grimacing in pain, pulling at the hardening bone. Tilga fought the urge to step back. Instead, she too knelt in the grass, her knife ready as she watched the human struggle with the foul anklet. One last look over her shoulder confirmed that the smoky woman had dispersed into the air, leaving nothing but dead earth and leaves as a reminder that she had indeed been real.

"What, or who, was that?" she asked, shifting on her knees closer to look at Sarafina's bondage, her small gutting knife ready to help cut away the clinging anklet. She could see the healer's hands shaking. The woman was rattled.

"And rightly so," thought Tilga, feeling the creepy jitters run down her back. Malevolent laughter still permeated the air.

Sarafina was finding it increasingly hard to maintain her composure. "I cannot . . . It's not . . ." Her fingers kept slipping, and she could not grasp the bone with any strength.

Tilga gently shifted her hands out of the way and taking the small knife, bent to the task of cutting at the slick green mass. The blade, a dwarf-made tool of expert quality was extremely sharp, but made no dent in the bone. Tilga stopped trying and squatted back on her haunches, studying the anklet with nervous disgust.

"Who was that?" she asked again, trying to keep any quaver out of her voice. All she could think of was Berold off alone in the forest, except for the mute, younger dwarf. She didn't like it. She didn't like it at all.

Sarafina rubbed her hands in the grass at her side. Taking a deep, calming breath to ground herself, she stood and gingerly put weight on the now burdened ankle, testing it.

"Unfortunately, Tilga," she said, narrowing her own green eyes at the last of the smoke, "that was my aunt. She goes by the name of Morauth."

A HISTORY LESSON

Master Blisk relished the summer holiday. His passion for Faltofar's history was only exceeded by his love of gardening, and on this crisp morning, he was blissfully happy. He'd been poking and digging in the earth since early sun's rising. His little cabin, nestled to the southern end of the forested region of Glennburrough, was an hour's walk to the common buildings where the children of the region were tutored, and just isolated enough that Blisk didn't feel the need to wear more than padding on his knees while in the garden.

"Just the way the One created us," he always said to himself.

Blisk was a naturalist at heart and found the warmth of the sun and the fresh air on his skin to be a balm to his soul. Being that he lived alone, he didn't have to explain to anyone his propensity to spend the majority of his days naked. So when the two dwarves walked out of the forest to the edge of his garden plot, he was at a loss as to how best to address them. Being naked and all.

"Um. Ahhhh. Right."

Blisk stood up quickly, feeling that to do so would at least lend him a slight amount of dignity. The trowel in his hand was the best he could manage for coverage, and he used it as a sort of loincloth, dusting the dirt from his knee pads with his free hand. He could not, however, cover his surprise. He had never seen a dwarf before.

The three men stared at each other as the sun took a short step across the sky. Blisk swallowed several times, ready to break the silence with an introduction, but the stern continence and low rumbling of the older dwarf made him second-guess himself. The younger dwarf, who seemed to have something wrong with his face, kept silent. Then, in utter humiliation, Blisk realized what afflicted the lad. What had started as a twitch in the youth's cheek turned into a soft snicker that erupted into outright, bent-over-double, thigh-slapping, eye-swiping laughter. The older dwarf's raised eyebrows, dissolved into deep scornful wrinkles around his narrowed eyes. He glanced over his shoulder at his companion.

"The company I keep." Disgustedly Berold reached over and hit Dundar on the head with his fist.

Blisk, who would never think of hitting anyone, wanted to hug the older dwarf, but instantly thought better of it. Standing taller, he used his best tutorial voice to address his unexpected company.

"Teodore Blisk, at your service, gentlemen," he said, rocking on his heels. "My home is just there. May I offer you a refreshment and repose from your journey?" As he spoke, he pointed toward the knoll where his cabin stood and realized, belatedly, he'd used the hand holding the trowel as his pointer. He quickly repositioned the tool.

Berold stood silently, sucking on his teeth. Tilga hated this habit of his, which he exercised when he was irritated.

"Tilga was right. I should have stayed put at the hearth," he thought to himself. "I'm surrounded by idiots."

Dundar blinked tears away. Suppressing the urge to burst into laughter again, he pinched his lips tightly closed and looked down at the ground. Dundar had only ever seen humans from a distance. None up close and certainly none naked. He thought the man rather spindly. In all aspects. Berold sucked on his teeth one last time and, giving what could only be described as a disapproving huff under his breath, spoke for both of them.

"Berold," he said, pointing at his chest, "and Dundar." He kicked the boy who, still slightly bent over, had snorted another laugh towards the ground. "Of the Forest of the Glenn."

Blisk swallowed carefully. Berold's introduction held more information than just the dwarves' names. Theirs was a social structure that went back much farther than the humans of Faltofar. Being the foremost historian of not just Glennburrough, but all of Faltofar, Blisk had a solid grasp of who stood before him. The dwarves of the Glenn were the oldest line of dwarves in the land. Dwarves did not participate in royalty, but their pride of ancestry permeated their beliefs and subtle hierarchy within their culture. In the darker history of Faltofar, the dwarves of the Glenn had served as the leaders of their kind. They had also rallied forces with those practicing the Light Arts, for the good of all. Blisk bent his tall frame in a bow. The dwarves before him deserved that and more.

"I am honored," Blisk said. "I, ah, would ask you to rest a moment or two here at my garden while I just, ah, ah, tidy up my home and prepare refreshments. Please join me at your leisure." With a nod of his head and a soft "gentlemen," Blisk turned on his heel and purposely strode out of the garden toward his house with as much dignity as he could muster. The dwarves watched his receding, white backside, then Dundar broke into a fit of laughter again.

"Oh, be done with it, boy," Berold said, settling his stocky frame on the bench. The human, halfway up the hill and silhouetted by the setting sun, did not look back. With a final hiccup snort, Dundar leaned against one of the garden's fence posts.

"We will go to the human's house," Berold said, not taking his eyes off the ridge where the figure had disappeared. "He's a Rememberer. Their best. And we could use some direction."

He sat back, the warm sunshine a balm to his aching body. He was getting older. By human standards far too old. But, by the seasons of earth and rock with which his people were bound, he was still young enough, even if it didn't feel like it today and even if his own people sometimes discounted him. Theirs was a much longer cycle than any human's life. Long enough for Berold to have his own memories of the darker days of Faltofar. Even if the others chose to forget, he knew what he knew. He believed his memories would serve to somehow keep his people safe, even when they stopped seeing and hearing him. He had fought against the darkness alongside those heroes cherished by the humans. Cherished and long dead. Berold had lived long enough to understand that even humans might be allies in dark times.

"By the One, I could use some of that tincture Tilga makes," he grumbled to his companion, rubbing the small of his back. He hated weakness of any kind. His body pain felt like a betrayal of sorts. The days hiking in the forest had challenged him physically. But, he knew from experience it was only a matter of time before he and the youth would grow stronger.

He looked up at Dundar without expecting any response. He rather liked the fact that the mute didn't speak. His personal sounding board. No one to talk back at him.

"Lord knows I have enough of that at home," he thought.

Dundar kicked a loose stone at his feet, glancing up the ridge.

"The boy holds his own," Berold thought, studying him out of the corner of his eye. "He's quick with the spear and alert. And he's the biggest damn dwarf I've ever seen."

Adjusting his suspenders, Berold stood.

"I'd say that's enough time for the human to dress hisself."

The younger dwarf shifted away from the fencepost and followed a pace behind Berold as they headed up the ridge to Blisk's house.

———

They had entered the human's cabin at his invitation without banter or small talk. Dwarves knew nothing of these human social games, and Blisk gathered this quickly. At Berold's request for information, the historian found himself back in the shoes of scholar and educator. He busied himself immediately with the tools of his trade: a map and a memory.

"The, ah, um..." Blisk ran his finger along the edge of a jagged line on the map, waving his other hand vaguely behind him. "I need the, um..."

"The Rememberer wants them." With a smack to the backside of Dundar's head to get the boy's attention, Berold pointed to a shelf at the edge of the kitchen. Dundar hurried to accommodate the human, bumping the shelf in his haste. One of the figurines teetered and would have hit the floor had Dundar not caught it. The ledge it had rested on was covered with a handful of tiny replicas of Faltofar's inhabitants, from sea snakes and massive giants to humans and dwarves. Each small statue, ornately crafted down to the last detail, whether snarling, sharp teeth, or glittering sword, would have been worth admiring had he not been preoccupied with what the human was doing at the table.

"Please, if you would be so kind."

Blisk's hand was extended behind him, grasping blindly. His impatient finger-snapping would have been irritating had the dwarves been any less passionate in their quest for knowledge. Dundar scooped the other figurines into his beefy hands.

"Zet zem yus yer," Blisk said, pulling the pencil from between his teeth and pointing, distractedly, at the edge of the table. He continued to thumb through a thick book bound in aged leather that smelled faintly of mildew.

"The history of Faltofar is grand and illustrious." He was warming up. "These creatures," he wrapped his long fingers around a powerful-looking figurine, half-man and half-horse, holding it to the light. It sparkled in the sunshine from the kitchen window. "Astoundingly beautiful." He pivoted the tiny statue this way and that. "The Sepheriis have inhabited Faltofar as long as your people." He shook his head, enchanted by the thought of the centuries. "Maybe longer." He set down the figurine and tapped it with the tip of his pencil.

"Their strength does not lie in numbers, but in the lightning-rod capabilities of their kind to draw energy from all sources."

Blisk looked back at the thick book, using the eraser to flip pages, stopping only long enough to slide his glasses further up his long nose. Focusing on the map laid out on the table in front of him, he absently scratched his head using the pencil as a makeshift tool.

"They are a magnet for both the good and the bad. Rendar and Morauth…" His words tapered off, and his eyes, magnified behind the thick glasses, blinked several times, pausing to sort through the information in his head.

The three stood looking at each other, the dwarves shifting from one stumpy leg to another, waiting for the tall human to gather his thoughts. Blisk blinked several more times, his finger tapping his lower lip. He almost hummed as he snatched up the Sepherii figurine to emphasize his words.

"You see," he said, swooping his hand over the map in mock flight. "This mountainous high country was where the final confrontation took place." He thumped the Sepherii down on the ridgeline. "And ended. A power so immense, it caused the deep rift in the valley below the North Country." His long finger pointed at a dark green swath that ran parallel to the mountain range.

"The Sepheriis were drawn into the battle. The weapon, the black blade…"

A breeze was picking up outside, and a leaf hit the window with a loud thwack. Man and dwarf alike jumped, a gruff yip emanating from Berold, a yelp from Blisk. As usual, Dundar remained mute.

Pushing his glasses back up his nose, Blisk refocused on the map.

"The Sepheriis couldn't, or wouldn't, use it. Rendar the Strong…" He stopped mid-sentence flicking the tiny statues around with his long fingers until he found the majestic form of a man holding a dagger. Triumphantly he held it up toward the dwarves. "It was Rendar who was given the magnificent obsidian blade by a Sepherii."

He brought the figurine close to his face, angling it this way and that. Light reflected off the dagger replica sending rays throughout the tiny room. Blisk thumped the figurine down on the map, where the word *Ledges* emphasized an abrupt elevation change. A cold wind of memory washed up Berold's spine, filled with images of the windswept heights, the sound of battle, and those last moments when

A HISTORY LESSON | 101

the human had to choose between power or peace, love or hate. His recollections brought the metallic taste of fear and, unconsciously, he wiped the back of his hand across his mouth. Blisk continued.

"When the blade struck Morauth, parts of the obsidian sheared off. One into Morauth, and the other pieces...?"

"She fell from the cliff. He shoved her." The old dwarf's eyes were glazed over, his memories trickling out in a whisper. His mouth snapped shut; a muscle twitched along his jaw. Both Blisk and Dundar absorbed what the old dwarf had said, and understanding suffused the younger dwarf's face. Berold had seen the battle with his own eyes.

Gingerly, Blisk picked up the figurine holding the dagger. He brought the small replica close to his blinking, owlish eyes then extended it under Berold's bulbous nose.

"The impact..." He hugged the figurine back into his chest, momentarily breathless. Then, without warning, his arms shot out over his head into a wide V. "The impact went so deep into the depths of Faltofar, the earth shifted and split for miles!" Dust motes dappled the golden afternoon light that slanted through the window, and the dripping faucet at the kitchen sink suddenly became the loudest noise in the human's tiny cabin.

"You know." Reverence and awe permeated Blisk's words and broke the silence. "You were there." He lowered his arms slowly.

Dundar, unused to such a passionate outburst, had inched his way back from the table and out of the reach of the human's long arms. Berold merely coughed and hooked his thumbs into his suspenders. Realizing he'd gotten a little carried away, Blisk sheepishly set the figurine on the edge of the table.

"Well. Yes, ah, there it is then. The Great Battle." Unable to help himself, he picked the figurine up again and set it on a white peak at the right edge of the map. Resting his hands on his hips, he admired his placement.

"I found a prophecy. A long time ago. A parchment, barely legible." Berold's stubby chin jutted forward, listening to what the tall human was mumbling. "Water damage. Withered with age and exposure." Blisk clicked his tongue and continued, talking to himself, oblivious of his audience.

"Something…Something…Sepheriis hovering over a cliff and two becoming one." He scratched his chin, staring at the map. "It just. I don't…can't find…" His words tapered off. Berold coughed again.

"Ah, yes." Distractedly, Blisk acknowledged the dwarves then, reaching to the side of the table, he began gathering the other figurines and placing them hither and thither.

"As you know, the battle had raged for years, and the world of Faltofar was filled with a myriad of lifeforms large and small, good and terribly evil."

He busied himself for a moment, making minute changes in each placement. Dundar bent closer to peer at a small, stubby figure, an almost perfect resemblance of Berold. The figurine held a studded club in one hand, raised menacingly in front of it.

"Yes, yes. That one represents your people." Blisk cocked his head, distractedly, his glasses perched precariously at the tip of his nose.

"The dwarves of the Glenn were the leaders of the Dwarf people. They joined the battle of good against evil in the last days of the conflict. Their support," he cut his words short, embarrassed, realizing his error. "Your support was the turning point in the struggle between the dark and the light of the One."

And that was the crux of the matter. The dwarves had fought for the good, but they had waited…and waited until the very last moment to join the battle. Their kind had distanced themselves from humans for centuries, believing that the source of evil and all that had ailed Faltofar originated from the tall tribe of humans. There had been many of the small kind who felt the humans deserved what they had created. What Faltofar would have become had darkness prevailed and had the dwarves not joined their forces for the good… Well, that was merely speculation. Berold wasn't interested in guessing; he had other things in mind. Facts. He needed to know the pattern of the history before the dwarves chose whether to fight. Again.

"All due respect, Master…Rememberer," Berold scowled up at the scholar, "but we's endeavrin' to understand what it means that I'se recently seen the Sepherii."

Blisk's head snapped up at this disclosure. His frown said more than anything he could have uttered.

Berold reached forward and, with a stumpy finger, slowly slid a glittering Sepherii across the map toward the immense snowy peaks where the human, Rendar, stood tall and majestic. As he did so, the figurine of a woman draped in dark robes with long flowing hair the color of a murky well, tilted and fell forward. The sword she held aloft sliced through the air, cutting Berold's finger deep enough to bring the deep blue of dwarf blood oozing to the surface. A drop landed on the map, directly in the crease of the Rift Valley, slowly spreading, as three sets of eyes watched the paper begin to buckle.

PAST, PRESENT, AND FUTURE

S tepping from the sunny exterior hallway into the cathedral-like quietness, a blast of cool air hit Argath. He blinked in the dimness, his eyes adjusting to the half-light that filtered wanly down from the high windows. The side door slammed behind him and, uncharacteristically, he jumped.

"I will grind my teeth to nothing if I keep this up."

He kicked a chair out of his way, grateful for the distracting stab of pain as his shin collided with one of the heavy, wooden legs.

"You push us too far, Liannan," he muttered, shoving the chair aside.

Stopping at the edge of the cavernous room, he placed one hand on the cool surface of the wall, flexing his fingers wide. Inhaling deeply and filling his lungs, he slowly exhaled through his nostrils, practicing the meditative breathing all Highlanders were taught from a young age. His hands ached from clenching his fists. His jaw ached almost as much. How ludicrous that he searched for solitude, if only for a moment, in the great gathering hall of the tribes.

"You push us too far, Liannan!" he repeated, his voice louder this time.

His hand remained on the wall, but slowly his nails gouged

into the brown rock, his fingers curling back into themselves. Illuminated by the light of a high sconce, the smooth stone surface, now cut by the grooves of his fingernails, mirrored the deep etching of weariness crisscrossing the warrior's face. A movement, perhaps just the air shifting around him, warned him he wasn't alone.

"You. Push us. Too far!"

His fist pounded into the wall, and small particles of masonry cascaded to the floor at his feet.

"Your emotions deserve another direction." Liannan's words, like the first flakes of snow preceding a blizzard, drifted down from where she sat at the high table.

Argath pivoted on his anger, his lithe body careening between the chairs, crashing against one of the heavy tables to stand below her.

"Are we but pawns in your game?"

He looked up at her with eyes as glacially blue as her own.

"Pawns?" she asked, twirling a ring on her small finger, her eyes unwavering. "Hmm." Her tapered hands drifted down to her long, flowing gown, adjusting a minute fold. Her skin was almost translucent, the blue of her veins an intricate pattern just beneath.

"So deceivingly weak looking." The thought surprised him. He no longer saw her as an ally.

Forcing himself to maintain his place at the base of the stairs, he observed her as she slowly stood and descended. Highlander men and women tended to be robust, their evolution molded by the harsh winters and isolation of the north country. Argath was large in stature, even by Highlander standards. Liannan was tall enough to look Argath directly in the eyes.

"Walk with me." It was not a question, but an order.

She glided away down the central aisle as her garment, of the finest wool, twirled about her form, undulating with a life of its own. A muscle in Argath's neck pulsed with the strain of refraining from a retort. She was still his superior in clan and in battle, no matter what she'd done. He'd stood by her always, witnessing her strength on the hunt and in skirmishes with other clans through the years. He had always respected her physical abilities. There had never been a time when he questioned her leadership.

Until now.

Liannan paused at the tall doors, the main entrance to the hall, her hands coming to rest against the solid wood. The hair on Argath's neck tingled as he watched the doors swing outward of their own volition, propelled by her whispered command. She lowered her arms and crossed the balcony. Resting her fingertips lightly on the railing, she surveyed the vast valley far below. He followed her at a distance, his leather over-gear tapping against the sword at his side. He waited, several paces behind her, watching her unearthly stillness with newly formed disgust.

Liannan was not her given name. In the dialect of the mountains, the name meant Protector. She was the descendant of regal women, all the foremost leaders of the north country clans, and all given the honorary title. There would be others after her. Strong women. Perhaps someone's wife, someone's sister, someone's daughter.

He swallowed hard, thinking of Arialla. Liannan's words broke into his thoughts, and Argath blinked away the image of his twin.

"What did you say?" He shook his head, trying desperately to clear it.

The breeze picked at her garments, the material fanning out around her, framing the silvery green of the distant forest.

"It is limitless," she said again, without moving.

In disbelief, Argath followed her gaze, watching the flight of a Swift Hawk, circling in an updraft in the distance. Then, his rage bubbling over at the thought of his sister's senseless death, along with all the others, he snapped at her.

"Lives have been lost!" His words were dagger-sharp with guilt. "Precious lives! Young lives. People with hopes for their futures." Spittle, laced with self-loathing and agony, formed at his lip, and he wiped it away in frustration. Struggling to control himself, he brought his voice lower. "You stand there, unrepentant."

He swallowed, recalling the smell of burning flesh and the sound of the agonized cries when the buildings had gone up in flames. God, the bodies. Their tortured faces. The plague had swept through the isolated high mountain village, but not all had been dead when the fires were lit. He had followed her orders. How could he live with that? How could he live when Arialla was gone?

"You stand there," he repeated, disgust contorting his handsome features, "lording over your domain. You speak of your power over the people." He paused. "Mother."

The sarcasm in the title drifted to the floor between them, like dust in an unused room. She had always been Liannan to him. He had never called her mother, never known her as someone to comfort him, or his siblings, in times of sadness or childhood worries. The loss of Arialla pierced his heart yet again.

Liannan made no response, her features motionless. Time inched forward, and the late afternoon sun shifted the shadows further along the terraced balcony. Voices from lower levels of the vast fortress drifted upward, sentries acknowledging each other, and the high laughter of a young maid.

"Listen to them, Liannan!" He flicked a hand toward the lower terraces. "You were named as their Protector. Does that mean nothing to you? Should not each life be held sacred? Should not each life be accounted for?" His words choked off. If he continued, he understood the sadness and anger inside could drive him to hurt her. His fighting hand had gone to the hilt of his sword. With utmost control, he loosened his grip but kept his hand resting lightly on the hilt. His other hand rubbed at his eyes, willing away the dust of exhaustion.

The feel of Liannan's hand over his startled him. Her cold blue eyes brimmed with unshed tears. It surprised and disturbed him.

"I know you grieve, Argath, not just for Arialla and the boy, but for all in that village."

His skin crawled at the sound of his sister's name uttered from the source of the order. Arialla lost. And the boy. God help them.

"I spoke not of limitless power over the people, but of the threat of pain and suffering inflicted on so many by a single force of darkness." Her eyes were now devoid of any sign of tears.

With bitter, cold intent, Argath gripped his hilt tighter, refusing to give in to the urge to yank his hand from under hers.

"Do you speak of yourself, Liannan?"

Power crackled between the two Highlanders, and the mild evening suddenly grew chillier.

It was Liannan's turn to rub her eyes. It was a human gesture, surprising and unusual in the regal woman, but it broke the angry tension between them. When she spoke again, there was a weariness underlying the steel in her voice.

"Her name is Morauth, and mark my words, my eldest, she will come."

Liannan laid her hands on either side of Argath, holding his arms gently. He could not remember her ever having touched him before. Let alone twice. Her fingertips were both cold and charged with untapped energy.

"You were born a Warrior of the Light, child." Her eyes dimmed, inwardly seeing the march of time. "There have been generations of such warriors. Some rose to the cry of the battle. For others, there was no need, and the centuries moved on.

"This will be your calling." Her hands drifted away from him, almost listlessly lost in the folds of her gown. "If I have my way, it will not be your undoing. Nor the undoing of anyone who follows the One."

Liannan's face settled into angles, once more a stone pillar, lacking emotion. Her lingering touch surged through Argath, sharpening his thoughts and sending adrenaline coursing throughout his body.

"It feels as if I could slice through the stone column with one stroke of my sword," he thought.

Involuntarily he shivered, taking a step back from her and moving his hand from the hilt.

His history lessons, Faltofar's past, scratched through his mind on some long-forgotten blackboard. Horrific stories of Morauth, the Destroyer. Morauth, the Dark One. Morauth of the bloody battle at the end of the Dark Days. He focused on Liannan's profile, not really seeing her.

"But how can such a vile being still be? She was vanquished during the great battle. The dwarf-forged dagger." He searched for its name. "The dagger of...Rendar?" He tapped at his forehead with one finger, a long-unused habit from his schooling days. "Did it not slay her and send her minions into darkness?"

Liannan merely stared out over the valley, perhaps lost in her recollection of the dark Sorceress. He had not expected a response from her and began his pacing again, remembering the old voices of his tutors. Every child had loved to hear the story of the battle. He recited the story now, almost by rote.

"The dagger pierced her heart through, bits of the blade shattering. She fell, was pinned to the ground, the black obsidian working its binding magic. From where she lay, a vast crack in the earth opened up, and the darkness was absorbed into the soil of Faltofar."

His pacing brought him back to Liannan's side. His hand swept across the panorama in front of them.

"That is how the great Rift was created."

Liannan's only response was to raise her arm slowly. As she did, the Swift Hawk they had seen earlier soared upward from the steep ravine below the terrace, landing effortlessly on her forearm. The bird leaned close to her, sliding its sharp beak slowly up her cheek, then sat back and cocked its head, unblinking eyes staring into Liannan's. After a mere moment, she shifted her arm upward in a silent command. The mighty bird crouched then launched itself. Its graceful wings unfolded, capturing an updraft that took it skyward.

"Your sister, Sarafina, comes." Looking up at the bird's flight, Liannan tipped her head to one side, the tendons in her alabaster neck stretched taut, her eyes momentarily closing. When she looked at Argath again, any sign of weakness was gone. "Let us hope she arrives in time."

ENLIGHTENMENT

Thom and Lilianna, freed from their chores, ran through the field adjacent to their home, waving their arms at their friend. With his back to the children, Torr did not return their greeting, continuing to high step away from them through the tall grass. Periodically, he arched his human form, raising his arms wide, ecstatically stretching and reaching toward the sky.

"Thom." Lili had stopped suddenly, her hand pulling on Thom's sleeve. "Stop."

They were still at least five stone throws away from the Sepherii. His leg completely healed, Torr pranced further away from the children. He seemed oblivious to their proximity, lost in his movements.

"Thom. He's...it's the Dance. Or, something like it." She frowned, not sure she could express to her brother what she meant.

And again, the Sepherii raised his arms high, his palms flat toward the sky, intently looking up. Glancing over at Thom, Lili could tell by his narrowed eyes that he was studying the Sepherii. She waited. Thom would tell her.

"The air is shifting above him, Lil. He's...it's as if he's playing with the light." She looked across the swaying grass at the Sepherii and the sky above him. She couldn't see anything moving but understood Thom was describing something to her that he could not understand.

"One of his hands is...is," Thom frowned. "It's light. And, the other is fading into, well, almost like a black hole." Lili's hand slid down the material of Thom's sleeve, intertwining her fingers in his. Slowly they moved forward toward their friend.

———

Torr looked toward the sky and knew he had been drawn forth from the solitude by the shifting will of Faltofar. The land was like an extension of himself, equally drawn toward the light of goodness or, just as easily, pulled into the blank void of dark evil. All power originated from the One, and his kind could channel either. History, life, and death, would repeat itself, as it always had, in its quest for balance.

"We are but pawns in the infinite circle of time."

He spread his arms wider, one upturned palm reflecting the summer sunlight, the other absorbing every imaginable shadow around him. When he brought his hands together, the clap reverberated through the air as loud as thunder.

"It has been a very long time since I have answered the summons to Faltofar."

He brought his hands down to his chest, studying the swirling ball of light and shadows that spun, restlessly, in his palms. Then, glancing over his shoulder, he finally acknowledged the siblings who nervously waited in the tall grass nearby. Their hair crackled and snapped, a conduit to the electricity that rippled through the air.

"It has something to do with the child."

Not wanting to startle them, he raised the brilliant ball of energy slowly, watching them closely before addressing the children as he would during one of their many lessons.

"One of you will catch this."

It was neither a request nor a command, merely an acknowledgment of what he now understood was inevitable. The prophecy would unfold in a child's game of toss. The ball spiraled through the air and, almost casually, Lilianna's hand shot up, catching it effortlessly. Sparks of light, like the firebugs the children loved to capture throughout the summer months, twirled around the girl, enveloping her in flickering points of brilliant light.

———

Through the lazy afternoon, the three made their way to the edge of the field where the woods and grassland butted up against each other. After all the sunshine, the cool shadows of the forest beckoned, but the dense woods would not allow for riders. Torr gave a small buck, teasing the children off his back. Thom leaped lightly to the ground. The girl's dismount was slightly more awkward, but she landed on her feet, only slightly wincing.

"Oh child," the Sepherii leaned forward and placed his hand lightly on Lilianna's wild red hair. "I am sorry. That was thoughtless."

Lilianna leaned into his muscular flank and smiled up at him.

Thom had already parted the tree branches and was working his way into the soft green of the forest understory. The others followed him to a clear area where a log lay half decomposed in the old detritus of the tall swaying evergreens. The children pulled food from a pack Lilianna carried on her back and settled contentedly on the fallen tree. Torr stepped softly across a small creek, bending to scoop water gracefully into his mouth. Their companionable silence, broken only by the soft sounds of eating, lasted only for a bit before Lilianna spoke.

"Torr?" She forced the stopper back into the leather bladder and wiped the back of her hand across her mouth. "How was it that you were hurt?"

In the soft light, Torr's frozen features were illuminated by the glow from his eyes. Thom shifted nervously on the log, suddenly very uncomfortable. He glanced at Lilianna, who remained perfectly still, staring back at the Sepherii with a poise Thom found disconcerting. The question hung between Sepherii and child. The wood underneath Thom suddenly felt unbearably rough, and he would have stood had it not felt as if he were sitting on the edge of a cliff. A cliff that opened onto endless air and a freefall into adulthood.

"Children, perhaps you are ready to witness some of the darkness that resides in Faltofar."

Thom watched the Sepherii cautiously, noting the regal, fearless profile of his sister. In the darker shadows of the forest, Thom could see several of the sparkles of light from the ball still glittering softly, caught in the strands of his sister's hair. Torr stepped forward, standing directly in front of them, folding one long leg under him, his eyes on the earth at their feet, his arms at his sides.

"Place your hands on my forehead and close your eyes. I will remember for you, and in this way, you can see for yourselves."

Thom and Lilianna placed their hands close together on the Sepherii's forehead. Torr's hair fluttered. An elusive breeze whispered down the children's spines. The Sepherii's memories came alive inside their heads.

Anyone watching the children from a distance would have noted confusion cross Thom's face at the same time that his sister began to smile. It was as if they saw two different scenes. While Thom was confused by the billowing haze around the Sepherii, understanding and awe bloomed on Lilianna's face.

"Torr? Are you in the air?" Lili's eyes flew open, her words coming out in an excited rush. "You can fly?"

The Sepherii merely shifted his bent knee. Lilianna quickly shut her eyes again.

The clouds became thicker, and moisture gathered on the Sepherii's coat, trailing droplets along the golden fur. He was alone, joy in his every movement. And then slicing pain along his leg. The air around him exploded with triumphant yowls. He began to fall. In the air around him, dark-winged felines, not quite his size but threateningly large nonetheless, soared and darted. Torr righted himself midair, rearing up, his sharp hooves slashing at the attacking pack. If one could smell evil, it permeated the Sepherii's memories in ghastly layers of decay.

It would have been an even battle had it been one-on-one, but the Sepherii was outnumbered. The wound on his leg, received in the first moments of contact, weakened him. Facing the ringleader, Torr did not see one of the beastly things hurtle out of the dense cloud behind him, curling into a dark, massive ball just before it hit him. The impact sent Torr spiraling down through the air - down, and fortunately, into the depth of the forest where he was hidden and protected by the towering green of the ancient trees.

The children opened their eyes, but neither pulled their hands away. The sounds of the forest were just as they had been before Torr's memories saturated their minds with vivid images and the overwhelming sense of evil. Every shadow around them now held a sinister caste. Lilianna shuddered, breaking the spell enough for Thom to move his hand over hers. Together, they pulled their hands away, and Torr raised himself back to his full height, crossing his arms over his chest. His eyes no longer glowed, but the look he gave the children was laced with compassion and the burden of witnessing the loss of their innocence.

Wordlessly, they stood and followed the Sepherii through the woods toward the meadow, their footsteps muted in the densely matted forest floor. Both children, lost in thought, jumped when Thom stepped on a slender branch, snapping it. Torr twisted his head around, his concern flowing into their minds. Their sheepish smiles acknowledged they were nervous, and Torr reminded himself to tread more lightly, both physically and mentally.

"After all," he thought, exhaling softly, "they are children still."

Sunlight, reaching the outer edge of the canopy, filtered through the branches, dappling patterns across their faces. Emerging into the field, all three blinked and stood quietly, waiting for their eyes to grow accustomed to the light. Standing in the open, surrounded by the swaying green grass of the meadow, Thom felt the heaviness of the unknown, the anxiety of a world with such evil, diminish. Quietly, Lili set her pack down and rummaged through it, pulling out her summer jacket. The cover was rumpled and had grass stains on one arm. Bits of straw stuck out of one pocket, but she ignored all of this as she slipped it on. The jacket was like a security blanket for her. Although she hadn't worn it lately as much as she used to, she rarely went anywhere without it dangling from her shoulders or elbows. The fact that she felt the need to put it on now was the only outward sign that Torr's memories had disturbed her too.

"Are you ready?" Torr asked gently, bending down toward them.

Thom nodded, not quite sure what he was agreeing to but trusting his friend completely. He reached up to where human form and horse merged, and leveraged himself onto the creature's tall, muscular back. Leaning down, he held his arm out to his sister. They linked wrists, and with a little leap and pull, she shifted her weight behind Thom, wrapping her arms around his waist, having tucked her worn jacket closely around her.

The Sepherii shifted beneath them, prancing in one precise circle. Then, facing the wide-open field, Torr tossed his head in acknowledgment of the moment. Both children instinctively leaned low as the Sepherii launched himself forward into a full run.

There wasn't much to it, Lilianna recalled when she thought about it later. It was the sound of the hooves that gave it away. Or, more precisely, the lack of sound. They were careening full tilt across the meadow, and then they were airborne. Holding on tightly, Lilianna rested her cheek against Thom. The muscles of Torr's back moved just the same whether he galloped above the trees and fields or on solid ground, but, especially as they flew higher, the air itself felt somehow different. Lilianna tried to focus on where Torr's wings were, but the sunshine reflected blindingly off their gossamer surface. The currents of light rippled in brilliant rainbow ribbons, making them difficult to see. She had never "not seen" something so magical.

Lili could sense Thom's excitement through his vest in the tight control of his movements. He was practically humming with the joy of the adventure. "Isn't it beautiful, Thom?" Lilianna tilted her head up to yell in his ear and saw Thom flinch.

"You don't have to yell, Lil!" he yelled, then caught himself with a laugh and, just for the sake of it, gave a loud "Wahoo!"

The Sepherii glanced back indulgently. Both children laughed with joy, entranced with the freedom of flight.

"Hold on tightly. Now you truly learn to ride a Sepherii."

Torr tipped ever so slightly forward, gliding through the air toward the ground again.

"Oh boy," Thom said, and Lilianna felt him clench his thighs. "Hang on, Lili!" He had the better view, and Lilianna did as she was told.

Torr's hooves moved rhythmically through the air, expertly navigating his landing. The dark, fertile soil muted the sound of contact into a repetition of deep drumming that brought them full tilt to the far fence of their property.

"Oh boy, oh boy," Thom exclaimed as he ground his teeth in determination.

"What . . . ?" Lilianna's arms wound more tightly around her brother.

With a burst of speed, Torr launched the three of them back into the air, his hooves flashing inches from the fence top. Lilianna's grip around Thom's waist loosened as they leveled off again, and he released his grip on the torso of the Sepherii to look over his shoulder at her. She patted his side, her eyes alight with the adventure.

"That wasn't so bad!" She exhaled breathlessly. Thom's relieved laughter drifted up and over their heads.

Torr quietly moved through the air, leaving the children to their thoughts. The dark greens of the forest of Glenn spread for miles off to their left. Their home and the outlying buildings were dark specks below them now, floating like little islands amidst the browns and softer greens of the pastureland surrounding them. Torr banked to the left, and they soared toward the distant crags that bordered the coastal region.

Lilianna had never traveled farther from her home than the town and her school. Her hair spun around her and into her eyes, and she tucked it back, distractedly. It almost hurt to look at the distant coast and the vast expanse of water, its surface glittering in the late afternoon light. She followed the white line of surf foaming along the shores as it disappeared into the distance. It seemed like the coastline went on forever.

"Like fancy lace on the hem of a dress." She smiled to herself, imaging the size of the giantess who could wear such a brilliant blue skirt.

Glancing over her shoulder, she could just make out the immense purple mountains that made up the North Country. "That is where my grandmother lives." The thought of Liannan was always disturbing. "Liannan." She tested the name softly to herself.

"That is how far my mother will have to travel alone." Her mother covering such a vast distance and being so far away gave Lilianna a momentary sick feeling in her stomach. Looking back at the terrain that lay behind them, she was startled when they touched ground again.

Torr had chosen a plateau far enough above both forest and coastline that the skeggulls drifted like dust motes below them. The birds darted in and out of their nests along the lower cliff face, the chaotic orchestra of their squeaks and squawks rattling small bits of rock off the pitted stone walls. Torr cantered to a halt, and the children dismounted, Thom first, then Lilianna, with just a bit of help from her brother.

"My legs."

Thom thumped his fists against his pant legs to bring circulation back to them. They both high-stepped and stretched to get feeling back in their exhausted thighs.

"If we are ever to travel any true distance, you will have to get used to using those muscles."

Neither child registered the ominous prediction implied in the Sepherii's comment, lost as they were in the beauty of the land and sea that spread out below them.

"Why here, Torr?" Thom had raised one hand, sweeping it in a gesture that encompassed the plateau and the view.

"It is a meeting place," Torr replied cryptically, his eyes glowing.

Lilianna walked away from the two of them to get both a better look at the terrain that stretched into the distance and to find privacy in which to relieve herself. Near the edge of the cliff, a tumble of rock afforded a small screen that Lilianna ducked behind. She felt so free and alive. Not even the wind, which usually grated on her nerves, could diminish her awe.

Finishing, she stood and extended her arms wide, mimicking the flight of the birds she could see below. The smell of the ocean reached her, and a light spray carried up from the crashing waves far below bathed her skin. She stuck her tongue out and licked the back of her hand, tasting salt. An updraft caught at her jacket. The material lifted away from her, except for one pocket. Something substantial bumped against her side.

"Ah, perfect." She sniffed, thinking she had a handkerchief. She had just begun to reach into the jacket when a shout from Thom on the bluff froze her fingers in place.

"What in the name of . . . ," she trailed off, scurrying back up the slight incline, her dripping nose forgotten.

At the top of the rise, Lilianna froze, her breath catching in her throat. Torr and Thom stood side by side. Even from this distance, Lili could see the tension that radiated from her brother. Surrounding the pair, four beautiful Sepheriis hovered just off the ground. In the span of time it took for her to clamp her mouth shut, a fifth Sepherii quietly descended from the expanse of sky above the plateau, taking his place to create a circle around Torr and Thom. Their hooves touched down, and instantly they became immobile as statues, save for the wind whipping their hair and tails.

"It is a scene from my father's book." She swallowed, wishing for just a moment she was back in the comfort of her family's cabin, flipping the worn pages of Faltofar's history.

This frozen tableau might have gone on indefinitely had it not been for a soft squeaking in Lilianna's pocket. With one finger, Lili pulled open the pocket and gaped down into the tiny, whiskered face of the titmouse.

"Why you little stowaway!" she whispered, reaching in and pulling out the shivering animal, putting her finger on the tip of its nose to quiet it. Its little paws pushed her finger away.

"SepheriiSepheriiSepheriiSepheriiSepheriiSepherii," tittered the mouse loudly, its whiskers quivering nervously. The wind, which had shifted yet again, sent the nervous squeaks of the titmouse in the direction of the circle. Lilianna looked back up. Six pairs of glowing eyes focused on her. Protectively, she cupped the tiny rodent to her chest.

A TORMENT OF THE SENSES

Sarafina reattached the dipper to the side of the well. She wiped the water from her lips with the back of her hand, still tasting bile. Nausea had come on fast, leaving her little time to reach a low bush at the edge of the yard and discharge her breakfast. Sometimes it happened that way. The visions could come swiftly. This one had doubled her over with the pain of loss and violent death. Not her children or Olitus, no, not this time. She offered up a silent prayer of thanks to the One.

"But who?"

Blowing a stray hair that drifted across her cheek, she turned back toward the shed. She had been on her way there to finish the preparations for her journey, limping slightly from Morauth's trinket that still wound tightly around her leg. No amount of effort on her part, or Olitus's, had dislodged the unwanted jewelry. She had known it would be futile, the magic too strong, but she had to try. She grimaced at the jolt of pain that shot up her leg and spat the last of the bitter taste from her mouth.

Swinging open the wooden door, Sarafina leaned against the doorway, giving her eyes a moment to adjust to the dimmer light within. A shovel leaned against one corner near the shed's entrance, gloves thrown carelessly on the ground next to the dirty blade. She had worked in the garden the day before, preparing a corner for early summer planting, instructing Lilianna thoroughly on the garden's management and care.

"The child will do well," she assured herself, thinking how much her daughter had changed over the last several weeks. The young girl was becoming a woman. She was thoughtful and kind. Her linguistic skills with the animals, all animals it seemed, would serve her well on their farm. Sarafina thought briefly of the ewe that was about to lamb, knowing she would not be there should anything go wrong. She had to believe Thom and Lilianna, and Olitus, of course, would manage.

Shaking her braid back over her shoulder, Sarafina brought herself back to the present and scanned the wall and the tack hanging there. Halfway to the back of the shed, a pack, larger than the one she had recently used for her overnight trip to the Holy Oak, dangled from a hook. Alongside it, a slightly bigger water bladder draped over a wooden peg. Sarafina's bedroll was already in the house, along with the journey cakes and dried fruit and meat she had prepared during the week. Her quiver and bow would supply her with the majority of her food along the two-week expedition.

She took down the pack and bladder and continued to the back of the shed, setting them at her feet to free her hands. She had fought off an anxiousness all morning, associating it with the angst she felt in leaving her family. She needed to focus the Sense on preparing for the weeks ahead. Taking a deep breath, she slowly scanned the walls and floor.

The shed got messier from here. Along the back wall, a shelf was crammed with tiny castoffs. Rusted hinges lay in a pile next to an old latch. A broken awl and leather straps floated above an array of miscellany: bits of an old plow, a dented feed bucket filled with metal shards, and a pile of odd, flat pieces of wood. She rummaged through smaller farm equipment and unused gear, not sure that she needed anything back here but feeling the urge to take inventory just the same. Olitus disliked throwing anything away, refurbishing materials down the road for his children or one of his men. Sarafina thought of this as his strange little quirk but admired his utilitarian ways. She sensed she would find what she needed.

At the back of the shelf, a glint of metal caught her eye. She moved aside a pair of climbing boots with crampons attached to them, leaning in closer. An old metal flask Olitus had carried with him in his bachelor days leaned against the back wall, its surface pocked with small patches of rust. Part of the metal was clear enough for Sarafina to see her reflection. She twisted her head to the side, raising her eyebrows and scrunching up her mouth, trying to lighten her mood. The metal distorted her face, casting her features into a clownish mask. She smiled and leaned in closer, then drew back with a start. Gone were her dark hair and olive skin, replaced with the fair complexion and blonde hair of her sister, Arialla.

"Oh, Arialla, no!"

As Sarafina watched, helpless to do anything, the face of her sister contorted in pain. The woman's eyes were bloodshot and kept rolling up in her head. Sarafina moved her hand, aching to reach out and help her sister. In doing so, she tipped the flask, and Arialla's features faded, replaced by another.

The tall form of Liannan filled the surface. Instinctively, Sarafina drew back. Liannan stood at the edge of an abyss. Air glittered and snapped around her from a bitter cold, like the fine-cut glass of a crystal goblet. Her face was as brittle as the snapping cold, her features chiseled by determination and disdain for any form of weakness. She raised one sharp fingernail, pointing it at Sarafina and slicing a line through the frigid air. Sarafina read her lips, knowing her mother's words were not directed at her.

"The blood of my enemies would suffice for wine."

The image distanced itself, and Sarafina watched Liannan step away from the sheer, icy cliff edge. The image shifted, and she now saw through Liannan's eyes. Liannan's formal guard stood before her. Their breath expelled in puffs of steam, and the air around them was dense with the sweat of exertion. Sarafina could feel their exhaustion . . . and their agitation. Her Sense told her they had been on the move since early morning to reach a village high in the snow-capped mountains. Sarafina leaned closer to the flask, her view shifting again to encompass Liannan standing before them.

"Burn it. Burn everything."

The finely crafted buildings behind her loomed vacantly in striking contrast to the whiteness of an encroaching blizzard. Their dark doorways and lightless windows were dark blots against the rusted metal of the flask. Sarafina could not see the occupants inside, but she could imagine the agony and loss. At Liannan's command, her silent companions moved off to do their leader's bidding. All except for one. Her eldest brother and Arialla's twin.

"Argath."

Her brother's name sent a great puff of dust billowing around the metal container. The walls of the shed seemed to close in further, and Sarafina, her hand at her mouth, stifled a sob.

"We do them a disservice without the burial rights."

Sarafina touched the cold metal of the flask and the image of Argath's equally cold, rebellious face.

"Oh Argath, take care," she whispered. No one questioned Liannan.

"We do all a disservice if we let any part of this contagion spread throughout Faltofar. Do not dictate to me what must be done for the good of our people."

Sarafina watched as her oldest brother pulled his hood up over his head and angrily stomped away. Alone, Liannan's face filled the metal side of the container, the glow from the growing flames of the buildings giving temporary color to the cold, regal woman standing at the edge of the snow-encased world.

The image began to waiver, and Sarafina felt panic rising in her. Helplessness and panic. What of Arialla and the child? She grabbed the flask and shook it. It shimmered, catching what little light permeated the shed, and then Arialla drifted back into focus. The encroaching flames flickered behind her, undulating like an eerie backdrop of death that had come to life. Her mouth contorted in a final plea: "Come, now." Just before the vision faded from the surface of the flask, Sarafina saw the tiny features of her young nephew clasped in Arialla's arms as flames engulfed them.

She bent double over the pack at her feet, holding firmly to the shelf, waiting for the walls of the shed to stop spinning. The dusty particles that seemed so much a part of the shed's interior slowed with her breathing, and in the dusky light she blinked back into the present, reassuring herself she was inside the shed, not lost in the cold, deathly vision reflected in the dim metal of the flask. She straightened to her full height, her jaw set, her lips drawn thin, determined more than ever to heed the call from Liannan if for no other reason than to lend support to her siblings. Her heart ached for Argath. For Arialla and the child. And what of the others?

A puff of air, winding through a gap in the shed door, twined through her braid, rocking her back on her heels. She knew better than to ignore the sign. Extending her hand, she moved it along the shelf, feeling the heat of attraction rise as she got to the flask. She grabbed it angrily, wanting to blame anything for the visions. Even the empty container. Fine, she would bring it. She grabbed her pack to shove the flask inside when her skin brushed up against an old pair of boots and rusted crampons. The container's metal nearly burned her hand.

"These, too, then."

She ripped the rusty crampons from the old boots. The clanking of metal on metal jarred her to the bone.

With her head aching and her eyes bleary from unshed tears, she made her way out into the yard, stumbling in the bright light. With her arms full of gear, she would have fallen had it not been for the steady hand on her jacket smoothly pulling her upright.

Sarafina's brilliant green eyes locked on the light purple of Olitus's. He held tightly to his wife's coat, keeping her vertical, taking in her pale, tight features.

"Fina?"

"Olitus, it's Arialla."

Sarafina couldn't finish and dropped the gear on the grass around her, her head down. Olitus's strong arms encircled her, and for a moment, she leaned against his warmth, his heartbeat against her cheek. She kept seeing the downy head of her nephew and his fevered red eyes.

"I need to explain." Her anguished eyes brimmed with tears. She rocked back on her heels away from him, distancing herself from his caring embrace.

"Arialla and . . ." she choked off a sob, "the new baby boy." She fought the despair that wanted to double her over. "They're dead."

Olitus wrapped his arms around his dark-haired wife and held her tightly. He could feel her wiry strength. There would be time in the near future when they would be apart and have to rely solely on their fortitude to get them through the further trials that lay in store. The time had not yet come, and he breathed in the scent of her, gathering strength and giving her strength in return.

The rustle of Cleo's feathers, as the bird landed on the roof of the shed, brought them back to the present. Sarafina shifted, and Olitus loosened his hold. He could feel her gather her focus, wrapping it around herself like a cloak.

"I must leave at once, Litus. I . . ." Sarafina's voice tapered off, her lips compressing, her eyes silently asking for his blessing. Unconsciously, her hand had gone to the small leather pouch dangling from a thong around her neck. Her talisman rested higher on her chest, ever-present. Inside the pouch, the small acorn from the Holy Oak nestled, a reassuring small lump.

It had been a week since she had been to the Holy Oak. A week since she had somehow, unknowingly, summoned Morauth. She and Olitus both understood that the omens predicting the return of the sorceress were far too real to deny. They understood, perhaps better than anyone else in Faltofar.

"Except for Tilga."

She would never forget the dwarf standing with her against Morauth. The ties that bound both their families to protect Faltofar ran deep in their veins. If it came to it, they would fight or die trying.

"As it was, so shall it always be."

The words were etched on her talisman in a long-dead language. She hadn't even realized she'd whispered them.

Olitus nodded slowly, his long fingers wrapping gently around her own. The weight of Cleo landing on his shoulder didn't lessen his apprehension, but the bird's presence reinforced his resolve to assist Sarafina in whatever way she needed him. He leaned forward and gently kissed her hand, releasing it. When he bent to the grass to pick up the pack, the water bladder and crampons, his eyes rested a moment on the dull metallic bone coiled around her ankle, an ever-present reminder of her recent family reunion. His eyes narrowed at the thought of the ghastly woman who had cast the spell.

Cleo had hopped from his shoulder to the grass next to the flask. She pecked at the metal several times, her head cocking one way and then the other, obviously fascinated with her reflection. Sarafina knelt, her fingers briefly skimming the bright feathers along the birds back before she picked up the weathered container.

Sarafina and Olitus faced each other a moment longer, both quietly memorizing the geography of each other's features. How long would it be until they saw one another again? Olitus leaned forward, his lips gently brushing the worry lines across his wife's forehead. He took the flask from her hand.

"I will fill this with Pago. It will serve to keep you warm some nights without me at your side."

He threw the crampons and bladder into the pack, hoisted it onto his free shoulder, and moved resolutely across the yard and up the stairs into the house. Sarafina, realizing she'd been gripping the acorn pouch, released it. It thumped lightly against her chest.

IN THE WIND

Lilianna gently reached down and stroked the titmouse's whiskers, softly shushing it. She chewed on the inside of her cheek, giving herself a moment to process the reality of not one, but six Sepheriis. Slowing her breathing, she waited, unsure what was required of her. The breeze around her had diminished to an eerie stillness.

"We are tethered to the clouds. A floating island, high in the sky." The thought made her wonder if their friend had isolated them here to hurt them? No, that didn't feel right.

"No. We are in this together." She wasn't sure if she had thought the words, or if her friend had spoken them in her mind.

A calmness settled over her. Almost detached, Lilianna studied the play of emotion crisscrossing her brother's face. His stance was that of an athlete readying himself for action. Perhaps a green, untried athlete, but still…It was one thing to befriend a single Sepherii, but to be surrounded by multiple ones was disconcerting at the very least.

Torr leaned into Thom, gently placing his hand on the boy's shoulder before moving away to join the circle of the others. At his touch, Thom relaxed slightly.

"Come, child." Torr's vibrant voice filled Lili's head. "He will be allright, as will you. Step forward and take your rightful place next to your brother."

The titmouse gave a startled squeak, and Lilianna realized it could hear the Sepherii. She stroked it reassuringly and tucked it back in her pocket.

She exhaled slowly, resisting the urge to reach out and touch the Sepherii as she passed through their circle. Her hands tingled.

The presence of so many of their kind rippled across her skin, their power intertwined with the salty updraft. The breeze lifted the Sepheriis' hair, exposing the perfect angles of their faces. Their tails swished in ornate patterns. The beauty of each one of them was distinct...and yet, they shared similar characteristics. Each had the same dazzling eyes as Torr, but their coats varied in metallic hues of golds, bronzes, and shimmering silver. The air radiated around them in ripples of tightly controlled physical energy – living, supernatural statues. Only their heads turned, slowly, following the girl's path into their midst. When she reached Thom, she nudged him with her shoulder, trying to lighten the tension.

"Lil, don't." The reprimand came out of the side of his mouth.

A skeggull drifted above the cliff edge and landed softly in the grass, followed quickly by more birds. If the Sepheriis noticed, they did not acknowledge them but continued to stare at the humans. More birds filtered down from the sky, landing quietly in twos and threes, folding their wings tightly around themselves. Their feathered circle spread out, surrounding the inner circle of Sepheriis.

"They have blue feet, Thom."

He glared down at her.

For a brief second, Lili thought she had seen a hint of a smile on Torr's face just before he spoke.

"The prophecy unfolds. A circle within a circle."

She shifted closer to her brother, the importance of the moment resonating inside her with the utterance of the word *prophecy*. Her fingers intertwined with Thom's. The combined voices of the Sepheriis wound through their minds.

"As in the old, let the new begin again. We are the six. We are the sign and the sum. We are the beginning, middle, and the end."

Torr alone spoke. "I am the Watcher."

"As in the old, let the..." Lilianna tried to repeat their words. As much as she wanted to retain what they said, she knew she would not, or perhaps, could not. Still, it seemed necessary. She tried again.

"The beginning, middle ,and the..."

Something about signs and sums of six. Her mind felt foggy, and Lili shook her head, trying to rid herself of a throbbing in her ears that mingled with the humming sound emanating from the Sepheriis.

Her thoughts drifted back in time. She had gone into the village to market with her mother. They had rounded the weathered corner of an old stall adjacent to one of the stone buildings, a creative masterpiece built by masons long dead. She recalled how intricate the structure seemed to her after the simplicity of their cabin. Melodic chanting from a group of women had filled the air. They sat in a circle, sewing, their faces lit by the late afternoon sunshine, enjoying the last of the heat reflected off the warm rock walls. Sewing and singing. Her mother's beautiful alto voice had joined in for a moment, acknowledging the ancient magic they wove with sound. Proudly, Lilianna had grasped her mother's hand tighter, just as she did now with Thom. The magical moment had ended as the sun tipped over the horizon, and the song had come to an end. But the women's joyous laughter had stayed with Lili. She smiled up at her brother. He held his free hand to his forehead, moving it from side to side.

"Thom?" He kept his eyes closed and did not respond.

She leaned in closer to her brother and waited.

The air in the circle around them seemed to thicken. Thom's eyes snapped open. He had felt the shift too. The vibration of sound began to pick up small flotsam of grass and earth. It swirled around their feet, then moved higher until it became necessary to cover their faces with their free hands. Cautiously Lili peeked through her fingers.

"Thom?" Squinting through the debris, Lilianna looked down at her feet, fascinated more than fearful by the fact that she was no longer standing on solid earth, but floating inches above the ground. She could feel the rising panic in her brother by the intensity of his grip on her hand but, after the initial shock, all she felt was calm. She drifted higher.

The titmouse, who at first had been so very nervous, seemed to be adjusting to its adventure. The little rodent excitedly exited Lili's pocket, scampering to the higher perch of her shoulder for a better view of the events. Her red hair now fanned out around her, and the mouse was kept busy dodging around and through it. Seeing the stowaway for the first time, Thom shook his head, trying to clear it of a vision he was having trouble processing.

"A titmouse?" His voice came out in a squeak.

Lilianna didn't answer. She found that she liked the weightless feeling, and the humming was somehow soothing. If she could just… concentrate…a…bit…more. Tilting her head, she tried focusing on the titmouse's whiskers, but all it did was make her go almost cross-eyed.

The Sepheriis grasped hands, their eyes radiating a deep blue. The skeggulls now stood as immobile as the inner circle of Sepheriis, their blue feet and legs tiny pillars of support.

"You must let go of each other," Torr said through the soft humming. "Have faith in the One that binds us all."

Lilianna let out a little yelp, and Thom realized he had squeezed her hand even tighter, trying to keep her anchored to the ground. Guiltily, he lessened his grip but didn't let go. How could he best protect her, protect them both?

"Thom, it's allright," Lilianna said. "Let go."

He barely heard his sister's voice as the magical wind increased around them, but her confidence enveloped him. As Lili looked down at him, her face radiated an angelic peacefulness. He closed his eyes against the unbelievable and opened his other senses to try to understand.

He could feel heat in her hand. It radiated up his arm, and with it came a wave of gratitude for his sister. Suddenly, he understood, and his apprehension drifted up and away. He opened his eyes to perceive light emanating from between their fingers. Beyond the circle of Sepheriis, past the stoic birds, the deep blue waters of the ocean glittered the same color as the eyes of the beings which surrounded them. He saw the pattern of circles within circles, and in a moment of complete clarity, he acknowledged what was inevitable. He, Lilianna, all of them, were part of the whole. In letting go of her, he was affirming his belief in her, in all of them.

The titmouse seemed to have come to a similar conclusion and showed its new enlightened state by jumping up and down on Lilianna's shoulder. "ThomThomThomThom!" it spun in a circle. "Letgoletgoletgooooooo!"

Thom heard only squeaks, but the mouse's enthusiastic message was clear. He released his sister's hand, accepting that in doing so he was freeing them both. He watched Lilianna rise higher. A soft smile spread across her face and her eyes, slightly closed, shifted skyward now. The titmouse stood on its hind legs, its whiskers twitching in anticipation.

"Anticipation of what?" wondered Thom, staring up at his sister. "What are we becoming?"

The humming grew louder and, as it did, Lilianna's body slowly began to rotate, each revolution moving faster until she became a blur of red hair. A cone of light, emanating from her center, twirled skyward, radiating across the sky. Holding his hand over his squinting and watering eyes, Thom saw a small dark shape drift up the funnel of light. Just as he realized the dark little mass was the titmouse, it caught the updraft and shot into the sky, disappearing from view. Lilianna's revolutions began to slow. Thom craned his neck in the hope of seeing where the titmouse might come down, but the tiny animal was gone.

"What if that had been Lil?" For a split-second Thom felt guilty. He had given value of one life over another.

The humming from the Sepheriis changed, growing softer. Their music seemed to cushion Lilianna as she drifted down to the grass, landing gently on the soft padded earth. Her brother moved cautiously to her side and knelt, resting his hand on her shoulder.

"Thom, I've had the best dream." She yawned loudly, knuckling her eyes.

Thom picked a piece of grass from her hair and scanned the sky. The clear blue expanse remained empty of any sign of the small mouse.

"It's all right, Thom," his sister said, blinking upward as well, her eyes glowing a soft blue. "He's the Messenger."

Lilianna's words reverberated across the plateau, stirring the Skeggulls into flight. Over the sound of their flapping wings, his sister's voice rippled, over and over, "...the Messenger, the Messenger,...Messenger...Messenger....enger...enger."

He extended his hand to his sister, who grasped it and slowly rose to her feet.

THE MESSENGER

Dundalee's hand froze, the Corianna seed she had been grinding settling to the bottom of the mortar. Late afternoon light glittered off the flecks of metal embedded in the stone pestle that lay forgotten in her hand. A noise, like scraping branches against a glass pane, had caught her ear. But there were no branches close to the house. Wiping her hands on her apron, she walked through the patch of sunlight to the far kitchen window. At first, she saw nothing more than the movement of swirling leaves near the garden bench, but as she began to turn away she noticed a small furry lump on the sill, one little paw plastered against the glass, its claws extended.

"Ah, well then," she said, tapping the glass where the little mouse's claws rested. The titmouse slumped forward.

"Oh my, you poor little one."

Careful not to dislodge the small furry body from its perch on the sill, Dundalee lifted the latch and opened the window, gently picking up the limp form. Running her finger down its body, she searched for any breaks. Her ministrations were met with a contented squeak, and the titmouse stirred and raised its head to look at her. Dundalee drew in her breath. Its eyes were rainbow-colored and glowed not unlike...

"Ah, little man. Are you the Messenger?"

The titmouse yawned widely and raised itself to its hind legs, its whiskers wiggling in importance.

"I see," said Dundalee, smiling gently at the animal balanced in the palm of her hand. She gently placed the mouse back on the sill. "I understand and commit to the One."

As if in response to her words, the wind picked up the last of the leaves from the patio outside. They whirled in through the open window, twirling briefly around the mouse, then whipped into the air, taking the little creature with them.

"Safe journey, Messenger." She leaned on the sill, gazing up into the branches and blue sky beyond until the mouse was entirely out of sight.

"I believe it is time to pack."

Gently she shut the window, pulling the latch into place.

Olitus stood at the fence, the sturdy structure of the coral lending him something substantial to lean on. He was afraid, but not for himself. He shoved away from the fence, his irritation an outlet for the knot that coiled in his chest like a Plythe snake ready to strike. He would move mountains, slay dragons and sorceresses to protect the woman to whom he'd pledged his heart and whose departing figure grew smaller and smaller across the field.

She would be gone long before the children came back from wherever their adventures today had taken them. He had no doubt the Sepherii had his agenda. Sepheriis always did, and he would never question Torr. Nor was he concerned for the children's safety. It was unfortunate their mother could not wait for them, but he and Sarafina knew time wasn't necessarily on their side.

"And perhaps it's better this way."

Distractedly he ran his hand through his hair and headed back toward the shed. He had kissed Sarafina goodbye, assuring her he would follow as soon as he had gathered his men. The dagger rested lightly against his hip, and he touched the hilt in acknowledgment of his responsibilities.

"I will do you honor," he whispered, sliding open the shed door and thinking of his brave forebears who had wielded the weapon before him. He was a strong man and had had his share of skirmishes over the years, but his stomach clenched in nervous anticipation of the battle to come.

"We will fight for Faltofar," he said to no one.

On the floor at the back of the shed, he moved the pile of odd pieces of lumber to one side and scraped away at the dirt with a trowel. Impatiently he slid aside the last of the soil with his hands until he found the small metal ring. He grabbed it with both index fingers and pulled. Slowly the trap door revealed itself, the stiff hinges making low, rusty groans of protest as he lifted the heavy wood. The last of the dirt drifted down onto the ground, and Olitus let the door fall away. Getting on his knees, he reached down into the previously hidden storage area. With a grunt he heaved one, then a second, heavy canvas sack up into the dim light. Slamming the door shut again, he hefted the bags to his shoulders and headed into the yard, dropping them on the grass at his feet in a distinctive sound of chattering chain metal.

Would that he could have suited his wife in the strong, dwarf-made armor. He resisted the urge to go to the fence and scan the distant field to see if she was still in sight, to offer her protection, even if ill-fitted. He knew it would do no good. As a healer, she had always refused to wear anything resembling battle gear.

"Go with speed and the light of the One, my heart oath," he whispered, his fingers working to untie the cord holding closed the mouth of the first sack. A glint of metal inside the bag caught the late afternoon sunlight. As Olitus began to pull out the contents of the canvas bag, something hit the side of the shed, like a clod of dirt being thrown.

"What in the name of?" he exclaimed, dropping the bag and standing. At the base of the shed wall, a small titmouse sat on the grass, waggling its snout from side to side. Olitus quickly stepped forward and picked up the semi-conscious ball of fur. It swayed in his palm, holding its paws to its head, its eyes closed, whiskers trembling.

"Poor thing. Who treats you thus?"

Olitus walked to the well and pulled the dipper from its hook, filling it from the bucket sitting on the ground.

"Here, tiny one. Drink."

While the little one satisfied its thirst, Olitus gave in and looked across the field to where Sarafina had departed. The horizon was empty, save for the sway of the early summer wheat. Newly revived, the mouse began pulling at the dipper, drawing Olitus's attention back down to it. The glowing orbs of the rodent's eyes startled him, causing him to almost drop both the dipper and the mouse into the bucket at his feet.

"Ah," Olitus said, regaining his composure. "I see."

Olitus studied the small animal in his hand a moment more. "Well, my little friend, you have been given a considerable task."

He nodded to the mouse as if it had replied. He took a deep breath, feeling the responsibility of what he was about to do settle on his shoulders. It felt heavier by far than the chain mail.

"Off you go, Messenger, to the next. And know that..." The enormity of his words caught in his throat like a chunk of stale bread swallowed without water. So many lives were at stake. "And know that I, Olitus of the Finn, descendant of Rendar, commit to the One."

The mouse gave a squeak and righted itself up on its hind legs. Olitus held his hand out at arm's length. Within a blink, a gust of wind blasted across the yard, hard enough that Olitus had to close his eyes to avoid the grit in the air. When he opened them again, the Messenger was gone.

Walking back to the canvas sacks, he reached in and pulled forth a war jacket. The metal, hammered by the most skilled dwarf crafts-man, was nearly impenetrable.

"The Messenger is timely," he said, hefting the armor up toward the blue sky.

The Rememberer finished his private history lesson for the two dwarves with a flourish of tightly rolled parchment held at arm's length.

"This is one of the only original written accounts of the Great Battle. The rest, as you see, is in the books. But these . . ." The parchment swung wide overhead, nearly hitting several hanging pots and a spare lantern in the close bachelor quarters. Both dwarves took a cautious step back, Berold mumbling in irritation at the human's long reach. Dundar, who, as usual, had not made a sound, stood closest to the door. He opened it wider, either needing more air in the small house or preparing for a quick escape from the crazy, stick-thin human. Blisk was oblivious.

"In here, somewhere here, yes…no, that's not the right… hmmm." He'd set the valuable parchment at the end of the counter, freeing both hands to rummage through the piles of paper. A welcome draft of air from the window above his sink caught the tube and it rolled off the counter landing on the floor with a hollow, musical thwump, heading for the open doorway. Both dwarves watched its progress, keeping one eye on the mumbling human. Nodding at Dundar to grab the scroll, Berold addressed Blisk.

"What's we need to know, Rememberer, is the signs again. It wouldn't be my first battle, and it won't be my last, by the Metal Gods," he mumbled, then more clearly. "But the Dwarves of Glenn have to have a sign and what you been telling us seems to be…"

A noise from the doorway stopped Berold from whatever he was about to say. Dundar had begun spinning around like a top, grabbing at something in his hair. Stunned and with his mouth hanging open, Berold scrunched up his nose in an effort to figure out what he thought he'd heard. Then the younger dwarf spoke again. And loudly.

"Off! Get it off! I hates rodents!"

Neither Blisk nor Berold made a move to help the younger dwarf, who had begun to leap around the room. Blisk, still lost in his history lesson, merely cocked his head sideways, his features glazed over in thought. Berold's eyes had narrowed at the realization that his mute companion had unmistakably just spoken—and quite clearly at that.

Angrily, and from a habit of years, he reached for his club, his hand encircling the shaft of the new, untried weapon, then thought better of it. The memory of the tussle with the boy-human, and the loss of his old, favorite thumper, added to his crossness. Growling an expletive about humans and their nosey offspring, he stomped swiftly across the cabin, focusing on Dundar, who was bent low and desperately trying to reach into the back of his shirt. With exact precision, Berold landed a kick to Dundar's backside, sending the dwarf flying out the door and skidding across the porch on his belly.

"You wasn't honest with me, boy!"

Dundar, winded, lay in a heap. The mouse took the opportunity to scurry out of the material, but before he could get halfway across the porch, the toe of Berold's boot landed on his tail, pinning him to the wood flooring. The older dwarf reached down and grabbed its tail, swinging the mouse midair like a furry pendulum, ignoring its angry squeaks and little claws. Dundar rolled over, scooting on his backside away from the upside-down mouse. He shrugged at Berold, a sheepish smile on his craggy, young face. Berold growled again, ready to fling the mouse off into the grass and launch himself at the boy.

"Wait!"

Blisk, who had finally come out of his fog, stood directly behind Berold. Both dwarves frowned at the human, who was frantically pointing at the little creature swaying upside-down.

"By the hammer of the Metal Gods," Berold said. Grabbing the swinging mouse with his other hand, he flipped it right side up and into the palm of his hand. It raised itself up, crossing its arms, whiskers twitching angrily. Dundar stood quickly, far enough away from any fist Berold might throw at him, but close enough to observe what he now realized was no ordinary rodent. The dwarves and the human leaned in to study the titmouse.

"Ah, yes, yes, yes!" Blisk said, rocking back and forth on the balls of his feet, an ecstatic expression on his face.

Dundar looked questioningly from Berold to the jittery human, then again at the mouse. The old dwarf squinted at the tiny animal and moved close enough that his bulbous nose and the titmouse's snout almost touched. Mouse and dwarf glared at each other.

Blisk, who had stopped rocking, reverently leaned forward and gently took the mouse, patting it gently on the head with his finger. Berold backed away and crossed his arms over his chest, unaware that he stood exactly as the mouse was standing.

"That, Dundar," the wise, old warrior said grudgingly to the younger dwarf, "is the sign I been askin' about." Nodding toward Blisk's hand, he scowled, "Meet the Messenger."

Blisk pursed his lips, a show of concern on his face. Berold knew what the Rememberer wanted to ask, but he hesitated. Once said, the deep magic could not be undone, and memories of those dark days haunted him still.

"The thing is, I know'd it would come again, and I'll be damned if the Dwarves of the Glenn will wait. Not this time," Berold mumbled to himself.

Uncrossing his arms, the warrior took a breath so deep his barrel chest jutted out past his belt. He bent forward, his nose, again, inches away from the tiny mouse. When he exhaled, the titmouse scrunched its face up, its whiskers vibrating in irritation. Convinced by what he saw, Berold stood to his full, short height.

"I commit the Dwarves of the Glenn to the One, Messenger." He spoke clearly, his words reverberating across the porch. The titmouse sighed loudly but lowered its furry arms to its side, somewhat appeased. Still, mouse and dwarf continued to glare at each other until Berold flicked his hand at the tiny Messenger.

"Shouldn't you be off, now?"

————

Tilga stopped scrubbing, her scalp tingling, the brush in her hand forgotten. Something had happened. The pots hanging above her sink had begun to sway so hard they clanked against each other, and she could hear shouts from the men outside. She felt it too, almost like someone was pulling on her ear, demanding her attention.

"What has that husband of mine gone and done?" she asked, wiping her hands on the towel by the sink. Scurrying to the window and throwing it open, she yelled to the first dwarf who ran past.

"What is it? What has happened?"

An older dwarf, hurriedly shuffling down the road beyond her fenced yard, stopped only long enough to shout his response. "We are summoned to war for the One." And then he was gone.

Tilga slowly closed the window, wringing the dishtowel around her hands.

A determined knocking distracted her from her uneasy thoughts. Tucking the towel in her skirt waist, she went to the heavy front door, opening it cautiously. Dundalee stood on the step. Tilga shook her head and began to close the door, but Dundalee, ignoring the poor greeting, leveraged her way through the narrow opening and into the house, taking Tilga by the arm.

"Come, come, Tilga, dear. No room for sore feelings. It's time to pack."

––––––––

Days later, when the wind finally stopped, the little titmouse had traveled far and wide. Like a colossal slumbering beast awakened from a long nap, the lands of Faltofar and its good people rallied to the cries of their leaders.

"We fight for the One."

In the dark corners across the land, something else also began to awaken. The angry, lost, and inconsequential shifted their downcast eyes up toward the smoldering skies, hearing the howling promise of power. They slithered, crawled, and hobbled out of the darkness toward their mistress's castle, leaving destruction in their paths.

THICKER THAN BLOOD

Nero rubbed harder. The Mistress was never happy, no matter how hard he tried to please her. Her leather boots, made from the hide of one of her many "pets," gleamed dully in the meager light. Looking out the high window, Nero could see only gray. The incessant fog that surrounded the fortress made him yearn for the lush forest around the village where he'd grown up. The thought of what he'd left behind made him sneer.

"The old fool has no idea how high I's can reach."

The rubbing of cloth on leather slowed to a stop as the dwarf lost himself in visions of grandeur. A beatific grimace spread across his bulbous features as he played out the torments he would inflict on those who had wronged him: his father, the villagers, the human healer most of all. Lost in his thoughts, Nero did not see the mocking kay flit in through the turret window until the bird was almost on top of him.

"Trouble double Nero Zerooooo," it cackled, flying so close to the dwarf's head that he involuntarily ducked, waving the stump of his useless arm over his head to brush off the offending bird.

"Be gone, you worthless flutterer!" the dwarf screamed at the bird.

The mocking kay had landed on a piece of metal jutting out from the wall. A chain attached to Nero's ankle looped through the circular end at the tip of the metal rod. Ignoring the boot he held between his feet, Nero stood and spat at the bird, then wiped some of the drool off his lips with the rag in his hand.

"Zeroooooo, Nero Nero."

The mocking kay fluffed its feathers and deposited a steaming green blob of bird poop on the floor next to Nero's feet. It splattered on Nero's pant leg, his filthy feet, and the boot he'd been polishing.

"Now see what you done!"

Nero moved as far away from the bird as the chain would allow. Squatting, he put the boot back between his feet and, with his one hand, began to rub the leather again.

"I'll tell her you dun it, I will," he mumbled, periodically scowling up at the bird. "I'll tell her you're the first one I want to... to."

Nero's rubbing slowly came to a stop again, images of the bird rotating on a spit over an open fire bringing a smile to his face. The creaking of hinges as the door to the turret opened brought him to his feet, and he blinked in the light from the doorway. A sentry gripped the door handle with a beefy, clawed paw, his hairy arm covered in dark armor. The white of sharpened teeth held in a perpetual grimace greeted Nero. The smell of decay wafted across the room, and the dwarf quickly tried to breathe only through his mouth.

"Stand tall, little man," barked the sentry, heeding his own advice. "She comes."

Nero felt the warmth on his leg before he realized he'd wet himself. Ashamed, he turned sideways, wiping quickly at the growing stain on his breeches. He didn't want her to think less of him. Perhaps she wouldn't notice.

"You fidget, midget."

Nero shifted from one foot to the other. Morauth smiled down at the dwarf, amused at her rhyming, but the smile did not reach the bottomless depths of her black eyes.

"Tttttt…trouble! Hahahahahhaaaaaaaaa!" cackled the mocking kay.

One sleek eyebrow raised as Morauth waved an indifferent long, elegant hand at the bird, who gave a little squawk and froze on his perch. For a split second, it balanced before teetering and falling dead to the floor at Nero's feet.

"Perhaps you should use that to rub my boots," she said softly. "The rag seems to be…" Her eyes slid down Nero's pant leg, where the urine stain had darkened the cloth through to his knees. "….Slightly used."

Nero swallowed and was about to respond when she abruptly turned away and glided to the window. She stood for a long moment, gazing out at the sullen sky. Nero held tightly to the rag in his hand, keeping his eyes on the bird. On anything but Morauth. The mocking kay's legs twitched, and Nero realized the bird wasn't quite dead, but in the throes of some painful agony.

"Won't be long, stupid feather brain," he whispered under his breath.

"What did you say, dwarf?"

Morauth's penetrating stare pierced Nero's brain, and searing pain brought him to his knees.

"I, I." He held his hand to his head. The pain was so intense, he bent and vomited, grateful he'd thought to shift away from her at the last moment.

"You disgust me," Morauth said, her red lips pursed together, exhaling through her nose, her fingernail raking the rock below the window. "My dear Nero. So much like 'Hero.'" Her cynical smile vanished within seconds. "You were so misnamed. Such a pity. I had such high hopes."

She pulled at her long dark sleeves, covering her wrists with the material. Despite having been warned by one of the sentries to keep his eyes averted from her, Nero had seen the scars there. It gave him a certain amount of pleasure to know she'd once been chained too.

"Never mind. You may still be of use." Her words tapered off, their meaning as comforting as the dampness oozing from the dark stone walls of Nero's cell.

The dwarf stood up but kept his head down. He wiped a corner of his mouth with the well-used rag, holding it to his nose first to see if it smelled like pee.

"I am plagued with idle necessities," she sniffed, her face suffused in a grimace. "It seems the time has come, my dear boy. Your papa has rallied the wee uglies of the Glenn to a fight they cannot win."

Her words sent a chill of hope through Nero. Forgetting the sentry's warnings, he beamed up at his mistress, his oath of loyalty ready. The stump of his arm ached with the memories of all the pain and insults he had endured as a child, surrounded by strong, complete young dwarves. They could toil in the mines. They could hammer metal. But he was just a crippled, useless nothing. Not even the human witch had been able to craft her magic into a useful potion to save his hand. He hated her for that. Nero's dirty face crinkled in a smile that resembled a snarl.

A draft from the window caught Morauth's dark hair, and it twined around her head. Silhouetted against the dreary light, Nero could have sworn he saw likenesses of snakes writhing and caressing her shoulders. The smile left his face and he stepped back involuntarily, his chain clinking loudly. Morauth looked down at the dwarf. This time her smile lit her eyes a dull red.

"Afraid, little Nero?"

She waited. Nero understood this was his opportunity to speak. He opened his mouth, but no words came out. Morauth began to laugh. The sound echoed through the stone chamber louder and louder until Nero couldn't stand it any longer and covered one ear with his hand. The stump moved upward, uselessly waving in the air.

"Ah, poor, poor, Nero. Cat got your tongue?"

A flurry of dark wings covered the windowsill, as the leader of Morauth's pets landed heavily on the sill, his girth blocking out what little light came from the opening. The dark, catlike creature whose wingspan, when spread, would surpass the width of the cell, perched precariously on the stone ledge, huge claws gouging into the rock, sending little chunks clattering to the floor. It growled, then settled itself more firmly into the framework of the window. Rather than fur, virtually impenetrable blue-black scales covered the winged predator. Its gleaming eyes hungrily devoured the dwarf. Yellow fangs glittered at the tip of its snout, and its pink tongue darted out, licking leathery lips in anticipation of a meal. Morauth extended her hand, scratching the cat under its chin, not taking her eyes off Nero.

"Speaking of kitties," she purred. "Sentry. Unchain our friend Nero. See that he gets himself cleaned up and ready."

She scratched the cat's chin one last time, addressing it directly. "Not just yet, my pet," she said, correctly interpreting its unblinking stare. "Ready your kind. We leave by the setting sun three days hence."

With a nod, the feline dropped from sight, the only sign it had been there were the deep grooves made from its sharp claws as it launched itself into the air. Morauth, lowering her arm, moved to the cell door, stepping delicately around the pile of vomit on the floor. Brushing past the sentry, she gave one last command.

"See that he cleans my boots thoroughly or cut off his other hand."

TALISMAN

L ilianna separated herself from the group at Torr's request. The grogginess had departed, leaving something else in its place.

"I feel grounded." She laughed at her own description, noting the irony having just floated in the air.

She walked next to Torr along the edge of the cliff, idly kicking small rocks off the grassy lip, wondering as they dropped from sight if any of the Skeggulls were silently cursing her from below. The breeze had come up again, stirring Torr's tail into a snapping ribbon of light and causing Lilianna's eyes to water.

"Didn't you wonder, Lilianna? When your brother first introduced me to your father – Thom must have told you of the exchange – did you not realize your father and I had already met?" Torr's question surprised her.

After the titmouse had been launched into the sky, the group of Sepheriis had slowly moved closer to the children, and Lili had felt the foggy dream state begin to fade. The Sepheriis' presence, rather than frighten her, gave her strength and a feeling of being part of something bigger than herself. She felt like she'd known them her whole life, and not just as images in a picture book. Thom had become more trusting of them, too. His eagle-like stare had softened, embracing the grandeur of the unique beings before them.

The squawking of the skeggells below them began to make her feel guilty. She stopped kicking the stones and faced Torr. The Sepherii's eyes no longer glowed but studied Lilianna kindly.

"Torr…" She licked her dry lips, not sure exactly what she wanted to express. She gnawed at the inside of her mouth, giving herself more time to say what she was feeling.

"When Thom rides on your back, he is like an extension of your body."

Torr nodded in agreement, a fleeting smile crinkling his usually stoic features. "Your father was just as skilled."

Lilianna's thoughts traversed along the plateau back to where Thom stood amongst the other Sepheriis, his hands tentatively touching their strong backs. She felt a deepening sense of peace and lost herself in the sensation for just a moment.

"You are of the line of the Finn clan, and as such, you are destined to protect the lands of Faltofar. Your line and mine are inter-twined forever." The Sepherii crossed his arms. "Whether we like it or not."

"I still don't understand." Lilianna's hand had wandered to her talisman, twisting it this way and that.

"The answer is at your fingertips."

Lili narrowed her eyes at Torr, the peace she had felt dissolving almost instantly.

"We are but tools to be used? You respond to my questions with riddles? And…" She paused, trying unsuccessfully to squelch her anger. "My bloodline gives me some responsibility I never signed up for?" She yanked at the talisman cord, the leather burning the back of her neck before it stretched and finally separated. She held the talisman in her hand, face-up, resentment crisscrossing her face, tears welling at the corner of her eyes.

"Explain it to me, because I seem to be missing something." The edge in her voice was new to her, burning in her chest and sending a fire throughout her body. It confused her that moments before she had felt such peace and now...now, she wanted to...She turned into the wind, gritting her teeth, a burning at the back of her throat. Her fists clenched around the talisman. It was that, or cry. And cry she would not.

"Study it, daughter of this land."

The Sepherii brought his stone-like face closer to Lili's fist. Rather chagrined, she opened her hand, and Torr's warm breath enveloped the cool disk. With a quick swipe at her eyes, she did as the Sepherii requested, studying the image engraved on the metal. The top half of the coin was filled with the trunk and branches of a beautiful tree. The leaves, made of tiny nicks in the metal, glinted in the sunlight. Beneath the tree, on the lower half of the sphere, two hands spread wide, the fingers grouped in patterns of two: little finger and ring finger, middle finger with pointer finger. The thumbs on each hand touched at their tips, like a bridge. Around the edges of the coin, in a language long unused, were the words, "As it was, so shall it always be."

Lilianna understood that the symbols, the tree and the hands, represented a combination of her parents — the joining of two lines. The Holy Oak was sacred to Sarafina's clan. Its knowledge and protection were rooted in the soil of Faltofar; no matter where any of their clan went, its members were connected. Although she had never seen a Holy Oak, she knew there was one in the deep forest and, of course she knew of the one in the legend of the great battle that had clung to the cliffs of the high country.

The hands of the clan of Finn were more of a mystery. She had always thought this symbolized their strength in protecting the people of Faltofar. They were leaders and warriors from the great battle. Her ancestor, Rendar, had been the one who had wielded the dagger that had caused mountains to move and had stopped the Dark Ones. The same dagger hung from her father's belt. The very same dagger that everyone assumed would go to Thom someday.

Torr's words brought her out of her reverie. "You traverse the correct paths in your thoughts, child. Symbols of your family on both sides, yes, but there is more. Look closely at the configuration of the hands. There is meaning in the pattern in which they are formed."

She moved her hands thoughtfully in front of her face, looking closely at the grouping of the fingers. She had toyed with the idea of their pattern but dismissed it as the artist's rendition of symmetry. Torr reacted in what could only be translated as a laugh, his head held high, his eyes staring out over the vast ocean.

"Symmetry is one way to look at it."

The sun had dropped low in the sky, and the path of sunlight glittered brightly on the horizon.

"If you count the grouping of fingers, by distancing the hands and separating the thumbs into their own single group, you come up with six."

Lili raised her eyebrows and waited. Torr stamped his hoof, his tail swishing in agitation.

"Thom is better at riddles than I am, Torr."

"Walk with me, child of the Finn," the Sepherii said apologetically.

Still holding the talisman tightly in her right hand, Lilianna placed her left on the arch of her friend's back, where horse and human torso met in perfect unison. The contact somehow soothed the angst she felt.

"We are the six." The Sepherii tipped his head back slightly, motioning with his chin toward Thom and the other Sepheriis. "The hands of a Finn have the ability to call us. Separate the two hands, Lilianna. Six groupings of fingers. Six Sepheriis." Lilianna looked down at her own hands.

"This number is powerful. The hands of man draw us, and we, in turn, draw energy. Both good and bad. Our kind made a pact at the end of the Dark Days with your forebear, Rendar. We are bound by this agreement to come in times of need."

"And, I am..." Torr paused and continued. "I am personally bound by my actions. A mistake I made a long, long time ago." His words ebbed slowly out, like a creek running its course to dry.

Lili shook her head.

"But we found you injured in the forest," she said. "If not for your injury, you wouldn't have been there."

They began to walk again.

"Not so, child. You are a descendant of Rendar. I heeded a call. It is my duty, of the six, to answer the summons. It is also my duty to train each generation." Uncharacteristically, he brushed hair out of his eyes in an almost human-like gesture.

For Lilianna, the seemingly-disparate pieces of a story, hers and that of Faltofar, were beginning to fit together and make sense.

"That is why my father knew you!" she exclaimed. "He trained with you as well?"

Torr nodded in agreement. "Every generation of Finnekin born has been trained. Every leader who wields the dagger of Rendar becomes versed in how to ride." He halted and crossed his arms. "My mistake was in assuming that leader was your brother."

Lost in thought, Lillianna continued walking, unaware that Torr had stopped. As his final words registered, she froze, absorbing what he had just said.

"Are you suggesting that I am...?" Her voice caught as another thought almost brought her to her knees. She began to feel sick to her stomach.

"Torr, did my father meet the other five?" The Sepherii gave no response. She felt a weight settling down on her shoulders and asked the question that was most on her mind.

"Has the time come again that humans are in need of the six?" she asked her friend.

"Not just humans, Lilianna Finnekin, but all of Faltofar."

Lilianna clenched her jaw tightly, brushing a stray hair from her forehead, exactly as Torr had done moments before. The sun had dipped lower, and the breeze voiced a whisper of coolness that penetrated the thin jacket of her childhood.

———

Thom watched his sister and Torr walk away along the edge of the cliff, their heads close together in conversation. He had no desire to follow them, to leave the other Sepheriis. His distrust was gone, replaced by absolute fascination. They had moved in closer, emanating a bright glow that was soothing. The kindness in their eyes softened the stone-like features of their faces. Each Sepherii he touched radiated sparks of energy up his arms, electrifying his whole body until he felt almost the same perfection he had felt when riding Torr. Any trepidation he had of them had disappeared completely.

"What amazing creations you are," he murmured to them. One of the Sepheriis, whose coat and hair was a shade darker than Torr, spoke for all of them.

"We are the six, child. You are a Finn and the descendant of Liannan. What has begun cannot be undone. The Messenger has been sent." The Sepherii who had spoken regally peered out over the plateau. The others said nothing.

Thom thought of his sister's little friend, the titmouse. He swallowed his concern for the tiny rodent, choosing instead to trust what Lili had told him of the dream she'd had inside the circle. The Messenger would be safe, protected. Thom had to believe.

He lowered his hand from the thick coat of the last Sepherii he had stroked and looked toward the higher end of the plateau where Lili and Torr had gone. Having been lost in his thoughts, he was surprised to see them almost back at the group of Sepheriis. Lili's face revealed an intensity that had not been there when they had walked away.

"What now?"

Hearing the concern and determination in her brother's voice reminded Lilianna that she was not alone in this battle at this life-changing moment. Her features softened into a calm resolve. She nodded to Torr, then addressed her brother, her words chosen carefully.

"Torr tells me we are...needed, brother. We leave immediately for home."

Seeing the questioning look on his face, Lili took a deep breath, feeling the weight of responsibility settle over her like an unwanted royal cloak.

"The five will join us later," she said, motioning to the other Sepheriis. "Their job is complete. For now. The Messenger was sent." She tipped her chin respectfully at the others. "We stay with Torr." Her voice rang with a strength Thom had not heard before.

One by one, the Sepheriis approached Torr, briefly touching hands and moving aside. When the last of the five had come forward, they faced Lilianna and Thom. Connected by some unspoken tie, the Sepheriis bowed forward on their long front legs. Then, in a unified, fluid motion, they rose to standing and lunged forward and off the cliff, soaring up and away into the dwindling, soft-blue light.

"Mount up?" Thom asked distractedly, shielding his eyes against the light radiating off of five sets of translucent wings.

Torr dipped his head and motioned for the children to join him. Giving the departing Sepheriis a final squint, Thom walked to Torr's side and with the precision that comes from long practice, pulled himself onto the Sepherii's back, extending his arm to Lilianna and pulling her up behind him.

"I will give you a history lesson on the way home," she said, leaning into her brother's back.

Torr launched off the plateau in the opposite direction from where the other Sepheriis had disappeared. With the beating of his wings settling into a rhythmic pace, Lilianna slowly let go of her brother's waist and extended her arms wide, her skin sparkling in the high clear air.

SARAFINA

The bowstring stretched tautly, its symmetric arc like a crescent moon. Sarafina fought the urge to release the tension of her hand against the bow. Of all the times to have an itchy nose. It was almost laughable.

Her eyes narrowed, following the movement in the thick bushes. Holding her breath, she quietly adjusted her angle, pulling further back on the bowstring. Slowing her breathing, she focused on the small furry silhouette of a rabbit in the understory. Just as she was about to release the arrow, twigs exploded around the small rodent.

"Fiddle." She lowered her arm, disgusted, as a hawk swooped up and away with her dinner. Closing her eyes, she rolled her head from side to side, fatigue making her movements less fluid than usual.

After more than a week's travel, she was tired and rather hungry. She had made good time, stopping only to replenish her water, fill her belly on berries, take short catnaps, and kill. Kill if she had to. To survive. Her eyes snapped open, and instantly her arrow was notched again, the bow resting against her shoulder. With a soft flutter of wings, the bird that had snatched her next meal had lit upon a branch above her, in full killable view. Its feathers fluttered in the soft breeze, and it observed her with piercing eyes. The rabbit, now dead, dangled from its talons.

"Ah, of course." Her words were laced with sarcasm as she addressed the Swift Hawk. Slowly, she lowered her arms, relaxing the tension on her weapon.

"Hear me." Her words, weighted with the stress of hard travel, dropped to the floor of the forest like stones. "Send greeting to Liannan. I have heard her command, and I come."

The branch bent and sprang back as the bird took flight. Several leaves detached and drifted down toward the healer. Her eyes followed the raptor's elegant path on the updraft, and a small smile of appreciation shifted across her weary features. The disappointment she felt at her loss of a meal dissipated. Sliding the arrow back into the quiver, she slung her bow over her shoulder in preparation to move on.

She froze at the shadow that crossed her path. Shielding her eyes with her hand, she frowned up into the sky, curious as to why the hawk had circled back. With a sweep of its expansive wings, the bird glided closely over her head. As it passed her, its talons spread wide, releasing its catch. The rabbit plummeted through the air, its body thudding softly on the forest floor at Sarafina's feet. The Swift Hawk let out one long cry and was gone. She bent and picked up the rabbit, a whispered thanks forming on her lips, then stepped back into the shadows of the forest.

FEATHERS AND FUR

L ilianna rubbed the cloth along the blade one last time. The sharpening tools lay on the floor next to her stool. The knife glittered in the afternoon sunlight, the metal sharpened to a tapered, paper-thin edge. Her father had always demanded they keep their weapons clean and sharp. The repetitive motion of the steel sliding back and forth on the sanding stone was such a routine, everyday chore that Lilianna had hoped it would somehow ease the chattering "what ifs" in her head.

Mosely, sitting in a sun puddle in the kitchen, lazily blinked at her. Lilianna could feel the cat's eyes on her.

"He does not seem fretful about anything." Standing up, she stretched the kinks out of her back, sheathing the small dagger, and crossed the room to scratch his chin. He batted her hand away and padded toward the kitchen.

"Mr. Mosely, you are ever wanting the next bit of food scraps." Walking to the door, she opened it just enough for the small feline and motioned to him. "Well, there are none, Sir Furry, so perhaps you should go pester Thom outside." Mosely took his time walking back toward the girl. She nudged his backside with the side of her foot, but the cat stopped halfway out the door to stretch.

"Come on, Mosely, be a good cat, and go on." Lilianna laughed and nudged him again.

Giving her a withering look of indignation over his shoulder, he crossed the porch and headed down the stairs. She waved at him and shut the door, her smile dwindling. She went back to the stool, plopping herself down on it and addressed her tools.

"Everything has happened so fast." She spoke softly, tucking the sharpening stone and rag in the storage box Olitus had built for the items.

Cleo, perched on a shelf above the stove, rustled her feathers, and Lilianna smiled up at her in gratitude.

"Dear Cleo. You watch over all of us, don't you, pretty bird?" Cleo dipped her head sideways, giving Lilianna a wink, and a tiny squawk, then began to preen. Cleo loved compliments.

"Where has my father gone, Cleo?"

Lilianna's question was more rhetorical than anything else. Cleo had never opened her thoughts to Lilianna, reserving her communications solely for Olitus. Still, their lack of communication had not stopped the two of them from having a wonderful friendship. Lilianna believed her father would not be complete without his feathered companion.

Cleo had saved her father's life more than once. In the evenings, sitting around the fire, he'd laughingly told story after story of the beautiful parrot coming to his rescue. If not for the bird's warning, a wild boar would have gutted Olitus on a hunting excursion. On another occasion, Olitus, far from home, had severely twisted his ankle, rendering him unable to continue. Cleo had sought out Sarafina and brought her to him. Lilianna would forever be grateful for the colorful bird's love of her father.

Sweeping up the dust from her sharpening work, Lilianna could hear Thom chopping wood at the side of the house. Their home felt empty. Her father was off somewhere, and Sarafina had been gone several days. It had been disappointing not to have been able to say goodbye and wish her the blessing of the One, but they had understood their mother's responsibility to Liannan. After the plateau, they now understood so much more.

"Liannan." Lilianna's face scrunched up with emotion at the thought of her mother's journey. "I thank the One that Sarafina is my mother, and not…" Guiltily, she stopped herself from finishing the thought.

Liannan. One of the most powerful leaders of Faltofar. Based on what Thom had told her, Lilianna didn't think she wanted to be introduced to her anytime soon, even if she was their grandmother. If Torr's words were true, though, she would stand before Liannan within a fortnight. Or sooner.

After dumping the dustpan into the garbage pail, she tucked it away, her thoughts drifting back to her father and his role in what was to come. She wondered again where he had gone. Cleo had ignored her question and continued to busy herself with preening. Mesmerized by the bird's colorful, shiny feathers, Lili stood admiring her, her hand idly playing with the hilt of the small weapon at her waist, when the sudden sound of Thom's voice raised in the yard jolted both girl and bird. Lilianna hurried to the paned glass, followed rapidly by Cleo, who landed on the windowsill next to the girl, jutting her beak against the glass.

Thom, who had stopped chopping wood, was running across the yard, ax in hand, chasing Mosely. The cat, his mouth full of something, shot under the fence at the far side of the yard, with Thom not far behind, frantically waving the tool. Just when Lilianna thought Thom was going to run straight into the gate, he threw the ax aside and vaulted over the fence, landing in the corral, directly in front of the cat and startling him into dropping his catch. Mosely arched and hissed, then, realizing he wasn't going to win the standoff, abruptly sauntered off, his tail held high.

Thom bent to the grass and picked up Mosely's discarded catch, but with his back to the house, Lilianna couldn't quite see what he held. She headed for the door, Cleo fluttering right behind her, and hurried across the yard. Thom slowly climbed back over the fence, cradling the object in his hand.

"What is it, Thom?" Lilianna had to yell over the noise of Cleo's squawking from the shed roof.

Mosely, who had jumped on the fence, alternately glared at Thom and the bird. Carefully, Thom extended his hands, opening them up for Lilianna to see what he held so carefully. A disgruntled, dazed, and muddy titmouse blinked up at her.

"Oh, you poor, poor dear," cooed Lilianna, gently taking the mouse from Thom. It squeaked in agreement and curled tightly into a ball in her palm.

"Not much of a hero's welcome," said Thom, rubbing the rodent behind a tiny ear, envisioning the little mouse being catapulted into the sky a few days prior. "Survived your journey, little guy, only to be beaten up by our housecat."

"Mosely, you ought to be ashamed of yourself."

Lilianna stood on her tiptoes and glared at the cat over Thom's shoulder. Cleo squawked in agreement. Mosely jumped down from the fence and casually strolled toward Thom and Lilianna, glancing up at Cleo and giving a swish of his tail. His route led him between their legs, where he paused and gave a little sneeze-hiss. Hunching forward over his front paws, he waggled his bottom at them and shot across the yard and out of view. Both children watched his departing backside and laughed. With a final squawk, Cleo launched herself skyward, heading in the opposite direction toward the far field. Cuddling the mouse under her chin, Lilianna addressed her brother.

"Where is Father, Thom? I haven't seen him since this morning."

Thom had gone to retrieve the discarded ax. He stood with his back to her.

"Cleo goes to join him, Lili," he said, nodding at Cleo, who was already across the far field. "There's a contingent of warriors just arrived from the far coast." He waved his hand vaguely toward the distant horizon line of tall grass. "They're camped at the forest edge in the long pasture. He is standing with their leaders now."

Lilianna looked in the direction Thom faced, knowing she would not be able to see what he saw. It was futile. Cleo was already a speck in the blue sky.

The wistfulness in Thom's voice mirrored her thoughts. When they'd come back from the plateau, days ago, their father had been preoccupied with minor adjustments to his armor along with cleaning and sharpening his weapons. Thinking about her parents – or herself and Thom for that matter – in a battle made Lilianna's pulse race. Weren't those stories just the things of legend? Tales from Master Blisk's lectures? She thought about what she and Torr had talked of on the cliffs high above the ocean. If what he had told her was correct, there would come a time when she would have to be very, very strong. She swallowed her unease.

She and Thom had both chafed at their father's orders: Do your chores, keep the farm in order, and stay put. She felt a shiver of premonition run down her back. The little mouse in her palm gave a shiver of his own. They hadn't seen Torr since he'd left them in the near pasture several days before. His words still rang in Lilianna's mind, and they would turn out to be about as contrary as possible to the orders Olitus had given them.

"Be prepared for my return. Look to the West at dusk each evening. Pack a sling duffle. You will need layers as well as water and some food, but keep it light." Torr had touched Lilianna's hair but addressed them both. "And, check your weapons."

Stamping one hoof to emphasize his words, Torr had departed quickly. Lilianna soon lost sight of him, but Thom had watched the Sepherii in flight for several more minutes.

"Would that I had your sight, Thom."

Her brother shrugged, sullenly staring across the field where Torr had disappeared days ago and where Olitus now stood, surrounded by his men. Cleo landed lightly on his father's shoulder, and Olitus's men respectfully acknowledged the brilliant bird.

"I'm tired of waiting, Lil. You know as well as I do, maybe better, that we . . ." He studied his sister for a moment before continuing. "You know as well as that they will need us."

With her free hand, Lilianna felt inside the belt of her summer skirt. The hilt of the tiny, freshly-sharpened dagger – a gift given to her two years ago by her father - rested against her shirt. She silently thanked him for the games he had taught her to play throughout her young life, recalling the heaviness of his bigger dagger when he had first handed it to her. It hit the targets differently than her small weapon. He'd taught her to hold it just so, and she had listened carefully to his instructions about stance.

"Stay on the balls of your feet now, girl. That's it!"

His training had continued in both winter and summer. When the snow was deep outside, the children had held competitions in sit-ups and push-ups, learned to wrestle, and leaped from one piece of furniture to the next until their mother had finally had enough. In summer, Olitus had applauded them both when they traversed the yard without falling, jumping lightly along the pattern of stumps he'd placed hither and thither. Back then, Thom's coordination had been slightly less than Lilianna's. She thought about how quickly and gracefully he'd hurdled the fence moments before. Thom was no longer an awkward boy.

A nip on her hand brought her back to the present. Coming out of her reverie, Lilianna realized Thom had moved across the yard back to the woodpile, leaving her to her thoughts. She frowned at the mouse, ready to scold it for biting her, but the words shifted to laughter as it mimicked eating with its little paws.

"Allright, little Messenger. Let's go get you something to eat and drink."

Walking toward the porch, the girl glanced up at the sky, searching for any sign of Torr and the others. "Be patient," he had said. "Be prepared."

———

They finished a light supper, leaving a dish on the kitchen counter for Olitus. Lilianna gave Mosely a warning glare as she covered the plate of food.

"Don't even think about it, you scoundrel," she said to the cat.

He ignored her, licking a speck of dirt from his paw.

Dusk had settled across the yard when Olitus came through the door, followed closely by Cleo, who landed softly on the chair near Lilianna. Thom had been stitching a seam in his leather boot but set it aside and rose quickly. Lilianna stood more slowly, studying her father's face in the shifting light.

Never one to be shy about his emotions, Olitus encircled both children in a bear hug. Just as swiftly, he released them. When he spoke, his tone brooked no arguments.

"Thom, you are my eldest. Protect your sister and guard our land and our animals."

When Thom started to speak, Olitus raised his hand and continued. "That is a command."

His hand rested gently on Lilianna's shoulder. "Lilianna, you have your mother's ways about you." And something more, he thought to himself. The sudden knowledge disturbed him, an icy premonition in his veins. It felt like fear, but he had no time for such feelings.

"Take heed of the animals' needs. They will tell you." He took a breath, scanning the room for his supplies, his mind already to his men, and the march ahead of them. "Work together."

Seeing the plate of food, he smiled a nod of thanks to Lilianna. Folding a chunk of cheese into bread, he took a quick bite, already reaching for his pack where it rested by the door. As he hefted it to his shoulder, the chainmail armor inside clinked. Olitus turned one last time, nodding at Cleo, and gave the children an encouraging smile.

"I will send word by Cleo periodically." And then he was gone.

Cleo made no move to follow, and Lilianna walked to the chair where she perched and patted her gently. As Olitus receded into the twilight, Cleo shifted on the chair, stretching her wings wide. Lili stepped back, assuming the bird was about to take flight, but instead, she craned her neck around, opening her bill. Plucking two feathers from her back, she cocked her head sideways at Lilianna expectantly.

"Cleo?"

The bird hopped closer and waggled her beak, rustling her

feathers and tipping her head back and forth. Lilianna opened her hand, and the parrot dropped the feathers into her palm.

"You will know when to use these, chosen one," the bird said, gracefully launching off the chair and out the door after Olitus.

Lili looked down at the vibrant feathers, turning her palm this way and that, stunned by both the gift and the communication.

"Thom, she has the most beautiful voice."

Thom stoically faced the growing darkness beyond the porch; she wasn't sure if he had even heard her.

IN THE GREAT RIFT VALLEY

Dundar dumped a fresh load of green wood next to the log where Berold sat. The old dwarf refused to acknowledge the boy, focusing his attention instead on a small stick he was sharpening into a fine point. Equally stubborn, Dundar retrieved his pack, pulling out a worn book and settling himself against a boulder across the smokeless fire.

The dwarves busied themselves, pointedly ignoring each other until Berold's curiosity got the better of him. Shifting his bulky frame along the log, he tried to position himself at an angle from which to read the title on the leather-bound book Dundar held. He finally gave up and addressed the younger dwarf.

"What's that you got there?"

Berold reached out, attempting to take the book, but the boy stood quickly, tucking it into his tunic and glaring at his companion.

"Nothin'," Dundar said, somewhat sullenly.

Berold sat back down on the log, his meaty hands resting on either thigh, thick as logs themselves. He narrowed his eyes at Dundar, then wiggled his nose as if overcome by an itch. Grumbling to himself, he picked up his sharpened stick and began picking at his teeth, not taking his eyes off the younger dwarf. Grudgingly, he spoke again.

"Allright. Allright." For emphasis, he took the stick away from his mouth and sent a long stream of spit into the fire. "I admit I shouldn't ah kicked ya in the arse, but ya haven't been upright with me, boy. Nor with the rest o' them." He pointed his toothpick at Dundar. "You're not a mute."

Dundar just stared at the older dwarf, waiting for him to finish. Berold, realizing he was pointing the stick at Dundar, corrected himself, and began picking his teeth again as he looked into the fire.

"Everyone's got the right to secrets, boy. I got a few of me own."

A hazy detachment came over Berold's features for a moment. Blinking back to the present, he addressed Dundar.

"Why'd ya volunteer to come with me?"

The younger dwarf settled back down against his rock, holding his hand over his chest, where he had tucked the book. Dundar licked his lips as if wetting them would give his mouth the elasticity to talk after so long. When he spoke, Berold had to lean in closely to hear him.

"You have a son," the younger dwarf mumbled, not looking away from the fire.

Startled by this change in the topic, Berold sat back, the crease between his bushy brows as deep as the Great Rift Valley.

"Aye, I have a son. Or had."

It was Berold's turn to lick his lips, but his was more out of a sense of a thirst that had gone unquenched for a very long time. A deep wistfulness in his voice betrayed long-buried emotion. "I ain't seen the boy for seasons."

He reached down between his feet and grabbed a handful of earth. Shifting it in his hand, the dark soil drifted back down, leaving flecks of mica in his palm that glittered in the low flames. "A lot of seasons."

A log shifted and dropped; sparks skittered upward. "There's been a lot of metal harvested from our mines since the boy sat at his home hearth," he said, referring to his son.

Dundar watched Berold in silence. The old dwarf set his jaw and squared his shoulders, looking up from his dirt-covered hand.

"I know me wife, his mother, misses him." He swallowed. "Misses him dearly."

Wiping his hands on his pants, Berold stood and crossed to his pack, pulling out portions of their supply of dried meat and hard biscuits. Coming back to the log, he sat down with a sigh, handing Dundar his half of the sparse meal. They chewed for a while in silence. Berold squared his shoulders and spoke again, his words laced with sadness.

"I'm not the old fool everyone thinks, boy." Berold spoke not out of some need for his validation, but more to organize his thoughts. He was used to Dundar not talking and easily fell into using him as a sounding board. "The Messenger is proof of that."

Bits of hard biscuit flew from his lips as he spoke. Licking the end of one stubby finger, he blotted the crumbs off his worn pant leg and sucked them off his finger.

"The Dwarves of the Glenn will be involved in what's comin'. Good or bad."

Frowning over the last of his jerky, he scrutinized Dundar. "What does me son have to do with you comin' with me?"

Dundar finished the last of the dried meat and took a sip from his water bladder. Staring into the flames, he spoke haltingly.

"My mother saw it," he said, taking another small sip and wiping his mouth with the back of one large hand. "She saw darkness."

His glance skimmed the face of the old dwarf, but it was so much easier to focus on the flames of the fire. He knew too well the loss of a loved one. The last of his mother's vision tumbled out of his mouth like boulders rolling down a scree slope. "And, your son in the middle of it all."

Berold's nostrils flared, and the glow from the fire reflected in his small, crinkly old eyes. He had not thought about his son in a long while. Or, he had tried not to.

"Your boy lost a hand, yeah?"

The bluntness of the question struck Berold like a rock thrown at his soul. The old dwarf's shoulders hunched over, the burden from a massive weighted memory settling there. Berold saw pity flit across the boy's face. He shifted angrily on the log, sat up straighter, and spoke.

"The child had an accident at the home."

His words sounded defensive even to himself, and he grimaced. Gathering his thoughts, he continued more slowly, trying to make Dundar understand.

"Him and me, we was always gettin' about together. On the day it happened, he was with me, doin' the chores. One of those good days to be out and the boy was not a handful. He'd wander around the yard, and I didn't worry none."

The dark memory crisscrossed his face. "That day, the day of the accident, I turned my back. I was choppin' wood. He went around the corner of the house. I heard him cry, and when I come runnin', it was too late."

Berold swallowed, his mouth dry. "He fell on a rusted piece of metal in the yard." Taking a deep breath, he continued. "The infection that came with it was the likes of which we'd never seen. Tilga tried. Your ma tried. No one could stop it."

Berold swallowed again, and Dundar extended the water bladder to him. The older dwarf grabbed it almost violently, took a swig, then corked it, and set it between them.

"My Tilga wrapped him up and took him to the humans. Said the human healer was the only way. When she came back, she had a special poultice. We used it for days, weeks."

The fire crackled and sent a spit of steam skyward. In the quiet that followed, Dundar could hear Berold's pained breathing.

"The infection spread."

Berold took the toothpick he'd picked up off the log and threw it into the fire. It flared brightly as he finished the story.

"The only thing we could do was cut off his arm at the elbow. The boy never quite forgave me and his ma. He weren't the same after that. Never quite hisself."

Berold's son had been older than Dundar by years, and the boys had never really known each other. Not surprising. He wouldn't have anyway. Living on the edge of the village and being a half-blood had kept Dundar separate from the other children.

Dundar hadn't volunteered to join Berold out of pity. Dundar's mother, Dundalee, had told him that his journey lay in the same footpath Berold would travel. Her sight and Dundar's yearning for adventure had been enough for the young dwarf to raise his hand and step forward when Berold asked for volunteers. As if reading Dundar's thoughts, Berold spoke slowly into the night.

"Your mother has a way of manipulatin' people into things, boy." Out of some twisted need for the younger dwarf to feel pain as well, Berold added, "No wonder your pa didn't stick around."

Dundar ignored the last comment, pulling his prized possession out of his shirt and flipping through the worn pages. He stopped at the front of the book. Words, written in mottled ink and faded with time and touch, coiled across the inside cover — the only evidence he had of his long-gone father. They read, *Blood of my blood. I will never forget you, son.* The sole signature was the single letter *A*.

———

The fire had dwindled to a low glow of coals that Dundar poked periodically, more out of boredom than any desire to rekindle it. The younger dwarf had taken the first watch. The solidness of the book against his chest reassured him that he was not so alone. Berold lay across from him, wrapped in his cloak and snoring softly, his big head propped on his knapsack. Occasionally the old dwarf would let out a long fart, which amused Dundar, but also made him glad of the fire separating them.

A shooting star across the night sky drew Dundar's eyes away from the fire. He lay his head back and waited for more. His eyes, no longer focused on the glowing embers, slowly adjusted to the darkness around him. And that was what saved him when the spear arced through the darkness. He saw it at the last moment and rolled sideways and across the fire into Berold. Both dwarves were on their feet instantly, their backs against each other, staring out into the pitch-black forest.

"What the devil?" mumbled a groggy Berold, swinging his new club in the air around him. The heft of it felt right.

"Somethin' out there."

Berold could hear the determination in Dundar's voice — his resolution not to be afraid. For a split second, Berold felt the weight of the youth's inexperience settle on his shoulders. When he saw the spear, he flinched.

"By the Metal God, it's a bunch of the Hairies," he whispered. Berold crafted his words carefully. He needed the boy to grow up quickly. "Stand ready, boy. They will come all at once."

As he spoke, three shadows emerged from the forest, eyes glowing with the distinctive night vision unique to their kind. Berold spun to face them, cursing under his breath.

"Be alert, boy! Their chomp is worse than their yappin'."

The trio slowly slouched closer, and Dundar saw what Berold meant. They stood a head taller than the younger dwarf; their long snouts erupted from faces partially shielded by metal helmets. Yellowed fangs, bared in grimaces of anticipation, gleamed dully in the reddish firelight. Their bodies, where not covered by armor, were matted in dark wiry hair.

The tallest of the three spoke, its words coming out in a guttural, raspy voice. "Dwarves," it said, licking its teeth. "I like dwarves."

Berold moved faster than Dundar would have ever expected, swinging his new club high and striking the leader a glancing blow to the head. The dog-man spun around, knocking the second Hairy backward. Its spear flew from its hand, landing on the ground past the dwarves' stack of wood. The third lunged forward, the tip of its weapon aimed at Berold's throat. Dundar, his knife in hand, moved forward quickly, slicing through the back of the attacker's leg, severing a tendon and dropping the beast to the ground. Berold swung around and, with a swift hammer stroke, bashed in the head of the one who had fallen. At the same time, Dundar's dagger sliced upward, stabbing the leader in the groin. With blood spurting from its wound, the Hairy backed away, howling in pain. Dundar was so intent on the bleeding beast, he never saw the chunky piece of wood. The last thing he remembered was the feel of the grass on his cheek as his face hit the ground, then nothing.

———

When he awoke, daylight was creeping through the boughs of the trees. He didn't try to move, merely blinked away the dirt, and took inventory of his brain cap. His head ached terribly, and he noticed his eyesight went in and out of focus. He listened for any sounds of battle, but only the typical noises of a waking forest met his ears.

With an effort, he forced his hands under his chest and slowly leveraged himself up to sitting. Two of the nasty creatures lay dead near him. The world tilted and twirled, and his eyes felt like marbles rolling around in his head. Where were Berold and the third Hairy? He staggered to his feet, fighting the urge to vomit, and made his wobbly way to the rock by the dead fire, sitting down heavily. Elbows propped on his knees, he supported his head in his hands and tried to think what to do next.

A whistling from the forest gave his foggy brain something to focus on. Using his hands to lift his heavy head up and back onto his shoulders, he blinked, trying to comprehend the two Berolds who had emerged from the thick foliage, spears in hand, metal helmets perched jauntily on their heads like thimbles. Slowly, the two dwarves merged into one. Dundar leaned sideways and vomited what little of last night's meal remained in his stomach.

"That's a fine way to say hello," Berold said, standing in front of him, adjusting his helmet.

Dundar looked up at Berold and asked dazedly, "What happened?"

Berold, seeing that the boy was up and alive, had sauntered back into the clearing feeling rather pleased with himself. He glanced over at the two dead bodies, his smile fading.

"These are guards from Morauth's army."

Dundar tried to focus. "Morauth?" Just the name made his headache worse.

Berold sat down next to the younger dwarf.

"Aye, boy. The one who follows the Dark Ways. She and her kind will come. These," he motioned with the spear toward the carcasses, "are the first. The scouts."

Berold adjusted the spear to study the sharp tip, bringing it to his nose and sniffing. His nose wrinkled, and he quickly moved it away.

"Dipped in Swilly Poison. Good thing we didn't get poked."

Dundar sat up straight, absorbing Berold's words. He squinted at the older dwarf, his brain formulating a question related to the ill-fitting helmet perched on his head. The two who lay dead near them still wore their helmets.

"Did you…?" Dundar swallowed the bile that threatened to come up again.

"Aye."

Berold took the helmet from his head. He needed the younger dwarf to understand, and he needed him to grow up quickly.

"He was lame. I chased him down like a scurvy doggin and finished him." Berold's voice held no remorse, just a new coldness that Dundar didn't know if he liked.

"He would'a gone back to the main body," Berold continued, trying to make the younger dwarf focus on the importance of their actions. Uncharacteristically, he grabbed the youth's chin and locked eyes with him. "We'd of not made it to the foothills, boy, before they'd have had us speared and gutted."

Berold patted the younger dwarf on the shoulder awkwardly, his gesture stilted from years of kind thoughts never shared. "Now lad, it's time we were off," he said gently.

He didn't stand right away but gazed off into the forest from where he'd recently emerged, giving Dundar a moment more to clear his head. He couldn't share with Dundar how old he suddenly felt. Too old to lead his people into battle again.

"But if not me, the leader of the Dwarves of the Glenn, then who?"

Clutching the spear more tightly, Berold jammed it into the ground and hoisted himself up off the rock. Picking up the helmet, he weighed the heft of it, thinking of his son.

"'Tis poor craftsmanship that made this piece of scrap metal," he said, and tossed it over his shoulder.

"Come on, boy. It's time to get'a goin'. We've got ourselves a battle to attend to." Berold extended his arm to the younger dwarf.

With an effort, Dundar concentrated on the arm in front of him, then slowly raised his own. The firm grasp around his wrist and the weight of the book against his chest gave him the strength to stand and pick up his pack. Slinging it over his shoulder, Dundar slowly followed the receding back of the old dwarf. The stark mountains of the high country loomed ahead of them.

THE HOMECOMING

The high tower that housed Liannan's private chambers perched almost precariously on the westernmost cliffs of the city ramparts. Liannan continued to stare out over the valley below, even after her daughter's arrival.

Sarafina had traveled a fortnight to get to the high fortress, and she was bone-tired and in need of the bathhouse. Nevertheless, she stood silently and waited for her mother to acknowledge her, absently wiping at a smudge of dirt along her high cheekbone. She shifted the bow and quiver on her shoulder, not ready to put her weapon down, somehow needing its strength and weight against her side.

Her pack rested just outside the chamber door, next to the sentry who stood watch. He had given her a nod, acknowledging her right to enter the private chambers, and frowned only slightly at the bow and quiver. She could not recall the man's name, but she knew he'd been a playmate when she was a child. She did not envy him, living in such proximity to Liannan. She thanked the One that her dark features had determined her future as an ambassador to the lands below.

The contrast between the two women was as stark as the difference in their bearings. Liannan's white hair glowed in the afternoon sunlight, while Sarafina's dark mass of hair hung lankly down her back, stray wisps escaping. Instead of the smoldering authority that emanated from Liannan, the younger woman radiated the kindness of one long used to helping others.

Liannan shifted her weight, placing both hands on the windowsill.

"You made good time," she said, still gazing at the horizon. "You are one of the first to arrive." Turning away from the window, she pointedly looked at Sarafina's disheveled appearance before she continued. "I would have expected nothing less from a daughter of my house."

Sarafina nodded but kept silent, studying Liannan quietly. As tired as she was, Sarafina's senses were on high alert. She could feel the anxiousness in the sentry outside, and Liannan carried herself even more stoically than Sarafina remembered. The two women scrutinized each other, looking for strengths and weaknesses in the subtle language of body lines. Argath's abrupt entrance broke their silence.

"Sarafina!"

Before Sarafina could do more than smile at her oldest brother, his massive embrace engulfed her. The leather of his chest plate pressed against her aching muscles and the small bruises from her rugged travel. She returned his hug, but Argath had felt her flinch and stepped back apologetically.

"Little sister, you are travel-weary."

He patted her disheveled hair and teasingly grazed a knuckled hand across the dirt on her face. His lightness masked an unspoken reprimand regarding Liannan's lack of hospitality. Brother and sister smiled at each other in acknowledgment of what remained unsaid. They faced their mother, honor and ritual taking precedence over family. Liannan's back was to them. She spoke with a more profound coldness than they had ever heard.

"Your sister is well met, Argath. By you and by me." She swept past both of them toward the chamber door. "And now, the family reunion is over. Make yourself presentable, Sarafina. We meet at last light in the High Chamber. The others will have arrived by then."

She glided out through the doorway, and the heavy wooden door swung slowly shut behind her. Sarafina felt the tension between her shoulders drift like sawdust to the floor. She stepped closer to her fair brother, who raised an eyebrow and lifted one shoulder in a shrug. It was Sarafina's turn to hug him.

———

Sarafina ran her hands down along the waistline of her gown, studying her reflection in the mirror. The feel of the soft wool seemed so foreign to her now. Her old chambers in the fortress had been prepared for her: the linens fresh, the heavy curtains aired, clean water in the basin at the vanity. The attendant assigned to her stood patiently by the robe and tray of soaps and oils laid out for her use in the bathhouse. She thanked the woman and dismissed her, more grateful for privacy than any assistance.

When she entered her chamber after her bath, she found three gowns hanging in her closet. She knew they had been made by the finest linen weavers in the lands of Faltofar, and any one of them would fit her to perfection. Whether war strategy or fitted bodice, Liannan had a way with details. Sarafina chose the simplest of the three and dressed quickly. The sleeves of her gown were just long enough to hide the dagger. She checked the tightness of the armband that held the sheathed blade against her forearm and took a final look at herself in the mirror.

She had left Argath with the promise to meet him in his quarters prior to attending Liannan and the gathering in the High Chambers. She wanted as much time with her brother as she could get.

Her talisman hung on a hook near the water basin where she had left it before going to the baths. She took it down and pulled the simple chain over her head as she headed to the door, reassured by the weight of the coin against her breast. Pausing in the hallway, she listened for the everyday noises of the keep, where her room was.

The rest of the fortress was eerily quiet, raising goosebumps along Sarafina's arms.

"The calm before the gale?" The old saying resonated with a truth she didn't want to dwell on.

Memory led her easily to the floor below, and her brother's chambers. A loud, single command in Argath's deep baritone greeted her soft tapping.

"Come!"

No sentry stood outside Argath's door, and if he had any attendant, they were not evident. Two overstuffed chairs faced a massive mantled fireplace where a fire crackled, warming the room. Argath leaned against the rock and motioned Sarafina to take a chair. She nodded and took the closest, sitting on its edge. Wordlessly, Argath moved to a side table that held several pitchers and gestured to her.

"Water?" she asked.

"Water or Pago. I have both here."

Argath's hand hovered expectantly, and Sarafina couldn't help but laugh.

"Since when do you drink Pago in the afternoon, older brother?"

Slowly, he poured the amber liquid into two goblets.

"Since the world turned upside down and I lost Arialla," he said quietly.

Sarafina accepted the goblet from her brother, studying his face. Age and experience had carved deeper etchings of lines across his forehead, and a smattering of gray at his temples framed his craggy features. Placing her hand over his, she stopped him from pulling away.

"Argath, I am so very sorry." Sarafina hesitated, trying to find the words to express their shared grief, knowing she could never comprehend the loss of a twin. Not completely. Argath nodded and slowly took his hand away from hers. The log in the fireplace crumpled, and sparks drifted up the chimney, but neither of them noticed, each lost in memories of their golden-haired sister.

Taking a sip from her goblet, she asked, "What of the others? Lionel? Theresea?"

Argath continued to stare into the flames, but acknowledged his youngest sister's questions about their other siblings.

"They fare well. Both continue to reside in the far Reaches with their growing families. Neither comes home much. There was never much need." He gave Sarafina a smile that was more a grimace. "Liannan hasn't held many nurturing family gatherings over the years, as you know." They both sipped from their goblets.

"They won't be here, Sarry," he concluded.

She smiled fleetingly at his use of her childhood nickname, covering her disappointment.

"Kindith Pass has been blocked by a massive avalanche, and there is no time to open the way."

Sarafina absorbed this information. Perhaps it was for the best. Maybe they and their families would be safe. She shivered, grateful for the heat of the fire and the warmth beginning to spread throughout her body from the Pago. It wouldn't do to have more than one cup before the meeting in the High Chamber, but how wonderful to ignore the coming storm for just these few minutes. She was exhausted. It did not take someone with the Sense to see her fatigue, and Argath moved away from the fire to lay a lap rug against her legs, taking the goblet from her hand and setting it on the table at the side of the room. He sat in the chair next to her and began to talk, the words spilling out.

"A plague of some sort ravaged the high country. It hit Lourdes Landing, where Arialla has," he licked his lips, then corrected himself, "had lived these past years." Argath's brow furrowed as he continued.

"Arialla and the new babe, all of them. Infected."

He swallowed, and Sarafina reached across the arm of the chair to clasp his hand again. Before she could touch him, he moved away from her reach. Unoffended, she put her hand back in her lap and waited for him to continue.

"Sarafina, you don't understand. Liannan gave the command to torch the village. We obeyed." His tortured eyes burned into Sarafina's.

No words were necessary to show her the rest; her mind filled in with vivid detail those moments she had not been able to see in the metal of the flask. Ribbons of flames, soaring high into the cold night, cries of agony as fire engulfed bodies. Some of the strongest villagers, those not yet gone from the fever, had staggered out of their homes, walking torches screaming for mercy. Sarafina lay back in the chair and closed her eyes. Tears streaked down her face.

When she spoke again, her eyes remained closed.

"Arialla came to me in a vision, Argath. She told me to come. To hurry." She opened her eyes, looking at Argath. This time, he merely flinched but didn't pull his hand away when she reached for him. Pain emanated from him.

"What are you not telling me, brother?"

Standing, Argath tilted his head back and finished the goblet in one great swallow. Carefully, he placed it on the mantle, running his finger along the hammered metal of its base.

"The finest in dwarf craft, don't you think?" he said softly, almost wistfully, controlling his emotions with an effort. Sarafina didn't respond. The healer in her began to assess her brother for signs of mental trauma. Argath's finger stopped its motion.

"Don't, Sarafina. I'm nowhere near my breaking point."

"I…"

Argath raised his hand, stopping his sister before she'd even begun.

"There was a time the dwarves came to our assistance. The tribes gathered, regardless of their differences." He shifted his stance, adjusting the weight of his thoughts. "The good versus the bad and all that." He faced Sarafina directly, his hand resting on the hilt of his sword.

"Liannan believes this plague, and the ills that pervade the lands of Faltofar, are signs of Morauth's… resurrection. The people do not believe our wise leader." He didn't bother to hide his sarcasm. "They think she has sat too long at the high table." His words were laced with bitterness that had been nurtured in doubt. "There is mumbling from here to the summit of the Blue Mountains that they will not abide a leader who burns alive her very own."

Sarafina understood the anger that flitted across Argath's face, visible testimony to his internal battle between loyalty and outright disbelief at the actions in which he had participated. Her skin crawled at the mention of Morauth, but Liannan was right. Argath needed to hear of her encounter with the dark wraith at the Holy Oak. Her hand went to the corded pouch around her neck, where she kept the acorn. Her talisman was there, but she'd forgotten the pouch hanging on the vanity mirror in her chambers. She lowered her hand from her neck.

"Argath," she began. A pounding on the chamber door stifled the rest of her words. Again, her brother gave the single word command.

"Come."

The door swung wide to reveal the same sentry who had guarded Liannan's door hours before.

"She summons you to the High Chambers," the man said without preamble. Argath extended his hand to Sarafina, who grasped it and rose from her comfortable sanctuary by the fire.

THE DARK CHILDREN

S arafina and Argath followed the sentry along the narrow corridors to the vaulted room of the High Chamber. They chose to enter through the side door, close to the high table where formality dictated they were to join Liannan. Argath had used this same entrance hours before in his search for solitude in which to think.

As the door swung open, Sarafina caught her breath at the number of people gathered. The grand hall was filled to capacity with Highlanders, both dark and light – those who had lived their lives in the steep, cold, self-contained mountain communities, and those, dark-skinned and dark-haired like herself, who had traveled to the lowlands as ambassadors for the One, and for their leader, Liannan.

The siblings made their way to the stairs leading to the upper terrace, briefly greeting those they knew, some with just a nod, others with a quick grasp of hands. All returned their greetings, but Sarafina noticed that none of them smiled.

At the top of the stairs, Sarafina glanced at Argath. A storm-cloud brewed across his craggy features. "This may not go as well as Liannan hopes," she thought.

Together they bowed, acknowledging her as their high liege lord, then took their places, sitting on either side of her. The volume in the chamber increased. The Highlanders knew they were about to understand why they had been gathered.

Liannan rising signaled to the assembled crowd they were to begin. Conversation decreased, and those who had been standing took their seats. Liannan deliberately slid her chair farther back, the squeal of its wooden legs across the floor loud in the quiet of the hall. Her slow movement around the table was calculated to draw all attention to her. Silently, she directed Argath and Sarafina to join her at the front of the terrace.

"I thank you for coming." Liannan's voice echoed eerily across the chamber, and Sarafina wondered what trick gave her the ability to project with such little effort.

"I know many of you have left your homes and lands unattended and wish to depart again promptly. I will endeavor to make this gathering as efficiently enlightening as I am able."

The last of her words reverberated against the stone walls of the full chamber, echoing upward into the solid beams of the rafters. Liannan scanned the hall, her slate-blue eyes taking in every man and woman. She let the moment lengthen, the thick fortress walls absorbing the very last of her words. When she continued, her voice resonated in an even more commanding tone.

"I ask you to rise, and in rising, acknowledge your pledge to my house and your commitment to the One!"

The rustle of linens and the clank of metal throughout the chamber muffled the sounds of grumbling, as the ranks of leaders and warriors slowly stood. Liannan's request for allegiance was not so strange as it was ill-timed. Her recent orders to burn the village, in which lived people who had also sworn allegiance to her, disturbed the gathering to their very core. Nevertheless, every man and woman stood.

"Good," she said, her hands minutely adjusting a fold of her skirt. "Let us begin."

The last was spoken softly, the words inching along Argath's spine. With an effort, he maintained his stance without looking at Liannan. Sarafina made no pretense, her head snapping around to stare at their leader and her brother beyond.

Slowly Liannan's thin, strong hand slid out of her long sleeve, wrapping around Argath's wrist in a vice he knew he could not break. Those in the hall were too far away to see him flinch. Her marble-like skin glowed in contrast with Argath's dark, weathered hand as she raised his arm, holding it firmly in her cold grasp. Sarafina looked away from the loathing she saw in her brother's eyes.

"I give you Argath, my right arm. His allegiance and his loyalty are no less than the strength with which he wields a blade!" Liannan's words resonated with the crowd and were met by nods of approval and softly shouted affirmations of "Hear! Hear!" She raised her other arm, having grasped Sarafina's wrist just as tightly.

In a split-second memory of long ago, Argath saw himself and his sister running from the high walls of the castle, free for just a bit from who they were and the family they had been born into. "Sarafina." He swallowed the whisper of her name.

"Sarafina." Liannan voice echoed his whisper. She said nothing else for a moment, merely gazing at the upturned faces of warriors. "No less important to the well-being of Faltofar."

The Highlanders shuffled and looked to each other. Sarafina inhaled, forcing a calm into her being that belied the distress she felt at being in such proximity to Liannan.

"There is doubt among you. These doubts are like an unfinished tapestry woven by rumors. Rumors that waft like snowflakes throughout these high mountains, like lost memories or dreams only semi-recalled."

Liannan paused, patiently watching the gathering.

"Poetic cow piss."

Her cold blue eyes slid briefly toward Argath, acknowledging his mumbled words. When she continued, her voice lost its softness, cutting across the gathering with the force of a sharp sword.

"You are generations removed from the dark times of Faltofar. But I serve as your witness to those dark days, and as your leader I must prepare you for what is to come," she paused, "should we fail." Her stare stopped the angry murmurs.

"Sarafina is my youngest." Liannan's grip tightened and Sarafina sucked in her breath. "Like many of you called here today, she is one of the dark children, sent as ambassadors from the folds of our high mountains to the lands below us. We have upheld this tradition for generations."

Abruptly Liannan dropped Argath's arm.

"I ask those of you not of the dark caste to sit."

A soft grumbling erupted again throughout the hall. Liannan's request was an order. They had been asked to divide themselves. Loyalty ran high in their blood, no matter the caste of their skin or the color of their hair. Slowly, those of fair hair and skin began to take their seats, leaving the dark-haired, olive-skinned chosen standing scattered throughout the hall.

Sarafina's hand had begun to lose feeling where Liannan gripped it, but she refused to pull away. A morbid curiosity wound itself through her mind as she waited with the rest of them. The room quieted.

With her free hand, Liannan reached for the chain that held the talisman around her neck. It quickly came free, and she held it forth to show the gathered crowd below them.

"Our talisman. That of the Holy Oak."

She let the coin dangle from its chain, where it gently spun. "Talisman" and "Holy Oak" echoed throughout the hall.

"The image of the Holy Oak...on one side."

More scowls and mumbling throughout the chamber.

"She's losing them," Sarafina thought to herself. Her wrist ached, and she was tired of the drama. Liannan felt Sarafina shift her weight and turned to look at her. Her cold, steel-blue eyes bore deep into her daughter, but her next words cut even deeper.

"On the other side, embedded in the metal, is a small shard of obsidian broken off from the weapon known to you as Rendar's Blade."

Liannan now had their full attention. She brought Sarafina's arm down to her side without letting go.

"This sliver," she turned the coin, staring at the metal a moment, "is one piece of the banishing blade that sent Morauth deep into the earth." She paused, then raised the talisman higher, delivering the gut punch. "It should have kept her there, but it has not."

Her words carried over the room, dropping to hit the floor like lead glass, shattering any illusions of safety and warm hearths. They began to understand they had been called here for the purpose of war.

"You." The talisman swung, gripped in her hand. Her arm swept from one side of the room to the other for emphasis. "You, standing, are the dark children. You are the link of this house, the heart of Faltofar, to the lands below and above. The power of the obsidian resides in your souls. Whoever holds the obsidian, all of the obsidian, pieced back together, wields control over you, and has the power to harness good or evil."

Sarafina felt sweat trickling down the front of her chest and along her side. She could hear in Liannan the echo of the same message Morauth had given her at the Holy Oak.

"*Our time has come, child,*" it had said, pointing the bone at Sarafina. "*I have waited far too long.*" A smile had spread across the wraith's face. "*Join me or die.*"

"*At least I give you the choice. The others are nothing. Pawns.*"

In growing horror, Sarafina finally understood what Morauth had offered her. A chance to be part of the alluring and immense dark power that would morph Faltofar into unimaginable chaos.

Without warning, Liannan flipped the coin into her hand and placed the side of the talisman embedded with the obsidian chip against Sarafina's forehead, wrenching her wrist to keep her close. The crystal stone burned intensely. Sarafina fought the urge to pull away, focusing instead on maintaining her balance as the room began to fade. Her breath came in small puffs of fear, and only Liannan's grasp kept her standing tall, her grip counteracting the powerful pain inflicted by the obsidian.

Sarafina felt every fiber in her being begin to vibrate. Her hair, loosened from its braid, coiled around her, snakelike. Her skin tingled with the tiny, disgusting feel of bugs crawling over her body. It was the same for the others. Those standing rubbed at their skin, moaning softly. Through her diminishing sight, the dark Highlanders seemed to ripple, their hair, eyes, and skin crackling with electricity.

The air above and just in front of the high table began to shift. The chandeliers that ran the length of the hall swayed and twisted, bits of wax crumbling onto the crowd below. In the rafters, shadows congealed, spreading an inky cloud that darkened the ceiling above. At the very center of the swirling mass, the image of a woman slowly emerged, her features solidifying into a face that resembled both Liannan and Sarafina. The only light that permeated the darkness was the woman's eyes – deep, vile green beacons aimed at the high terrace. Morauth's face broke out into a slow, hissing smile.

"Well met, sweet sister." The endearment came out in a hiss. "Child."

Morauth nodded first at Liannan, then Sarafina. She completely ignored Argath, who, like the rest of the fair ones in the chamber, had doubled over, clutching his abdomen.

Blinking her eyes, Sarafina tried to dispel the fogginess in her mind that worked to take away her identity. In desperation, she reached for Argath as seething anger and the urge for violence saturated her mind. She wanted to kill.

The image of Morauth grew stronger. Her face leered at Liannan.

"This time, we shall see where true power resides." Morauth studied the Highlanders who stood below her, baring her teeth in obvious enjoyment. "Vengeance has such purity, don't you think, Liannan?" she purred. "Isn't it time we met again, sister?"

"Enough!"

Liannan released Sarafina's wrist and pulled the talisman away from her forehead. She turned the coin over, holding it aloft, and pointed the image of the Holy Oak directly into the smoky image of

Morauth. The apparition seemed to draw back, but even as she began to fade, her parting whisper coiled and struck like a viperous snake.

"I will see you soon, child."

Sarafina shut her eyes, her head filled with the memory of their encounter at the Holy Oak, and Morauth's message.

"Tell Liannan I am back, child." Laughter, oozing with hatred, bubbled forth from the smoke. "Better yet, give this to her as a gift from me."

Sarafina began to fall. Argath struggled weakly forward, catching his sister just before she hit the stone floor. With her in his arms, he watched in disbelief as a coiling white mass separated itself from her ankle. It slithered quickly toward Liannan, who stood at the front of the terrace with her back to them, waiting for the room to come to order. He lunged for the slithering bone, but his arms were full.

"Liannan!" Her name dribbled from his lips in a garbled mess. He held tighter to Sarafina, helpless to do anything else but watch as the thing arched to strike.

Liannan turned. She swung her talisman and tossed it through the air. The coin arced, trailing a rainbow of color reflecting off the metal from the setting sun outside the High Chamber windows. Daggers of light shot throughout the hall, dispelling the smoke. The chain caught the creature around the neck, spinning the talisman around it once, twice, three times. Weighted by the metal, it fell to the floor, a mass of writhing bone blackening and curling to dust. Within moments, it was reduced to nothing more than ash. Acrid green smoke drifted upward from the pile, mingling with the last of the dark cloud that had been Morauth.

Liannan moved to the burnt mound, looking down at it with mild curiosity. Deliberately she placed the toe of her boot at the center of the pile and methodically ground what was left into the stone. When she removed her foot, the talisman lay on the floor, dusted with ash, but intact. She bent and picked it up by the chain, dangling it from pinched fingers. She studied the coin a moment before pursing her lips, expelling one short breath that blew the last of the ashes from the gleaming metal. Then for the last time her arm extended above the filled room. The talisman swung back and forth, slowly coming to a standstill. As it swiveled, the shard of obsidian sparkled darkly.

"To the One." Her words were a summons to war.

The high windows rattled with the Highlanders' response.

"To the One!"

SMALL POWERS

"Tilga," reproached Dundalee. "Now is not the time to get fussy over your attire."

Dundalee continued to wind her way through the dense forest, somehow avoiding the branches that snagged Tilga around every tree trunk. Disentangling her shawl from a branch once more, Tilga fought the urge to snap at Dundalee.

"How in the name of the Metal Gods does she wander these woods without a single hair out of place?" she mumbled. She tucked a stray curl up into her cap, hiked up her skirt, and hurried to follow.

The women carried little more than their water flasks, tucked into the deep pockets of their skirts. Dundalee had assured Tilga that all they needed were a few of the dried herbs from her kitchen, a small, personal item of Berold's, and the shawl Dundalee had given her. A light leather purse bounced at Dundalee's hip, filled with Tilga's items along with some of her own.

Ducking under another branch, Tilga heard voices in the distance. She froze, listening. Dundalee, several branches ahead of her, had also stopped, her tiny turbaned head tilted to one side.

"Ah, yes. Just so," Dundalee said, pointing through the woods as if this would enlighten Tilga.

"We will be a bit of a shock to them," she said, tilting her head the other way. "But perhaps, not so much."

Dundalee looked back at Tilga expectantly. Tilga raised her hands and eyebrows in a gesture that implied, "What?" Dundalee motioned her to move closer, parting a sizeable green branch just enough for them both to see the clearing beyond where they stood.

A massive group of men was gathered on the far side of the meadow. Armor clanked, and the glint of metal weapons winked, blindingly, at the hidden women as the army milled around. Tilga drew in her breath. She had never seen so many of the tall humans. Their ugly, long limbs made her skin crawl.

"You don't mean for us to go out there, do you?"

Dundalee gently placed her finger to Tilga's lips, gesturing for her to be quiet. Offended, Tilga continued, in a forced whisper.

"Why in all of the realms would we show ourselves to them?" she demanded.

"Why, dear, we won't show ourselves to all of them," Dundalee said cryptically. "Just the important ones."

Dundalee busied herself rummaging in the purse at her hip, shifting her hand around and gazing into the dark opening. She mumbled under her breath, something about the right herbs, and then pulled out what she had been looking for with a flourish.

"There." She smiled at the fragrant bouquet in her small hand. "This should do the trick." Parting the branch again, she peeked out at the gathered men. "Now, we wait a bit."

Olitus paced back and forth at the edge of the clearing. He was anxious to get moving. Sarafina was easily a week and almost another ahead of him. After listening to his men speak of the atrocities they had encountered in their travels to reach him, Olitus wanted nothing more than to take action. His responsibilities were to the people of these lands, but a world without her was unimaginable. He summoned his first in command, Dideon.

"What is holding these troops from departure?" Olitus spoke softly. It would not do to let any of the men feel his anxiousness.

He did not fool Dideon, however, who scrutinized Olitus's face before responding. The two of them had been on many forays in the past, and Dideon was well aware of his commander's nuances.

"We are minutes away from the march, Olitus."

Dideon ignored his pacing superior and studied the dense forest. A shadow drifted along the grass at their feet, and both men tilted their heads up to watch Cleo pass overhead.

"It will be slow-moving, Olitus. Your bird cannot carry us on her back." His words were said to lighten the tension, but the humor fell on deaf ears.

"Would that she could," Olitus said, following the flight of his colorful companion.

Suddenly Cleo veered toward the woods on the far side of the clearing. Something in her abrupt change of flight made Olitus cautious. He motioned Dideon to join him. Together they moved across the field. Cleo had landed on the branch of a large evergreen and was making small, insistent noises, fluttering her wings and side-stepping up and down the limb.

The men stopped several paces from the edge of the forest. Dideon's hand rested on the hilt of his sword, and Olitus had drawn his dagger. When the vegetation below the pine where Cleo perched began to move, Dideon quietly drew his sword. Slowly Dundalee parted the branches and stepped into the sunshine, followed quickly by Tilga. Olitus put his hand on Dideon's arm and spoke softly.

"Stand down. I know them."

Dideon did as he was commanded, never taking his eyes off the two dwarves.

"Dundalee." Olitus bowed his head slightly to the turbaned woman and her companion, recalling happier times in the presence of the tiny sorceress. "It has been a very long time." Olitus spoke with respect, sheathing his dagger, and stepping closer to the women.

"You are not one to wander these woods without reason. And, I am in no position for small talk." Olitus hesitated, then added. "Forgive me that I am so direct." He studied the other dwarf-woman, racking his brain for a memory of her as well.

Ignoring Olitus for the moment, Dundalee's sparkling eyes flitted up into the tree above them, her features breaking into a radiant smile as she undulated her hand, mimicking the flight of a bird. Cleo launched herself from the branch and soared down, landing on Dundalee's extended arm and prancing happily up to rub her beak against Dundalee's cheek.

"Hello, pretty. So lovely to see you again, too." Cleo pecked lightly at the turban covering Dundalee's hair. "Stop, you silly feathered beauty." Dundalee gently moved Cleo's beak away. "In due time."

Tilga, who had been standing just behind Dundalee in the shadows, moved forward, watching the men cautiously. She couldn't help but think again how awkward the humans looked.

"Like trees in a drought. All trunk, no leaves." The sturdiness of Berold flashed through her mind, but she quickly extinguished thoughts of her husband.

Olitus glanced over his shoulder at the sound of his men readying themselves for travel. With an effort, he shifted his attention back to the dwarf women before him. He knew Dundalee would not be here, at the edge of this meadow, for no reason. He also knew she did not choose her companions lightly.

"Her name is Tilga, wife to Berold, leader of the Dwarves of the Glenn," Dundalee said, all business now. Gently she moved her arm upward, sending Cleo in the air to land on Olitus's shoulder, then handed Tilga the tiny bouquet of herbs. She began to rummage through her purse, pulling out a hammered metal wristband Tilga had grabbed from Berold's possessions just before they departed the village.

"Hold this a moment, dearie." Dundalee handed the jewelry to Tilga. "And while you're at it, think of your man."

Quickly Tilga pocketed the herbs and took the wristband from Dundalee, clasping it close to her chest as she continued to stare distrustfully at the two humans.

Olitus's eyes narrowed. He was torn between his desire to give the command to his men to get moving, and his curiosity as to why the she-dwarf was standing before him. Dundalee, ignoring the men, unwrapped the turban around her head. Tilga held her breath, fascination keeping her quiet for a change as her companion unwound the colorful fabric. She had never seen Dundalee without her head covering and was surprised at the flowing mass of hair that cascaded down the woman's back, almost touching the ground. It was the color of late fall sunshine, gold tinged with red.

"You are in need of assistance, Olitus Finnekin. I think I have just the solution to help you in the movement of your troops." Dundalee held the beautiful material in her hands, giving it a snap as she walked back toward the edge of the forest.

"If you would follow me," she said, looking over her shoulder at the three of them. "Tilga, your shawl, please."

Glancing through thick lashes at the men, Tilga hesitated then hurried to join Dundalee, taking her shawl from her shoulders and handing it to the other woman. Olitus and Dideon followed them at a respectful distance.

At the edge of the woods, Dundalee stopped. She took a corner of each piece of material and tied them together. A flick of her wrist brought Cleo back to her arm. Gently she offered one of the untied corners to the bird, who flew up into the limb of a tree and busied herself creatively entwining one corner of the material into the branch. The other piece hung low, dangling almost to the ground. Dundalee patiently watched the bird, ignoring the others. With a satisfied squawk, Cleo finished high-stepping far enough along the branch away from her handiwork to admire it. Again Dundalee flicked her wrist, and the parrot dropped down, grabbing the other untied corner of fabric and swooping back up to attach the fabric high in the opposite tree. When she had successfully tied this end off, the two pieces of cloth now stretched to their limit. The effect was that of a stage curtain, the opening in the middle showing a backstage of trees.

"There," Dundalee said, turning with a beatific smile to the others.

Three confused faces looked back at her.

"Ah yes," she said, wiping her hands together. "Patience, patience."

Reaching out to Tilga, she motioned for the small bouquet of herbs.

"And, dear, Berold's bracelet, please."

Tilga looked at the ornately hammered metal in her hand, remembering it on her husband's arm through their years together. She had to believe Dundalee had something positive in store with her magic. She handed the woman the bouquet and the jewelry and stepped back. Something about Dundalee always gave her the jitters.

Holding the piece of jewelry in one hand and the herbs in the other, Dundalee addressed Olitus, her smile fading.

"You must move them quickly, Olitus. You and I both know time is precious."

She winked up at the bird. When she spoke to Olitus again, any sign of humor was gone.

"Now. Have faith in the One and…" A squawk from Cleo interrupted her. "Yes, dear Cleo. And faith in your pretty bird. Time and space are malleable. Follow her lead."

Moving to the opening between the two shawls, Dundalee held Berold's wristband up before her and began circling the herbs in the air around it, chanting softly to herself. Not taking his eyes off the woman, Olitus spoke to his second in command.

"Go, gather the men. Now. Bring them here. We move immediately."

Dideon glanced at the dwarves one last time, pivoted on his heel, and quickly made his way across the field. Olitus and Tilga stood quietly, watching Dundalee work her spell. Olitus found himself relaxing just a bit. To have such a one as this tiny sorceress on his side enforced his belief in himself and his men. The last of Dundalee's singsong spell filtered up into the branches of the tree.

The quiet surrounding them was only broken by the noise of the men coming across the clearing.

"With Tilga's blessing, you will take this wristband and return it to its rightful owner," Dundalee said. Delicately, she stepped forward and placed the jewelry in Olitus's outstretched hand, before moving to one side to join Tilga. Waving the bouquet at the opening in the material, she said, "The way is through there."

Olitus stared at the opening.

"Oh, for goodness' sake!" Dundalee looked up at Cleo. "Dear, would you mind?"

Cleo launched herself into the air, circled around Olitus, her wings caressing the top of his head. She shot through the opening in the shawls and was gone.

———

Dundar splashed more water on his head. The cold trickle down his neck dispelled the last of the fogginess he had felt all morning. Berold stood just downstream of the other dwarf, tying off a rabbit to his pack. He'd snared the small animal moments before but would wait to cook it until their evening meal.

They'd stopped at the edge of this large clearing, safely sheltered by a rocky outcropping, to fill their water bladders in preparation for the steep climb ahead. The crisp late morning air carried the scent of the snow from higher up in the mountains ahead of them.

"It's not the smell of my forest, but it's a clean one," Berold thought, staring up at the massive range.

His eyes scanned the meadow for any signs of movement. Since they'd encountered Morauth's scouts, every fiber of Berold's being was on edge. The forest seemed to be crawling with all sorts of nasty little beasties.

"The woman has a way of bringing out the worst in Faltofar, I'll give her that," Berold thought as he hiked his pack to his shoulder, but not before flicking a slimy black slug off one strap. The rabbit swung gently from a string at the back of the pack, and a drop of blood dripped into the soil at Berold's feet.

"There'll be a lot more of that before this is over," he mumbled to himself. The blood slowly soaked into the wet earth.

Dundar had slung his pack onto his back and joined Berold by the rocks. As they stepped away from the rocks, a movement at the edge of the forest caught Berold's eye. Grabbing Dundar's arm, he pulled the boy quickly back to the rock face, plastering them both against it. Cautiously, they inched around the corner enough to see but not be seen.

"Well, I'll be damned by all the metal of the earth," Berold said, narrowing his eyes at the improbable image that greeted him.

Hundreds of men, led by Olitus holding his dagger at the ready, marched from the trees directly toward Berold and Dundar. Berold recognized the dagger instantly.

"Only a descendant of Rendar would have that in his grip," thought the old dwarf, his brain quickly processing whether the army was friend or foe.

The humans advanced across the meadow, fanning out around their leader who moved as if magnetically drawn to where the dwarves remained hidden. Every man carried himself ready for an attack, but their expressions were slightly dazzled by the magic trailing after them into the bright meadow. Their leader held something metallic in the hand not gripping the dagger. It glinted in the sunshine. Berold rubbed the underside of his nose and studied his bracelet. Following his gut instinct, he stepped forward, pulling Dundar with him and away from the rocks that concealed them. They faced the incoming wave of humans. Berold held his hands away from himself, opening them to show he held no weapon. Dundar did the same, standing resolutely by the old dwarf's side. The younger dwarf's calm strength was not lost on the seasoned warrior.

Within moments a half-circle of towering humans surrounded the dwarves. Their leader stood several steps ahead of his men and eyed the dwarves cautiously. He cleared his throat, glancing around the meadow and down at the bracelet in his hand.

"I am Olitus of the Finn. You must be Berold. I believe this belongs to you."

Olitus extended his hand, placing the jewelry in Berold's palm. Berold nodded his thanks, waiting for the human to continue. He could tell the man was slightly shaken. Traveling by magic was not a pleasant experience. Berold had only done it a single time, and that had been more than enough, in his opinion.

Surprisingly, it was Dundar who broke the silence, taking a slow and deliberate step forward to address the leader. "I am Dundar, son of Dundalee. I believe my mother had something to do with this?" he asked bluntly, gesturing to the silent army of men.

Dideon felt his commander tense and stepped forward, his hand hovering at his hilt. Olitus raised a warning hand, shaking his head. "No Dideon. All is well. I am just surprised."

"Well met, Dundar, son of Dundalee." Olitus acknowledged the younger dwarf, instantly liking the tall youth. Formality dictated that his response reveal his lineage as well. "I am Olitus, son of Guyeth, descendant of Rendar. And yes, your mother's magic got us here so," he paused, searching for the proper word, "promptly."

Olitus sheathed his dagger and, with a respectful nod to Berold, addressed his attention to his men, giving orders for some to guard the perimeters of the clearing while the rest checked their gear. Glancing up at the high mountains at the edge of the meadow, Olitus finished his directions with a warning.

"Make ready your heavier layers. The going will get cold as we climb. We leave before the shadows touch these boulders." Olitus motioned to the warrior next to him, and, together, they moved closer to the dwarves.

"My second, Dideon."

Distractedly, Olitus scanned the rock behind and above the dwarves, finally finding what he looked for.

"And this," Olitus said, gesturing with his hand toward the rock, "is the lady Cleo."

Cleo had landed quietly. She peered down at them, giving a low squawk. Olitus acknowledged her and continued.

"I have a message from Dundalee for you." Olitus chose his words carefully. "She said to tell you, 'They are on the move. The tunnels are in good repair.'" He waited for some reaction from the old dwarf, but the face before him maintained its craggy stoicism. "That was all she said," Olitus finished, somewhat annoyed at being a courier and receiving no other information.

Berold pursed his lips and nodded, still reticent to acknowledge the human, but knowing they were in this together.

"To the One," he said grudgingly, staring at Olitus.

"To the One," Olitus said, staring down at the dwarf. "Right." Olitus exhaled, then tipped his head at the dwarves. "We leave within the hour. You are welcome to join us. I could use someone at my side as knowledgeable as you, Berold of the Glenn."

The men still close enough to overhear Olitus glanced back at the old dwarf, dawning respect on their faces. There was not a warrior among them who, having read books on the Dark Days and the final battle, didn't recognize the name of the seasoned warrior before them. Olitus offered his hand, where it hung midair for a brief moment before Berold reached forward and wrapped his own beefy grip around the human's, in the universal bond of warriors united for the One. From the top of the rock, Cleo gave a loud, pleased squawk. The sound was gently picked up by the breeze, drifting high above the trees.

———

Miles away, Morauth brushed her hand past her ear, looking around for the perpetrator. "Awful birds. They make the most irritating noises." She frowned, spitting out a single, final word. "Parrots."

She stood on a rise of land, regally staring at the swell of recruits making their way toward the main body of her army. The ancient ruins of her castle loomed in the distance, now a day's march behind them. Her followers increased by the hour. They slithered, stumbled, screeched, and crawled their way from across the lands. The ground rumbled, squeezing every angry, lost, forgotten, and unforgiven creature from dark bogs, deep caverns, and desolate crevasses. One side of her mouth rose slightly with a hint of a smile.

"Oh, yes," she whispered to herself. "Rendar." She touched the small ruby ring on her finger, twirling it. "Would that you were here." Her nostrils flared, catching the dank, moldy smell of bodies long unused to the light of day. "Liannan will rue the day she buried me in the bowels of this forsaken land."

THE REMEMBER'S MAP

B lisk stood at the door of his cabin, admiring the view from his porch. The land sloped green and rippling down toward the garden. The fresh summer air felt good on his long limbs. He'd been up before dawn, bent over the oversized map of Faltofar as he riffled through his volumes of history. His back hurt, and he rubbed at it, lost in thought.

"I'm missing something," he mumbled, his hand shifting down to scratch the cheek of his right bum.

He'd tried wearing clothes for a bit after the dwarves had surprised him weeks ago, but the feel of the cloth on his skin irritated him. Looking back at the maps, he shrugged, thinking of his garden and the peace it gave him. The maps and the remembering could wait. He needed to be out in the open air.

"It's not like I'm offending anyone," he said to himself, motioning around the empty cabin. Grabbing his gardening hat off its hook, he placed it snugly on his head, wiped a smudge off the mirror over the sink, and addressed himself in the glass. "The One gave us our parts, and our parts should feel free to feel free." With a happy little laugh, he readjusted his hat to a jaunty tilt, giving his reflection a wink.

He stepped out on the porch and took a deep breath, enjoying the freshness of the new day. Plucking his hat off, he stretched his arms overhead, then bent at the waist and tried to touch his toes. His spine cracked and popped, but the pain was less as he stood upright, raising his arms again over his head. The relief brought a smile to his face, which quickly disappeared when he realized he had an audience. Standing not four feet from the bottom of the porch were two dwarf women, their faces emotionless. Blisk closed his eyes for a moment, hoping that when he opened them, the women would prove to be merely an illusion of his tired brain. It didn't work.

With as much dignity as he could muster under the circumstances, he lowered his arms and bowed to the ladies. When he stood, he held the hat strategically in front of himself.

"How may I be of service, ladies?" he asked, clearing his throat loudly. He noticed the pretty one stood with one eyebrow raised, a slight smile on her upturned face.

"She's enjoying this," he thought glumly, wondering if he would ever get back to a peaceful summer of gardening.

"Master Blisk, I believe."

Dundalee delicately pinched fabric at the front of her skirt, lifting the hem so as not to trip and made her way up the porch stairs, brushing gently past Blisk. For a moment, Blisk didn't know if he should follow her or stay facing the other dwarf woman. He opted to back up slowly and sit in his old wicker chair.

"Come, Tilga," Dundalee's lilting voice drifted from the cabin's interior. "Let's give Master Blisk a moment to gather his thoughts. We shall make a bit of tea, I think."

Blisk sat back warily as the second woman hiked up her skirts and stomped past him. Then he stood quickly and grabbed his overalls, which hung from a peg on one of the porch posts. He had to drop his hat to work himself into a pant leg, and hoped the women were too busy in the kitchen to notice him hopping around.

Buckling a strap over his shoulder, he entered his cabin. Steam rose from the teapot as Dundalee poured hot liquid into three cups.

"How did you brew that so quickly?"

Dundalee ignored his question and merely handed a brimming cup to him with a smile.

"We haven't time for trivialities, dear Master. Your map of Faltofar there," she motioned primly with her cup, "is why we are here."

Dundalee blinked sweetly up at Blisk, who stared back at her, mesmerized. "I am sure you do not mind."

"I'm sure I don't mind," Blisk said, blinking back. Tilga narrowed her eyes at this exchange.

"Yes, very good. Now, if you would, Master Blisk, stand just there and sip your tea." She waved her hand in front of his face and motioned toward the shelf filled with volumes of books. "It is very good tea."

Blisk's eyes opened and closed slowly, less of a blink now, and stepped back toward the shelf, all the while mumbling to himself.

"I'll just stand over here and sip my tea. It is very good tea, you know."

"Quite," said Dundalee, focusing on the map.

Tilga put her hands on her hips, studying the dazed expression on the human's face. It wouldn't do to laugh, but she was sorely tempted. The bean pole looked like an outright idiot.

"What did you do to him, Dundalee?"

Tilga walked over to Blisk, snapping her fingers in front of his face. Blisk ignored her, blissfully bringing the cup to his lips and sipping.

"Nothing that can't be undone, dearie." Dundalee hummed happily under her breath, tracing her finger along the Great Rift Valley. "We have a bit of work to do, Tilga. Finish your tea, my dear. I am in need of the leaves."

Dundalee tilted her cup back and downed the last of the liquid, then, upending the cup, she tapped the leaves onto the map at the point where her finger rested.

"Yes, right about here."

She extended her hand for Tilga's teacup. Tilga quickly drained hers and handed it to the tiny sorceress, who dumped the residual leaves on top of her own. Setting the cups aside, Dundalee placed her index finger in the center of the pile of dank leaves and began to stir the clump in an ever-widening circle, softly chanting words to herself.

Tilga stepped back from the table, almost bumping into the tall human, who stood happily humming. Suddenly Dundalee's finger came to a halt. The tea leaves, which had been a wet mound moments before, now lay in a dry pile. Deliberately Dundalee bent forward over the map and pursed her lips, giving one short blow that scattered the leaves across the map's replica of the Great Rift Valley of Faltofar.

———

Night had fallen as Morauth drifted through the trees, taking stock of the army huddled in groups throughout the woods. The mass of misfits continued to swell in ranks throughout the inky black night, their snorts and gleeful cackling echoing through the darkness. They had gnawed at leashes that bound them, broken locks and bars that held them, burrowed out from under the weight of the cast-off detritus of Faltofar's villages, joining other like-minded creatures, instinctively answering their sorceress's summons. Now, they cowered away from her in awe and terror as she passed by. It amused her. Both the size of her army and their unease of her were pleasing.

"Even the nasty little dwarf," she thought, leaning against a tree near Nero. Tethered by a chain around his neck, the dwarf had stretched the metal links to their limit, scavenging the dank earth for burrowing grubs. Dirt rimmed his mouth, and a soft, incessant babbling dribbled from his lips.

"Here, little morsels. Don't hide from the Nero. Your friend just wants to talk to you. No, don't wiggle away, come play!" Finding another grub, Nero shoved it into his mouth, alternately giggling and chewing.

"Disgusting," Morauth said, averting her face with a sneer of contempt. Her flying cats, at least those not patrolling the skies, draped lethargically throughout the trees. Their wings wrapped like blankets around their dark, feline bodies, and their glowing predatory eyes dotted the night sky.

"My lovelies. It won't be long," she purred. "Soon, you will have your fill."

Gently she ran her hand along the chain wrapped around the tree, caressing the metal as one would something cherished and alive. When she reached the end that led to Nero, she gave it a flick of her wrist. The movement jerked Nero from his knees onto his back, blood oozing from the cuff around his neck. He lay blubbering and choking on the grub he'd been chewing, a glimmer of sanity reflected in his eyes for just a moment.

"Me mom never treated me in such poorly ways."

His eyes glazed over almost immediately as he rolled to his stomach and returned to scratching in the dirt.

Morauth caressed the metal between her fingers, toying with the idea of dragging Nero painfully upright. She adjusted her grip and was about to whip the chain again when the air around her shifted. Angrily she spun around, watching the trees begin to sway from a wind that had sprung up.

"Who dares?" she whispered, the dwarf forgotten, her eyes glinting a dark red.

The sentries around her clambered to their feet, and the cats in the trees began to unfurl their wings. Terrified shouts carried throughout the woods as the wind started to blow harder. The noise and movement ricocheted all around them, surging gusts moving faster and faster.

The wind, targeting the canopy's topmost branches, sent a shower of leaves and twigs cascading through the air and down to the forest floor. Tree limbs, bent beyond their flexibility, snapped, creating jagged spears in the high bows. Morauth's pets, yowling in outrage and pain, tried to take flight, only to be forced back into the lashing treetops. Only Morauth stood untouched, the air around her calm. Baring her teeth, she glared at her motley army as it staggered this way and that, fighting the wind, searching for shelter against the onslaught.

The booming sound of wood splintering gave the briefest warning as an immense evergreen tottered and fell, taking two more trees with it. The cries of the dying trapped under the massive foliage filled the dusty air. More trees fell in the distance, toppling vast swaths of the forest and killing more creatures.

Nero cowered in the dirt, his arms covering his head, his yowling intermixed with the screams of those around him. Rocks and leaves shot past Morauth, the earthly bullets pummeling exposed arms, heads, and slithering bodies. In a matter of minutes, the windstorm had created havoc, injuring or killing a significant portion of Morauth's army.

"Enough!" Morauth screamed, jerking the chain so hard it flipped Nero backward several feet, where he landed with a dull thud.

As abruptly as the wind had started, it began to die. Her teeth gritted in a snarl, Morauth scanned the trees around her. She stepped closer to the dwarf. Seeing that he still breathed, she dropped the chain, already forgetting him. Brushing small bits of dirt from her robe, she narrowed her eyes at the destruction, assessing where best to use her sorcery to keep alive those not mortally wounded.

"A pity to waste my energy on healing."

A final gust of wind swayed the tree next to her, pulling a low branch to its limit. When it snapped back, the tip of the limb struck her cheek, gouging a single deep cut across her face. She reached up, tracing the wound, then delicately and with bloody fingers, she peeled off a damp leaf that had plastered itself to her forehead. Turning it over in her hand, her smirk morphed into a deep, curdling laugh. Walking back to the whimpering dwarf, she kicked him viciously, flipping him over on his back.

"You seem to have friends in high places, dwarf." Her lips curled downward as she dangled the leaf in front of his face. Imprinted on its green surface was the image of a smiling Dundalee.

The troop of humans had stopped on a rise hundreds of meters above the forest floor. The army was now spread out. Those needing water unstrapped their bladders from their sides; others reworked bindings that had come loose on boots or gear.

Olitus stood separate from the main force, at the edge of the drop-off, looking down on the valley. Dideon finished speaking to one of the men and joined him, just as Berold and Dundar reached the small summit. The older dwarf walked purposely over to them, followed by the silent younger one for whom Olitus felt growing respect. The head of the humans' army had spoken briefly to Berold about the advance scouts Berold and the young dwarf had encountered. Encountered and killed after traveling a considerable distance from the Glenn in a very short amount of time.

"And on such short legs," Olitus thought. Even in war, there had to be moments of humor. If only to keep themselves sane.

He covered the smile that threatened to cross his face. Dwarves were a proud breed, and the last thing he wanted was to displease their leader. The old dwarf didn't mince his words as he hoisted himself up the rocky summit to the humans.

"There. That is where we need to camp for the night." His stubby finger pointed to a saddle in the hazy distance further up the ridge. Olitus studied him, a quizzical look on his face, but said nothing. Letting out a big sigh, Berold explained himself.

"There's caves. The old ways that are kept for emergencies." Berold glared at Olitus and Dideon, shaking his head at the idiotic humans. They had to have it spelled out for them. "That'll be where the Dwarves of the Glenn'll be joinin' us."

"Berold, I want to thank you for your support." Any thing else Olitus was about to say was cut short, his focus distracted by a change in the evening light. A darkness had formed in the valley below, building up over a section of the forest. Within moments a storm cell of angry black clouds congealed, the mass circling faster and faster, the sound of wood splintering as trees toppled to the forest floor.

"That has magic written all over it." Words of agreement and shouts of amazement followed. The men not close to the edge had run over, gawking down at the chaos. The storm picked up force, flinging whole trees hundreds of meters. But not even a puff of air disturbed the men and dwarves where they stood. The destruction was fast and immense, ending as quickly as it had begun. In the quiet of the aftermath, Olitus spoke.

"I will hope that whoever created that chaos is on our side." There were mumbles of agreement. "Back to your preparations."

Olitus's men moved away from the edge, small groups debating what they had just seen. He studied the destruction a moment more, running his hand unconsciously through his hair. Then, resting his hand lightly on the hilt of his dagger, Olitus turned once again to the dwarves. He had to trust in the One.

"So be it, Berold of the Glenn." Respectfully he nodded at the old dwarf. "Dideon, rally the troops. We march for the saddle immediately." He glanced one last time down into the valley, and at the dissipating storm cell. With a nod to his three companions, he moved away from the vista point and headed for his men.

CLOSER

W hen they left the great hall, Sarafina, after a much-needed rest, had returned to Argath's chamber and shared with him what had transpired deep in the old forest under the Holy Oak.

"I, somehow, brought her back, Argath," she said, rubbing at her skin where the anklet had been.

Argath, pacing behind her, stopped at his sister's pronouncement. "She carries her own guilt," he had realized.

He contemplated her, all too familiar with the notion that haunted her. "No, Sarafina. This was not of your doing. This was, is," he corrected himself, "inevitable." He held the chamber door open to the hallway and motioned for her to lead the way. Their boots echoed eerily along the empty corridor that led to Liannan's chamber.

Argath's recollection of Morauth in the High Chamber was blurry at best, laced with overwhelming nausea. His conviction that the sorceress had to be stopped, however, remained as clear as ever. In the time it took Sarafina to acknowledge the sentry stationed at the door, Argath adjusted his tunic and his commitment to Liannan. He had been wrong about his mother.

"You still do that," Sarafina whispered out of the side of her mouth. Argath frowned at her, shrugging in confusion. "Fidget before we see her." In response, Argath pushed the door to the chamber open and nudged his sister ahead.

Framed by the archway that led to her private balcony, Liannan faced her children. Her hair, silhouetted against the evening light, shifted around her shoulders with the soft breeze. "We cannot wait for reinforcements. She is on the move. We leave at first light for the Ledges. The Highlanders have rallied to me. It will have to be enough."

Argath and Sarafina exchanged a look. Anger permeated Liannan's words. Decisions made from high emotion were decisions made from weakness.

Even so, for the first time in a long while, Argath found himself in agreement with his liege lord. Regardless of Liannan's motives, the sorceress's powers were wreaking havoc across Faltofar and she had to be stopped. Argath watched the conflicting thoughts traversing his sister's face, understanding that she had a better idea of what, and who, they were about to challenge.

Liannan crossed the room and picked up her staff, which leaned against the fireplace. The sharp edges of the clear crystal that adorned the top of the thick wood glittered ominously, sending shafts of light around the chamber. She retraced her steps, ceremoniously placing the staff at arm's length in front of herself and directly between Sarafina and Argath.

When Argath stepped forward, wrapping his hand around the staff, he watched his younger sister closely, wordlessly encouraging her. She acknowledged him with a nod, knowing he understood her internal battle with her own conflicting emotions, torn between rushing home to protect her family and her commitment to the people of Faltofar. It wasn't really a choice, but the distance she navigated across the room somehow seemed longer than the weeks it had taken her to get to the high country. Her hand grasped the staff between Liannan's and Argath's.

"To the One."

"To the One," they responded in unison.

First light came far too soon. Sarafina had slept perhaps an hour, spending the darkest part of the night by the fire, working the points of her arrows into lethal sharpness as she thought of her children and Olitus miles away. When the patch of light from her chamber window had stretched mere inches, she rose from her comfortable seat and readied herself. The click of her chamber door shutting behind her sounded like a final note of a song that had been her life. This day would bring a beat far different. The cadence of war drums.

Her Sense was silent.

"Fitting that I do not know." She ran one finger along the stone wall into which the stairs were carved. The dense rock of the fortress seemed symbolic of all that the humans had endeavored to create.

"A safe world in which to raise our young."

Thom and Lilianna's faces drifted across her thoughts. She stepped down the last flight into the courtyard, lifting her face to the early morning light.

She pulled her outer layer closer, shifting the weight of her quiver of arrows. She had dressed for the cold that would greet them as they made their way upward through the mountains. Winding her way amongst the huddled groups of villagers, she nodded to those she knew but did not stop. She could feel their eyes on her. She was one of the dark children. She was Liannan's dark child.

A ripple coursed through the massed warriors, and like a slowly waking giant, the body of the army mobilized. Liannan was nowhere in sight, but in the distance Sarafina could make out Argath at the head of the Highlanders. He was the first to move through the massive gates and beyond the safety of the high walls. She felt no need to join him at the front. She preferred losing herself amidst these strong, proud people of her youth, focusing on placing one boot in front of the other and following the person ahead of her.

Thoughts of Morauth sent chills along her spine, settling in her stomach. She pulled her layers closer around her. Their destination, the Ledges, was where the final battle so many years ago had taken place. She touched the back of her neck, feeling the tattoo marking her as a healer: an Ouroboros, imbedded in her skin, its symbol that of infinity and the cycle of life and death. She recalled the words spoken and repeated endlessly through generations of healers. In a sense, it was their mantra. She had been taught by the healer before her, and that healer had learned from those that had come before her.

"There is strength in the belief of the Infinite."

Her thoughts drifted to the bravery of the one called Rendar. Not of her line, but that of her husband and her children. "Such courage." She looked around at those marching resolutely next to her. "We are the army of the One. We will prevail. We must."

What would their ancestors think of this moment?

She tried to picture what Rendar must have looked like. The forebear of her husband and her children. He had shown such bravery at the limit of his strength, forcing himself up from the frozen ground to fight hand to hand with Morauth. A struggle to the death, cutting her deeply with his dagger and sending her spiraling hundreds of feet down from the Ledges. The magic surrounding Morauth had protected her from death, but there were worse things. The evil energy had created fissures in the blade's hard glass, and shards of obsidian had separated from the knife, one puncturing her hand, another piercing her heart. When she hit the forest floor, a section of the splintered glass pinned her to the ground. The impact, so intense it had shifted the earth, creating the Great Rift Valley and Morauth's permanent prison.

"Or so we thought," Sarafina snorted, then coughed as a slap on her back jolted her from her dark thoughts. The sentry, whose name she still couldn't recall, stepped closer, acknowledging her with a small salute.

"Sarafina, dark daughter of Liannan." Her head snapped up, and she coldly studied the man. He smiled gently at her, softening her mistrust. "The One will prevail, always. As will this mallet."

Hefting the weapon to his shoulder, he left her with a nod and a wink, striding ahead through the crowd. Within moments she had lost him in the marching mass of warriors. "I still can't recall his name," she thought.

Taking a deep breath, she hoisted her quiver higher on her shoulder, stepping in line with more purpose than she had felt in days. Worry would not determine the outcome of this battle.

———————

Streaks of red and orange coursed across the sky, bathing slumbering men and their piles of gear in its predawn glow. Berold wove his way through the snoring troops, nodding to the early morning watchmen. They did not follow or question him, assuming he was headed to the low rocks and shrubs for privacy.

The only person Berold wanted at his side was the descendant of Rendar. He had communicated with the human the night before and was not surprised when Olitus stepped from the shadows of a boulder and quietly joined him. Berold acknowledged him with a grunt, and together they moved silently up the rise. At Berold's direction, they headed along the base of the cliff band, away from the temporary camp.

The sky was quickly morphing from its early morning golden display to the soft blue of summer as they worked their way over a jumbled pile of scree until stopped by a huge boulder. Laying a firm hand on Olitus's shoulder, Berold motioned the human to stay put. He edged his way around the huge rock, stopping on the other side to look up. With his hands on his hips, the old dwarf let out a long, low whistle that mimicked the Mourning Hawk. Its echo bounced off the cliff walls, answered moments later by a similar call. Berold stepped back into view and motioned Olitus to join him. Coming around the boulder, Olitus found himself just below the dark entrance of an enormous cave.

"Your people's form of travel?"

Berold merely sniffed a response, his eyes never wavering from the cave opening. When he addressed Olitus, it was quietly, from the side of his mouth, his lips barely moving.

"Have your dagger in your hand, human. Not all dwarves are fond of your kind."

Olitus slowly drew the dagger from its sheath, poised to use it if necessary. Berold snapped his eyes away from the cave and glared at him.

"What?" Olitus's face scrunched in confusion. For a moment, he looked like a little boy who had failed at his exams. Berold exhaled in disgust.

"Not as a weapon, lad. They'll need proof a who y'are." He nodded toward the dagger, pointing at the jeweled hilt, then swung his stubby hand around and up toward the cave, where hundreds of stout dwarves had silently emerged from the darkness. "Show um the hilt."

Olitus turned the dagger in his palm and raised it high over his head, watching the line of small men above him. The movement began with one of the nastier looking ones at the front. A fist raised. Others followed until every dwarf stood, one arm raised straight above, stubby fingers gripped in a vice. When their meaty, clinched fists came down in unison against the metal of their chest plates, it sent a cascade of rocks careening off the far side of the cave opening.

"I'd say we's got ourselves an army." Berold exhaled through his nose and pushed past Olitus. "Time to go."

———

Morauth's dark army, its numbers now cut by at least a third, had left behind the demolished forest and begun moving. They raked claws against trees left standing, tore tufts of green grass and budding flowers from the damp earth, screamed their vengeance at their enemies, and tried desperately to avoid Morauth. In the coldest hours of the night they traveled, their route taking them up the steepest side of the mountain range, higher and higher and away from Olitus's troops.

Her flying pets had been ordered to carry those that slithered. The slimy, slow ones were often the most toxic, and Morauth had no intention of leaving them behind. The sorceress's strength seemed limitless, inspiring her followers. She stopped for neither water nor rest and ate only small bits of some dark red meat, her white teeth gleaming in the darkness as she delicately tore at it. Throughout the night, she spoke to no one other than to give commands, floating up each rise, a soft smile creasing the corners of her mouth. Her eyes, however, reflected only the darkness around them.

The captain of her guard had been given his orders. Any weak link was to be disposed of as he saw fit. They had torn one of their own kind limb from limb only hours before when he'd lagged behind due to a broken leg caused by a falling tree. The meat was fresh, and it had given the rest of them the sustenance they needed to reach the Ledges.

One of Morauth's special guards, tasked with transporting the gibbering little dwarf, pulled himself up the steep terrain with the last of the troops just as the night sky began to slip away, leaving room for a cold, bleak sun. Reaching over his shoulder, he grabbed Nero by a bulbous ear and flipped him to the ground. The dwarf hit the trampled snow on his side, a whimper slipping from the corner of his mouth, but lay still where he had landed.

"Nasty dwarf. Me done with you," said the hairy guard, looking over his shoulder to see if either his captain or the sorceress were nearby. Seeing neither, he kicked the dwarf in the side and spat at his head. Nero buried his face in the icy ground.

"I'll show them. They'll all pay one day, they'll see. I will, yes, I will." His crazed laughter dribbled down his chin leaving slimy tracks of dirty spittle.

The Ledges, which had been created by an extended outcropping of Granidian rock, ran almost to the summit of the Dark Tooth, the most towering peak in the High Range. Windswept and bleak, it lacked any signs of the greenery of the lands below. Nothing grew here, with the exception of one ancient relative of the Holy Oak. And even its gnarled branches, which twisted gracefully counterclock-wise, molded by the gusts of wind that carried snow flurries across the unfertile ledges, were bare of leaves. The ancient tree had grown roots that burrowed deep and far into the rock and ice, stretching down toward the lower lands of Faltofar, its energy spent in holding on. These partially exposed roots, so thick they defied the strongest winds, had kept the Holy Oak perched there for centuries, perhaps witnessing and waiting as the struggles from below climbed to meet Faltofar's oldest life-force.

Nero, who had landed near the tree, crawled to one of the roots and curled himself into its base. The guard grabbed his filthy jersey to stop him but let go when Morauth commanded him otherwise.

"Leave the little runt there. Perhaps the tree will take pity on him."

The guard scratched his belly, consoling himself by yanking the chain attached to the dwarf, beginning to coil it around a root that humped up from the ground.

"Don't. We won't be here long. That is where we are going." For emphasis, Morauth's long finger jabbed the air, to the final ledge above where they stood. "Where would he go, anyway?"

She glided away, already forgetting the dwarf. Sheltered by the root, Nero's voice was muffled, as a calculating look crossed his face.

"I'se a dwarf. Powerful dwarf. I'se a dwarf. Powerful dwarf."

CREATURES BIG AND SMALL

Lilianna shifted her weight from one leg to the other. She'd been standing on the fence rail for over an hour, challenging herself to remember old songs and stories of Faltofar's past and then filtering through them for any clues that might help her in the days to come. Her conversation with Torr on the cliffs above the ocean made her question everything she thought she knew about her home and her family.

"All we do is wait." Loosening her grip on the rail, she jumped down, frustration apparent in the slump of her shoulders.

Thom stood by the shed, tossing rocks in the air and using the dwarf club as a bat, aiming at an improvised target. Lilianna could tell by the thumping sound of stone against wood, first the club, and then the target, that his skill had improved. She wondered if the new game would make him reconsider the club over his sling as his weapon of choice.

"I wonder if impatience improves one's aim," she thought with a cynical smile.

She glanced at Mosely, who had parked himself on the fencepost next to her. He also seemed to be scanning the field, but Lilianna guessed he was searching for the titmouse. The little animal was usually never far from the girl's pocket, but it had scurried off several hours before, obviously intent upon a mission. The mission usually involved food.

Lilianna and Thom had decided to share one pack, and the duffle sat next to the door of the cabin. The livestock were fed and corralled. The garden had been watered, and the fencing around it shored up recently by Thom's handiwork. They had even found a way to automate the distribution of food and water should they be forced to leave for a duration of time. Anything to keep themselves busy.

Lilianna idly played with her talisman, running her fingers over the imprint of the tree and the hands. She walked along the grassy edge of the fence to the shed.

"Tell me again," she said as she leaned against the warm, wooden wall. She sometimes envied Thom's ability to see so far, but at least he was always generous in his descriptions. Or, almost always. Thom stopped mid-swing, the rock thudding to the ground at his feet, and gave his sister a disgusted grimace.

"The dwarf lady waved something in her hand and pointed at the trees. Her scarf or shawl thing was hanging there. They went through the gap and were gone."

Lilianna's hopeful face just increased his frustration. He shook his head and kicked the rock on the ground.

"That's it, Lili. Nothing more. They were there; then, they weren't." He stomped off toward the front steps of the cabin.

Lilianna picked up the rock he'd dropped and threw it as hard as she could at the target. It connected with a satisfying smack at the very center. Searching the ground at her feet, she was disappointed to see no other rocks around her and walked into the field to retrieve the one she'd thrown. Focused on the ground in front of her, she didn't see the beast careening out of the sky.

"Lili!"

Thom's scream and an uncanny yowl from Mosely were her only warnings, aside from the moving shadow that engulfed her own.

Instinctively, she tucked and rolled, coming up several feet away, her small dagger gripped tightly in her hand.

The razor-sharp claws of the catlike creature penetrated the ground like missiles, pulling up chunks of earth where Lilianna would have been. Its yellow teeth bared and it hissed, obviously disappointed its surprise attack had been foiled. Lilianna shifted her weight, centering her balance, her dagger aimed toward the big cat's chest.

"You're one of the big nasty things who hurt my friend."

The air around the girl shimmered, her growing power rippling toward the scaled monster. She shifted the dagger from one hand to the other, watching and waiting for its next move. As the winged animal squared off to her, coiling its muscular body in preparation to launch itself at her, she caught a movement out of the corner of her eye. Her dagger wavered, and both cats launched themselves. One at her and one -

"Mosely, no!"

The tiny cat shot across the yard, his tail fluffed to its fullest. Hissing and spitting, he arched to his full height, his small body separating Lili from the larger cat. For a split second, they were nose to nose, then Mosely spun and shot between its legs. The monstrous feline snapped around with a whip of its tail, its outstretched wings billowing up the dirt in a circle around it. Lili jumped backward and watched in disbelief as its huge front paw, claws extended, cut through the air toward their housecat. Mosely darted sideways, luring it closer to himself and further away from Lilianna.

"Mosely, run!"

Mosely, his ears flat against his skull, ignored his mistress. Yowling a cat taunt, he danced around and under the bigger flying cat. Thom, now breathless at his sister's side, held his slingshot at the ready, tensely watching for an opportunity to let the rock fly.

The beastly cat's scales glittered darkly in the late-afternoon light. Angry sprays of spittle erupted from its slavering mouth each time Mosely ran under its legs. The little cat's strategy seemed reliant on his speed. With each zig, Mosely zagged the attacker further away from the children.

"Thom, he's going to get cornered between the shed and the coop!" Lilianna waved her dagger helplessly in front of her.

Just then, the beast saw his chance and lunged for the cat, teeth gnashing in anticipation.

Lilianna whipped her arm back and let the dagger fly. It arced through the air, the gleaming tip making contact with the animal's leathery hide and penetrating the creature's foreleg. It paused mid-lunge and shifted its weight, shaking its paw in irritation.

"Thom, we've got to help him!"

Thom raised his arms, aiming the slingshot at the flying cat's eyes, the most vulnerable spot amidst the scales. But he never got the chance to fire. Mosely, faster than either of them could imagine, darted around the corner of the shed, pursued closely by the gigantic winged beast. Lili's dagger stuck out of its leg like a worthless toothpick.

A guttural dying howl from the far side of the shed ripped through the quiet summer air.

"NO!" screamed Thom, his shoulder slamming into the side of the shed as he reached its protection seconds before Lilianna. With his slingshot ready again, they cautiously peered around the corner. "What the…?" The rock fell from the sling with a small thud.

The flying feline lay on its back, its entrails ripped from its belly. A furred beast, twice its size, loomed over the vile, winged animal. It tipped its head back and gave one long yowl before sitting back on its haunches, its paw still on the bloodied scales.

"Mosely?" Thom and Lili squeaked in unison.

The huge cat, purposely ignoring them, casually lifted his paw, giving it a lick, before beginning to clean the blood from his whiskers. Slowly, he began to shrink.

"It's… He's…?" Thom trailed off, his jaw hanging open, and his arms limp at his side.

Lilianna took a step closer, staring at the carnage her extraordinary cat had created with a swipe of his huge paw. The creature was definitely dead. The smell of rot from the animal's exposed entrails made her gag. Keeping her lunch down with an effort, she backed away, her heartbeat finally beginning to slow. Thom had shut his mouth, but he now rubbed one hand over his eyes, trying to better understand what had just happened. They looked at each other.

"You okay?" Their questions overlapped in unison.

Mosely, now back to his normal size, padded toward them, his tail high. Lilianna knelt to Mosely's level, tentatively reaching for him and picking him up. Holding him in front of her face, she addressed him with respect.

"Mosely, you are an amazing cat, aren't you?"

Thom scratched the cat under his chin. Mosley allowed Lilianna to hold him for a moment before he wiggled to be free. She gently lowered him to the ground, and he made a dignified departure across the yard. Their disbelief bubbled up in relieved laughter.

"I fail to see what is so very funny about any beast such as the one dead in this yard."

The children jumped, startled for the second time in the day. Torr's voice reverberated in their heads, just as his hoofs touched the earth on the far side of the carcass. He crossed his arms, nostrils flaring. The other Sepheriis landed around him, their hooves pawing at the ground, their faces disdainful but alert. The children ran around the dead body. Torr bent and enveloped them in his arms.

"Well met, Thom. Lilianna," he said, releasing them gently. He glanced at Mosely's handiwork. "The dark creatures grow bold. The danger to Faltofar, and to you, has become too real."

Torr walked over to the pile of scales and shriveled wings. "How is it that this abomination lays here, splayed open?"

Mosely had disappeared, leaving the children to try to explain.

"It was Mosely, Torr."

The Sepherii looked back at her blankly.

"Our cat," Lilianna finished with a small laugh and a shake of her head, signifying her disbelief.

Thom added nothing. He bent over the gigantic, scaly cat's carcass and grabbed the hilt of Lilianna's dagger, pulling it free.

Wiping the blade on his pant leg, he handed it to his sister with a nod, silently acknowledging her marksmanship. She re-sheathed it at her waist.

Torr had moved back into the circle of Sepheriis. The elegant beings danced from hoof to hoof, their coats radiant, their eyes charged with determination. The time had clearly come for them to join the fight.

"Your packs?" Torr asked.

Thom ran to the cabin to retrieve the duffel. It bounced against his side as he hurried back to the Sepherii. Handing the bag to Lilianna, he grabbed Torr's side and swung up onto his back, taking the bag from his sister so she could mount behind him. They slung the duffel easily between them, leaning forward expectantly. Torr lunged into the air, followed quickly and quietly by the others.

Settling the duffel more tightly in front of her, Lilianna looked down and back, shuddering not from the crisp air but from the recognition that she should have been dead. Silently, she thanked their little house cat, who sat in the middle of the yard, gazing up at her.

THE LEDGES

The Highlanders moved higher into the mountains. Long experienced with the hazards of their land, they trod carefully, avoiding the tell-tale soft, crystallized snow that blanketed the deep blue crevasses. One misstep and a body would slide instantly down into the icy depths, embraced by the mountain forever.

Sarafina sat on a snow-encrusted rock and adjusted her crampons, silently thanking Olitus for his packrat tendencies. She snuffed out thoughts of her home in the warm lower lands, forcefully keeping her mind in the present by checking the straps for tears in the leather, and tightening them, one by one, around her boots. The Highlanders were quiet. Tension and the unspoken, seasoned preparation of trained warriors permeated the air. This would be their final rest before the march to the summit. She'd pulled up her hood, but even still, snowflakes found their way onto her eyelashes. Blinking them away, she stood and slung her pack onto her back, readjusting her quiver and bow. Others around her began to rise, determination and frost giving their features an otherworldly pale cast.

Liannan had finally decided to show herself. Their leader had emerged from the whiteness as if the snow flurries had solidified into the form of a human. Seeing her, the company's spirits had lifted immediately, not so much evidenced in exchanged encouragements, but in the way they carried themselves toward battle. Liannan stood now, staff in hand, on the next rise up from the body of the army, talking to Argath.

No one bothered Sarafina as she waited silently for what she knew was to come. She had finally seen it, or some of it, the night before in the hearth fire of her room. At any moment, Liannan would motion for her to join them. And over the rise from where her mother and brother stood, Sarafina would face her darkest fears in the form of the sorceress, Morauth. Beyond that, the Sense had been vague, showing her everything and nothing.

"The future is always mutable. There is hope in that," she thought.

Liannan looked down the ridgeline, signaling her to join them. And then, from every corner of the snowfield and through the white blizzard that swirled around them, all the demons of hell broke loose.

Out of the sky, dark torpedo-like beasts dove into the High-landers, their sharp claws leaving trails of bloody, torn flesh and screams of surprise and pain. Yapping, doglike beings erupted from behind icy boulders, their ugly snouts and vicious gaping mouths grinning from under metal helmets as their spears arced through the air, finding targets through gaps in the Highlander armor. Slithering, brainless blobs bubbled up from semi-hidden crevasses, their poisonous slime burning steaming paths in the snow as they wormed their way up the hillside.

With an angry howl that came from the depths of her being, Sarafina tossed her pack aside and cinched her bow and quiver tighter to her. She pulled her dagger from her sleeve and, dodging a spear, scrambled through the chaos, her arm slashing a path toward Argath and Liannan. Pivoting away from an oozing slug, she landed on the hand of one of the dogmen, purposely grinding her crampon into his furry wrist. Her knife sliced across his neck, blood fountaining forth with his dying exhale. She twisted sideways to avoid the majority of the blood and realized her foot was stuck in his flesh.

"Phhh, these crampons," she cursed in frustration. Preoccupied with freeing herself, she did not notice one of the slug-like creatures working its way toward her. Too late, she saw its tail as it whipped across her free foot. A portion of the bulky outer casing shimmered an evil green. She swung around, cutting it in half. The thick leather across the top of the shoe began to melt.

"Damn." She pulled harder, struggling to dislodge her dog-encrusted boot before the acid slime got to the flesh of her other foot. Grabbing a handful of bloodied snow, she worked quickly to wipe away the hissing goo, keeping as much snow as possible between her hand and the slime to protect her skin. It was inevitable, even with the battle raging on around her, that a foe would notice her predicament. One of the hairy beasts, his lips parted in a grin that framed yellow, sharp teeth, stomped toward her seeing an easy kill. Just as he got close enough to strike, Sarafina yanked her foot hard enough to free herself. She rolled away, and the spear tossed by the beast landed where her foot had been just a second before. When she came up, they were nose to nose.

"Perfect." Sarafina smiled up at the beast, who frowned at her in confusion.

Her hand smashed into his face, smearing the poisonous ball of snow she still held in her hand into his eyes. He staggered back, his eyeballs already melting down into the cavity that had once been his cheek. She tossed the rest of the grimy mass away from her, wiping her hand into the snow at her feet. Her fingers burned, but she ignored the pain and hurried toward the higher ground.

The sound of metal on metal, angry growls of determination, and the rattling gasps of the dying surrounded her. Dodging the swing of an ill-timed club, she reached the ledge not far from where her brother had stood moments before. As she searched for a handhold to leverage herself up, she heard Argath, who had seen her coming, yell her name. She jumped as a hand grabbed her leg, her dagger slicing sideways, stopping inches from the familiar sentry's face. He propped his mallet against the rocks.

"Go on! Hurry!" His name came to her finally as he cupped her foot to leverage her up onto the rocks where Argath now knelt.

"Thaddeus, my thanks!" she exclaimed as she grabbed her brother's hand and scrambled up next to him.

As Argath extended his free hand to Thaddeus, one of the flying cats rocketed down toward them. There was no time for Sarafina to unsling her bow.

"Argath!" Sarafina ducked sideways to avoid the heavy blade of her brother's sword as he rolled to his back, slashing upward, skewering the feline's soft underbelly and dropping it to the rocks. With the momentum of its fall and his hands still wrapped tightly around the hilt, Argath swung himself back to standing, jabbing the blade deeper before stomping his foot on its chest and pulling his weapon free. Sarafina grabbed Thaddeus's hand and pulled him up to join them. With their backs to each other, the three wielded sword, dagger, and steel mallet with renewed energy.

The Dark Army kept coming.

Liannan had moved further up the snowfield, her staff above her head, the crystal a welcome beacon of hope. Those in its circle of light found themselves protected from the onslaught of Morauth's army. The sorceress's minions hung back just out of the light, snarling, yapping, and hissing their fury. Those who had challenged the circle of light and stepped into it had burned. To a crisp. Still, Morauth's army, more vast in size, was able to force the Highlanders up the ridge even as Liannan continued to shout words of encouragement. Those not protected by the light from her staff fought ever harder, their space narrowing.

Several of the armored dogmen, jabbing their way through the throng of thrashing bodies, closed in on Thaddeus, Argath, and Sarafina, who were now the last line of defense outside the glow of Liannan's crystal.

"Argath! Thaddeus!" Sarafina yelled. "Avoid the spears at all cost!" She jumped, sidestepping an arrow, and brushed hair out of her eyes with the back of a sweaty hand. "The tips are coated!"

Her brother ducked a thrown rock, swinging his sword to chop the head off of a long, slippery creature that had the unfortunate timing to poke its head up over the cliff band where they now fought. "I'd like to avoid everything!" he yelled back.

Seeing a break from their attackers, he grabbed Sarafina and yanked her toward the summit where Liannan stood, shoving her in front of him.

"Go!"

The three of them scrambled up and into the safety of the crystal's light, which continued to expand slowly across the bloodied snow. Liannan shifted the staff from one hand to the other, resolutely moving upward. Sarafina, followed closely by Argath, carefully wound through the other Highlanders to stand beside her at the summit. With a nod, Thaddeus left them and joined those at the perimeter of light, facing the throng of evil, leering faces just beyond.

"To the One." Sarafina's chest heaved from exertion, her whispered prayer a puff of steam in the cold air as she scanned what was left of their companions.

Morauth's followers paced, slithered, and stomped back and forth along the perimeter of the crystal's light. The surprise attack had taken its toll, cutting the Highlanders' numbers by at least half. It was not good odds. There were far too few of them left.

From the far side of the ledge where they stood, a frigid updraft sent snow particles into the light from the crystal. The Highlanders stood silently, their stoic and determined faces a sea of macabre, blood-splattered masks. They gripped their bloodied weapons in hands made frigid by the icy wind, glancing bitterly at the creatures outside of the circle of light. Morbid curiosity enveloped Sarafina as she squinted her eyes against the white flakes. But, on the other side of the rise, the Ledges were empty.

"Where is she?" Argath's voice crackled with fury.

"So," Argath looked at Liannan, "where is this dark sorceress who sends her peons to do her destruction?"

The only spot clean of blood on Argath's sword glinted dangerously as he lowered it to his side.

With a hand on his arm, Liannan silenced him, nodding toward the ledge below them. From out of the curtain of snow, Morauth slowly emerged, her dark hair undulating around her head. The shuffling noises from both armies slowly died down, as the air around them snapped in the deepening cold.

"She is but a darker version of my mother." Sarafina gripped her knife tighter.

Morauth calmly scanned the gathered armies and casually stepped farther away from the edge of the ledge, dragging something in the snow at her side. It wriggled and cried out, but she ignored it. With her free hand, she pulled out a knife from the folds of her long, dark cloak. Liannan, her face etched in icy determination lit by the crystals' glow, looked away from her sister, scanning the faces of the loyal Highlanders.

"Argath," she said in a low, calm voice, staring up at the crystal. "She has a dwarf. A sacrifice of sorts. I cannot save him and protect our people."

Argath's eyes narrowed, and without a glance at Liannan, he separated himself from the rest of the Highlanders, moving down the slope. Sarafina quickly sheathed her dagger, pulling her bow from her shoulder. When she stepped forward to join her brother, Liannan's staff barred her.

"You are one of the dark children, Sarafina. Be careful of the," Liannan's features turned icy, "direction of your choices. Morauth's power is tempting." Liannan's cold, blue eyes bore into the equally cold, green eyes of her daughter. Sarafina pushed the staff away and cautiously moved down the slope, notching in an arrow as she came to her brother's side. Together they stepped out of the protective circle of light. Morauth's army howled in triumph and surged forward, but a single command uttered from their dark leader stopped them.

"Leave them TO ME." Morauth's voice ricocheted off the rocky outcroppings. Her army slunk back, and the siblings continued down the slope.

"Yes, come closer, children."

As the distance narrowed, Morauth's features came better into focus. Her face was creased in a soft smile. A narrow, red cut below one eye contrasted with her marble-white skin. The dwarf cowered at her feet, his face stuck in the snow, snuffling incoherently.

"Have you come to join me, Sarafina?" she purred. Her dark mass of hair swayed in the wind, the tips of each thick strand snapping venomous teeth. "The world will be ours very soon."

Nudging the dwarf with her boot, she added, "All that is required is the blood of an innocent, given willingly."

The sorceress lifted her boot and slowly leveraged Nero over with a tap of her toe. He lay quivering, his eyes pinched shut, his arms wrapped tightly across his chest, the empty sleeve where his lower arm had been, flapping in the wind. Sarafina could feel the tension in Argath, his sword point moving slowly in front of Morauth.

"Your brother has a weakness for dwarves, I think!" Morauth said with a cutting laugh as she sneered from Sarafina to Argath.

The sorceress's army sniggered and yowled, but a glance from her silenced them.

"Your life for his?" One finger tapped gently at her cheek, a mock frown crossing her features. "Argath, isn't it?" she murmured, addressing Argath for the first time as she twirled her dagger over Nero. "You certainly would fulfill the," she paused, searching for the proper word, "position."

Suddenly, like a striking viper, her dagger tilted forward toward Argath's chest, vibrating with violent magic. A green light exploded from its tip, penetrating his tall frame, just as a bolt of white light shot down the hill from Liannan's staff. The rays collided in sparks of green and white, showering the tall Highlander as he toppled to the snow.

Sarafina, bow held high, whipped around to see Liannan's cold features lit up with rage. The white light protecting those around her was gone, directed in that one bolt to save Argath. Morauth's army gleefully now encircled the exposed Highlanders. Sarafina spun around again, aiming her arrow at Morauth's face. She could do nothing for them, but perhaps she could save her brother. The sorceress stood there, one eyebrow raised.

"What will you do, Sarafinnnaaaa?" Morauth spoke her name in a soft hiss.

A deafening howling on the ridge above them drowned out Sarafina's reply. The dark army had moved in closer, confining the last of the Highlanders into a tight wall around Liannan. Swords and spears clashed, and the cries of all manner of creatures fighting for their lives filled the air again.

The Highlanders were far outnumbered, but the snowy terrain was familiar ground. They held their position while the evil army slipped and slid along the ridge, some losing their footing completely and careening past Sarafina and over the abrupt edge. A detached part of her brain enjoyed their dying cries as they hurtled into the vastness. Still, the battle was weighted against those who fought for the One. It would be over soon.

Sarafina, her bow and quiver unwavering, stared at her aunt, her face emotionless. Morauth's sharp, white teeth glittered between her thin lips.

"Ah, you have strength, child, and a will that would be of use to me. At my side, of course." And then she began to laugh.

The sound at first soft and low gradually increased. It seeped under Sarafina's skin and dove into the depth of her soul. Her arms began to grow weak, the arrow point wavering. A ringing in her ears stilled the sound of laughter for just a moment. She closed her eyes, swaying.

"NO!"

Her eyes flew open, fighting back. She wrapped her defiance around her, desperately trying to block the spell. "Just enough to… a….chance…to…think." Her lids dropped lower, and her muddled mind deceived her into thinking her husband, her love, Olitus called out to her. Then, she heard his voice again, stronger this time.

"Sarafina!"

She blinked blearily up at the ridge, her mind struggling toward the surface. She felt Morauth, inside her head, pull away. The sorceress had heard the voice too.

Olitus, surrounded by his men, his forces swelled with as many dwarves, swarmed up the ridge. Berold led his people, plowing through the mass of Morauth's followers, his club swinging a swath of destruction. With renewed energy, the Highlanders rallied, sand-wiching Morauth's army between the ranks of the armies of the One. The fighting was vicious, brutal, and quick. The men and the dwarves, although tired from the climb, were fresh and eager for the fight. Inspired by the vitality and the determination of the seasoned dwarf, their battle cries joined those of the Highlanders, reverber-ating across the windswept snow and cascading down to the small gathering at the edge of the cliff.

"Take command!" Olitus yelled over his shoulder.

Dideon nodded.

Olitus, signaling Berold to his side and flanked by their core fighters, detached from the primary battle. He fought the urge to run full tilt down to where Sarafina stood, motioning those following him to move cautiously. All of their lives – Sarafina's included - depended on quick thinking and deliberate action. He lowered his hand, watching Sarafina sway.

"And even then, it might not be enough to save us."

Morauth stood frozen, her head tilted to the side, a sneer of dismissal making her lips appear like a slash of blood across her features.

Olitus felt the shift in the sorceress before it happened. With a soft scoffing snort, her smile faded, and the hand holding the dagger swung high and through the air. A whisper of magic oozed from her red mouth. For a split second Olitus thought he would lose the most precious thing in his world, but the evil woman had something else in mind. A stream of dark light shot from the tip of her dagger's blade, wrapping a coil around Argath and Nero like a lasso. Backing away from Sarafina, Morauth glided closer to the edge, dragging human and dwarf with her through the snow. The dwarf struggled weakly, but the human lay motionless, the snow piling up against his limp body while drifting flakes covered his pale face.

Cowering away from the unconscious human, Nero struggled in vain against the magical bonds. Bubbles of spittle formed at his mouth and his good arm punched and clawed at Morauth's robe. She kicked the dwarf away from her, and he slid against a rock, the contact strong enough to knock the wind out of him.

Olitus came to a stop at Sarafina's side, locking eyes with her for a split second. Berold flanked her on the other side. She no longer swayed, and her aim was steady, the arrow pointed once again at Morauth.

Men and dwarves fanned out, alert for a word from their commanders. The blood-curdling noises of battle along the ridge above them permeated the air, as did the stench of death. A concoction of sweat, blood, and fear. But within moments, the metallic clang of metal on metal and the angry shouts of success and loss tapered off, supplanted by cries for mercy. The army of the One had triumphed.

Those who had gathered along the edge of the Ledges below the main force registered the shift above, but for them the scale had not tipped in anyone's favor. It was deathly quiet. Deathly quiet, save for Berold's quick intake of breath as he realized the dwarf at Morauth's feet was his son.

3 0

A WILD RIDE

L ilianna felt alive. Alive and determined to stay that way. Every muscle in her body felt charged with pent-up energy. Her legs ached from squeezing tightly to Torr, and her eyes watered, even narrowed against the wind. She hunched over the cumbersome duffle bag, the land below them a blur. Torr had never flown this fast with the children before. If not for the reality of their situation, she would have shouted for joy with each gust of wind. But his urgency resonated through her.

The Sepheriis created an arrow pattern in the air. Torr led at the point in front with two Sepheriis on either side and two slightly behind him. The last of them, the sweep, flew at a distance behind Torr and the children. The light around them had shifted throughout the afternoon. Due to the sun's angle, or perhaps from her newly-honed perception, Lilianna could finally see their magnificent wings. They spread out at least ten feet on either side, translucent and deceivingly fragile-looking. When they had first ridden Torr to the high plateau, it had seemed like he had merely galloped into the air. Now, she could finally appreciate the unique magic of these beings.

"They're stunning," she said quietly, unconsciously squeezing Thom tighter.

"What?" he yelled over his shoulder, squirming at the pressure.

Apologetically, Lilianna loosened her grip but didn't reply. The wind made it difficult to speak. She occupied herself in looking around, glancing back at the Sepheriis behind them. This time she squeezed Thom so hard it made him grunt.

"What Lili?" His ribs were starting to hurt.

He shifted his weight, scowling back at his sister. Instantly, his irritation dissolved. Two of the evil, winged cats followed closely behind them, their mouths open in delighted yowls, flapping lips spraying the air around them with poisonous spittle. Squeezing his thighs tighter, Thom released his grip on Torr's waist and pulled the slingshot from his belt, where it hung next to the old dwarf's club. Lilianna leaned sideways to give him a better shot, concentrating all of her energy on mentally sending Torr a warning. The Sepherii interrupted her.

"I know. Hold on tightly, both of you! We will outmaneuver them!"

Thom wrapped one arm quickly around the Sepherii, his slingshot still held tightly in his fist. Lili grabbed Thom.

The Sepherii dove downward, streaking toward the earth then abruptly banked to the left and rocketed straight up. The small duffel bag slid from Torr's back, spiraling down through the air. Watching it, Lilianna felt a moment of sick vertigo. What if that had been one of them? Without missing a winged beat, the Sepherii bringing up the rear snatched it before it could fall further, slinging the bag over its shoulder.

Speeding skyward with the sun directly in her eyes, Lilianna felt the surge of power vibrate through Torr and under her skin. Vertigo disappeared, replaced by determination. She leaned tighter into Thom, giving herself enough room to pull her dagger loose, and scanned the space around her for the flying cats. Keeping in formation, the Sepheriis dropped down toward the ground again, their unified movement efficient and precise. They skimmed the treetops, the Great Rift Valley fanning out below them, green and lush, and uniquely different from the rest of Faltofar.

Suddenly, off their left flank, the scaled cats appeared again, rocketing toward them, claws extended, gaping mouths wide with triumphant howls. Unshaken, the Sepheriis moved as a unit, dodging to the right and upward. Abruptly Torr banked to the left, giving Thom a clear shot with his sling. A yowl from the closest cat testified to the boy's marksmanship, and Thom gave a jubilant hoot as the beast dropped through the air, pawing at its eye socket. His triumph was short-lived. The second feline spiraled from high in the sky, striking the Sepherii holding the duffel bag, its claws raking dark streaks across the human torso. The golden being's pained cry reverberated in Lilianna's head. Despite the injury Torr had sustained just before she'd met him, she wanted so much to believe the Sepheriis were immortal, impervious to pain and suffering. She leaned sideways and vomited.

Again Torr pivoted, his muscular body arching with the effort to change course so quickly in midair. The others followed, maneuvering around the flying cat, circling it and giving no room for escape. Only the long hours of practice kept the children astride.

Conscious of his precious cargo, Torr hovered at a distance, his fists held high. The others tightened their circle, their sharp hooves slashing and cutting through the creature's scales. The injured Sepherii struck the final deathly blow, sending the beast plummeting down, where it disappeared into the forest.

There was no sense of triumph in the six. Quietly, they circled over the green canopy, searching for any movement. The injured one detached himself from the others and glided just above Torr, gently handing the duffel down to Lilianna. She could have cared less about their gear, feeling guilt that perhaps the Sepherii had been injured because of the burden. Still, she nodded her thanks and squished the duffel tightly between her and Thom. Hearing a squeak from its interior, Lilianna pulled the cord loose and peered inside. The titmouse blinked up at her.

"Unbelievable. You rascal."

The Sepheriis again moved into formation with Torr in the lead.

Their mood was somber, and the message clear: the act of killing another life force was one of necessity and no more.

Taking advantage of the opening, the little mouse poked its head out, curiosity making it brave. Its whiskers were plastered back against its cheeks, and its ears low on its head, like a skullcap.

"You're a natural." She patted it lightly. Who was to say what creature immense, or tiny, could be the next hero?

She sheathed her dagger, shifting the duffle slightly so the tiny stowaway could lean further out without falling. The line of mountains looming in the distance grew higher as they flew closer. The little dagger rested snugly and reassuringly against her skin.

TWO INFINITY

The line of dwarves and humans parted, freeing a space for Liannan. Morauth stood calmly at the edge of the cliff, watching with a predatory gleam in her red-rimmed eyes. The smoky wraith, awakened by Sarafina at the Holy Oak in the deep forest, was now gone, replaced by a tall, very real sorceress. She smiled as Liannan came to a stop, unaware or, more likely, unmoved that the majority of her army lay dead or dying on the ridge above them. They had served their purpose.

"Sister." Her voice dripped with sarcastic venom. "This climate doesn't suit you. You're so very pasty white. So," her smile broadened, "inhuman."

Argath had begun to moan and shift. Morauth flicked a finger at him, and his mind and limbs slid back into oblivion. Nero cowered nearby, averting his face from Morauth and the others, a look of calculation crossing his dirty features. He mumbled softly to himself, but the sorceress took no notice of him.

"Well, shall we get down to the business at hand?" she asked, sneering at the line of humans and dwarves facing her. Along the ridge, anguished pleas for mercy from the mortally wounded filled the air. The warriors of the One, humans and dwarves, walked among those almost gone and dispensed with them quickly, ending their suffering. Morauth's minions that still lived were efficiently gathered into small, manageable groups.

"Sister." Liannan raised her hand toward Morauth in a gesture of peace, but her sister saw it otherwise. Suddenly, and with unimaginable speed, the sorceress's arm swung wide, her magical blade cutting through the air, pulling Argath and Nero up from the ground. The sharp edge of the blade stopped inches away from their exposed necks. Argath moaned softly, his eyelids fluttering, his body twitching with his unconscious struggle to survive.

"Which one shall it be?" Morauth asked sweetly, her eyes sliding from one captive to the other, then back to her sister.

Her hand hovered closely in front of Nero's face, close enough for his crazed mind to focus. A beatific smile spread across the dwarf's features as if he had just solved an impossible puzzle. His mouth opened wide, lips pulling back from gleaming white teeth just before they sank into Morauth's flesh. To the bone.

The garbled, triumphant laughter that bubbled bloodily from the corner of the dwarf's mouth was drowned out by Morauth's curdling scream. She let go of both of them, flinging Nero away from her. Deep, red blood trailed after him, splattering Argath, the snow around the human, and the ice-covered rock where the dwarf landed. Blood dripped from Nero's mouth, and a small piece of white flesh dangled from his whimpering lips. Lost in his madness again, the dwarf began to draw pictures with the blood in the snow.

On hands and knees now, Argath shook his head, clarity dawning on his blood-splattered face. Morauth held her injured hand out in front of her, anger and disbelief erupting in sparks. Then like a striking viper, her other hand snaked out around Argath's throat. His strength returning, he fought back, his own strong hands pulling at her supernatural grip.

The distraction was just enough. Dundar, standing at the front of the line of dwarves, lunged. The impact of his body against Morauth loosened her hold on Argath, and he dropped to one knee with a dull thud, gasping for breath, leaving the sorceress and the halfling, their limbs entwined, to stumble and slip toward the edge of the cliff. Intent on freeing herself, Morauth viciously sliced her dagger upward, cutting into Dundar. Silhouetted against the white-blue backdrop of sky, they tottered on the edge in a morbid embrace.

With an otherworldly howl, Nero lurched forward, throwing his weight against them both. Time slowed with each windmill of their arms and then sped up as, like some macabre dance of marionettes, the three toppled over the ledge and out of sight. Dark red and blue drops of blood dotted the trampled snow where they had stood.

Men and dwarves alike rushed forward, stopping several feet from the flaking, snowy edge to cautiously peer over. Sections of ice and rock crumbled and cascaded down some twenty feet, piling up where the three had landed on a ledge below. Morauth had already gathered her supernatural strength and stood, swaying with each gust of wind. The crackling cold air around her rippled. Dundar, obviously stunned, with blood seeping from a wound at his shoulder, crawled away from her toward the tree. The seedling of the supreme Holy Oak, which had embraced the cliff edge with its massive exposed roots for hundreds of years, offered a sanctuary the halfling so desperately needed. In the center of the ledge, Nero lay face-down in the snow, unmoving.

Morauth's unholy laughter trickled from her parted lips and filled the air. She looked up and wagged a long, dark fingernail at Liannan, who had come to the very edge of the ledge above, the waning light of the crystal the only thing giving any color to her emotionless face.

"Here then, sister," she yelled above the wind, "is my sacrifice to all that is unholy and dark." Morauth stepped around the limp, unconscious dwarf's body, following the dark drops of blood to where Dundar now lay against a root of the tree. Holding her dagger aloft, she shouted in triumph. "A much better sacrifice! A half breed!"

Her cackling laughter snapped and twisted in the ice particles around her. Dundar blinked up at her blearily, weakened by the dagger's poison that had begun to course through his body, and too dazed to defend himself.

Sarafina gulped in the cold air. Her dreaded Sense had shown her nothing of the outcome of this day. Nothing. In desperation, she reached for Liannan.

"Help us," she whispered.

The arc of Morauth's dagger began to slice down through the air, aiming for Dundar's chest. Then, from out of the cold white horizon, a hurtled stone the size of a cliff swillow's egg ricocheted against Morauth's raised hand, jolting the dagger from her grip. Six Sepheriis rose to the cliff edge, level to where the sorceress stood. She whirled around, her teeth bared, and red eyes filled with hatred. Torr returned her stare with determination…and pity.

"Lili, get to safety!" Thom yelled, jumping from Torr's back and landing squarely on the ledge. He had already loaded another stone in his sling, and the thud of the dwarf club against his hip assured him that it had not been dislodged.

Ignoring Thom's entreaty, Lilianna shoved the titmouse deep into the duffle bag and maneuvered one leg over Torr's back. She tensed, waiting for her opportunity to jump as the Sepheriis banked to come around again. She could feel a force surging from them into her, power that was both exhilarating and nauseating. Ignoring her jittery nerves, she scanned the ledge for solid footing then lept from the Sepherii's back to land between Thom and Morauth. Olitus stood looking down at his children, disbelief and dawning understanding mixed with fear playing across his face.

"The prophecy," he whispered, then shouted louder for those around him. "The prophecy! We will vanquish the dark sorceress together!" Olitus, Sarafina, and the others quickly fought for hand-holds to lower themselves down the cliff wall. A piece of ice broke off under Olitus's cramping fingers. "Or, die trying," he thought.

Cradling her injured hand close to her chest, Morauth sucked in air deeply, ignoring the shouts of the men and dwarves.

"Brats!" she exhaled through clenched teeth, her cloak whipping around her. She advanced on Lilianna, any sign of weakness from her fall gone. "Who are you to challenge me?"

She lunged for the girl, but only grasped at air. Lilianna, moving with uncanny speed, dodged and twisted around her to where Dundar lay curled in the snow. Morauth spun in a circle, her voice rising in a screaming chant, her hands wide, searching. In answer to her summons, the dagger flew up out of the snow and into her grasp.

Dagger in hand, she pivoted and with a malicious smile made a slicing motion in Thom's direction, hurtling another curse into the wind. The sling in Thom's hand began to wither, melting around his grasp.

"No!" Falling to his knees, he struggled to pull his hands apart, but the sticky mass held firm. Morauth's laughter filled the air.

With an angry cry from the ledge above, Liannan pointed her staff at her grandson, sending a bolt of white-hot light through the air. For a brief moment, the slingshot turned a deep brown, then broke into pieces and drifted to the ground, freeing Thom's hands. Defiantly, Thom stood again to face Morauth, but she had turned her attention back to Lilianna and Dundar.

Sarafina, halfway down the ledge, desperately searched for another handhold. She glanced over her shoulder toward her children and Liannan's quiet voice suddenly resonated in her head and throughout her body.

"The acorn, Sarafina. Now. Lilianna needs the acorn."

Grabbing the thong around her neck with one free hand, Sarafina pulled hard on the cord. It snapped free.

"Thom, here!"

The small leather pouch soared through the air, past the heads of the men and dwarves clinging to the rocks. When it landed just beyond Thom's feet, the acorn rolled free of the pouch and dropped over the edge.

"Oh, please." Sarafina's voice filled with despair. "For the love of the One."

Sarafina shook her head in disbelief, then again in wonder, when seconds later, the acorn shot upward into the air, landing at Thom's feet. Tiny paws, followed by a whiskered nose poked up from the edge, and the titmouse quickly pulled itself up and stood, hands on its hips, surveying the scene. The little hero, obviously pleased with its handiwork, scurried away. Thom swiftly scooped the acorn up from the snow and pulled the club from his belt.

"Return it to the tree, Thom."

Liannan's commanding voice cascaded down the ridge, where Lilianna hovered over Dundar's unconscious body. "Courage Lilianna. I am with you. We are one." The last echoed as a whisper in Lilianna's ear. *One. One. One.* It echoed in Lilianna's head.

Taking a deep breath to center himself, Thom tossed the acorn into the air and swung. "Lili, catch!" he yelled.

Lilianna tilted her chin up, a small, determined smile crossing her features. Her hand shot out, and the acorn smacked into her palm.

"What is this, worthless child's play? A game of catch?" Morauth growled.

She closed the distance between the girl and the halfling. The sorceress raised her dagger, her eyes sparkling in anticipation.

With one arm wrapped protectively around Dundar's shoulder, Lilianna reached behind her and pressed the acorn into the bark of the tree. Over the sorceress's shoulder, the six Sepheriis quietly hovered, their wings barely moving. Torr dipped his head in acknowledgment, his eyes filled with sadness and pride.

The ancient magic worked instantly, bringing the slumbering giant to life with a loud, eerie groan. Its strong oak branches creaked, swinging and twisting branches taking the sorceress by surprise as they wrapped themselves around her outstretched arm. Morauth pulled against the dense wood, but her contortions did nothing to diminish the strong bind of the tree. Lilianna moved slowly back-ward out of her reach, dragging Dundar's limp body with her.

Ten feet above the ledge, Olitus let go of his handholds. He hit the ground and rolled to his feet. The others quickly followed their bodies thudding into the snow around him. Grabbing the jeweled hilt of his dagger, he aimed and threw.

"By the power of Rendar!" he bellowed, running toward his children.

The dagger spiraled through the air, its hilt a pinwheel of jeweled color. His aim was true, and the sharp point skewered Morauth's wrist, pinning her to the trunk where Lilianna and Dundar had been. The mighty oak shuddered, and its branches, now coiled tightly around Morauth's arm, hardened and slowed to their natural, immobile state. Morauth's dagger fell from her hand, landing in the snow at her feet.

The sorceress, her eyes flashing, swung her other arm wide. The howls turned to a sing-song chant of magic, and one-by-one the army around her froze, every human and dwarf on the ledge marbleized into statues, some crouching low, others frozen in their sprint toward her, precariously balanced on one foot, arms extended midair holding worthless weapons. Only their desperate eyes moved, their groans of panic frozen behind immobile lips. Nothing shifted on the ledges except the glittering, cold snow . . . and Nero. The grimy little dwarf slowly stood up, gaping at the chaos around him.

"You have not defeated me," Morauth shouted as she glowered at them and struggled to free herself. The jeweled hilt of Rendar's dagger sparkled against the white of her skin. She did not try to touch it but glared defiantly up at the Sepherii. Licking her bright red lips, she addressed Lilianna, lowering her voice to a silky, melodic chant.

"Pull out the blade, child."

Lilianna, her arms frozen in a hug around Dundar, heard Morauth but did not respond. Her limbs had begun to tingle; she tentatively wiggled her fingers, then her arms. The sorceress's enchantment was selective.

"The power could be yours for the taking!"

Gently, Lilianna lowered Dundar to the snow as Torr shifted above them, his translucent wings descending and rising once. The air around them sparkled into absolute stillness, crystal flakes of cold shimmering down like broken glass.

Lilianna's head tilted sideways, trancelike, studying the dagger and the beautiful black blade imbedded deep in her aunt's bloody wrist. Slowly she moved her hand to her talisman, looking away from Morauth to Liannan.

"Forgive me, grandmother," she whispered sadly, standing up and moving stiffly toward the tree.

Torr's wings spread wider, his chin dipping down, eyes distant. A triumphant smile crossed Morauth's face as Lilianna stretched up to grasp the hilt. Before she could reach it, she was violently shoved aside by Nero, hitting the ground hard enough that her head spun.

"NO!" he howled.

Reaching past the branch that held Morauth, he grabbed the hilt of the dagger and pulled. Blurrily, Lilianna scrambled halfway up, kneeling on one knee, blinking the snow out of her eyes. The blade came free, its jagged edge glinting in the dull gray light as the dwarf swung and plunged it into the sorceress's side. Stunned, Morauth gaped at the blood seeping from the new wound.

"Worthless, disgusting dwarf," she snarled through clenched teeth. "Take your fate into your own hand, then."

Her free hand moved through the air, making a stabbing motion. Nero, helpless and horrified, felt his arm shift the blade around before thrusting the knife into his own chest. Stunned, he fell backward into Lilianna, toppling them both to the ground. Lilianna forced her way out from beneath his bulky weight, her astonished face reflecting the terrible reality of the injured dwarf beside her in the snow.

"Stop!" she shouted up at Morauth, who shrugged and defiantly leaned against the tree, the spell withering with her disregard.

Nero frantically pulled the blade free, shock giving his features the same bluish tint as the blood that covered his tunic. Desperate to save him, Lilianna pressed her palms on the wound, trying to staunch the flow of blood. A gurgling death rattle escaped the young dwarf's lips. Her chest tightened in sorrow, and tears rolled down her face. Angry cries echoed along the ledge, none louder than Berold's, who struggled fiercely against his magic confines, unable to help his son.

"Child?" Morauth cooed softly. "Shall we rule this world together?"

Angrily Lilianna wiped the tears away, leaving a blue streak across her cheekbones.

"Child?" It was a question and a command.

Lilliana looked up at the sorceress. Her skin turned pale, almost matching that of the tall, evil woman who beckoned to her. The girl shut her eyes and bowed her head. The snow swirled around her in tempting patterns that painted a compelling future. The moment stretched for an eternity until Lilianna slowly opened her eyes and, through frozen lashes, looked up at Torr. Straightening her shoulders, she stretched her arms out in front of her and placed her bloodied hands together in the pattern imprinted on her talisman—fingers grouped in twos, thumbs touching.

"Yes, that's it!" Morauth's voice rang with success.

It was immediate; a surge of energy vibrated from Lilianna's center and moved almost lazily to the tips of her glowing fingers. The snow around her and the dwarf began to undulate in a spiraling mass, surrounding them in a curtain of white before dropping back around them. Soft moans escaped from the frozen mouths of those closest, their distress evident in their unblinking eyes.

Reaching across Nero she dug her hands deep into the snow. Ice and rock crackled beneath the surface, and the tree tilted, a root groaning in protest. The ledge shook like a colossal animal readying itself for a tremendous leap.

Bent over the dwarf's body and buried to her elbows, Lilianna was oblivious, engulfed in the power that surged through her. Slowly she sat upright, her arms clean now, the snow where her hands had been outlined in a soft blue of dwarf blood. In her grasp, she held a dark sliver of obsidian long buried at the base of the Holy Oak. Morauth's smile grew wider.

"Well, well." Morauth sneered at Liannan.

Sitting back on her heels, the girl gently pulled the dagger from the dying dwarf's hand. Glancing at Morauth, who nodded encouragement to her, she placed the piece of obsidian against the dagger's blade, and its light grew stronger. In seconds, the pieces had morphed together. Laying the sharp edge along the soft part of her palm, she calmly cut into her skin. A thin line of blood trickled from her wound, and a single drop landed on Nero's chest. She studied it for a moment, then gently touched the red dot and blended it with the dwarf's blue blood.

"That's it. That's it, child."

Running her finger along the side of the obsidian blade, Lilianna performed the magic that would complete the bind of glass to glass to metal, reuniting the pieces. Morauth's evil smile spread wider with confidence. Speaking softly, Lilianna studied the glowing blade.

"No."

Morauth lips parted, her confident smile wavering. Lilianna rose, pointing the dark obsidian at the sorceress, who backed into the tree, moving as far away from the sharp tip as she was able.

"No." The single word from the girl was no longer a whisper. Angry lines dribbled down the sorceress's face, comprehension beginning to melt her icy, smiling veneer. When Lilianna continued, her voice carried sharp and clear to everyone on the ledges.

"I invoke the oath of the six. I invoke the power of the Holy Oak and all that is sacred to the honor of the One."

Morauth's dark red eyes widened in growing horror as Lilianna moved toward her. The girl adjusted her grip on the dagger, her focus so complete she barely acknowledged Liannan, who had materialized at her side. Now within reach of Morauth, Lilianna repeated the words Torr had taught her high on the cliffs.

"The time has come to reunite you with your Father!"

Torr rose higher in the sky, separating himself from the other Sepheriis, the burden he had carried now revealed. His daughters stood below him, and he had given the child, his heir, the tools to destroy them both.

Lilianna lunged. The black blade punctured through the cloth, skin, and bones of the sorceress. Morauth swayed in disbelief. A dark mass began to congeal where the obsidian had penetrated. It grew, morphing larger and larger. A tongue of black smoke billowed outward from Morauth, winding its way, almost caressingly, toward Liannan. The wraith looked up from her chest and exhaled. Her voice, already barely audible, was laced with poison as it intertwined with the last echoes of Lilianna's.

"I will not go alone this time, sister! There will be no darkness without the light."

Liannan calmly studied the billowing cloud beginning to envelop her, repeating Morauth's pronouncement.

"There will be no darkness without the light."

Turning to her granddaughter, she extended her staff.

"Grandmother, I...," Lilianna began.

"No, child. Take it."

Lilianna wrapped both hands around the shaft of the staff and stepped back, stemming her tears. Liannan, whose form had begun to shimmer and fade into white mist, nodded her head toward Lilianna.

"Again, child, the oath of the six. Finish what has begun."

Liannan's soft voice reverberated inside Lilianna's head. She could feel Torr soaring above her with the other Sepheriis. He echoed Liannan's demand.

"Child, fulfill your destiny. My daughters shall come home. This you can do."

Lilianna tilted her face skyward and extended her arms, the staff now high above her head. Taking a deep breath, she spoke the incantation that would send both Liannan and Morauth back to the land, their homeland, that they had never truly known.

"By all that is holy to the One, I invoke the oath of the six! I am the voice of the One!"

Streams of light from the crystal shot through the white smoke and mingled with the vaporous blackness. The mass began to rise skyward to where the Sepheriis flew in a circular pattern above the tallest limbs of the tree. Black and white intertwined, becoming a column the color of slate. A blast of blinding snow from the wings of six Sepheriis erased the last of the sisters. A final gust of wind and the Sepheriis too were gone. All except Torr. Lilianna alone heard his soft voice.

"Take heart, child. You have accomplished what you were meant to do." He descended to Lilianna's eye level, one hand touching her gently on her blue-streaked cheek. In his other hand, he held Liannan's talisman, extending it to the girl. "You are the hope and the light of Faltofar. Take it." And then, he was gone. Quietly, Lilianna placed the talisman around her neck.

When the army of the One, freed from Morauth's magic, realized they could move, stunned silence gave way to shouts that began to ring out all along the ledges. Slowly Argath stood, supported by Thaddeus, who had scrambled to his side.

Scattered across the snowy ground, puffs of smoke rose from the bodies of the creatures who had pledged alliance to Morauth, their physical forms curling and twisting into nothingness, their anguished cries cut short as they disappeared. Astonished, the Highlanders on the ridge watched their enemy vanish. Then, realizing their victory, they began to cheer, waving their weapons skyward, unaware that they had lost their leader.

Olitus and those close by surged to Lilianna, Dundar, and Nero's limp body. Berold, elbowing his way through the humans, was the first to reach his son. He knelt and gently lifted the smaller dwarf into his arms, brushing hair from the younger dwarf's eyes. Nero moaned softly.

"Boy," he whispered, bending close, a tear dripping off his nose. "Ah, my boy, you were brave to the last." The old warrior stifled a sob, recognizing the all-too-familiar signs of a life ebbing away.

Nero's chest rose and fell. A gurgling line of blood escaped one corner of his mouth. With the last of his strength, he raised his one hand, grasping Berold's sleeve.

"Father."

Engulfed in the strong circle of her father's arms, Lilianna shifted, searching for her brother across the ledges. He stood with Sarafina in the space where Liannan had faded to nothing, understanding dawning on their faces. Lilianna swallowed the bitter taste in her mouth and shifted her gaze from her family to the bloodied battlefield. Blue and red blood intermixed in a disturbing palette of death. Gently she moved her father's arms away and walked over to the old dwarf.

"Found. And lost." Berold carefully laid his son back in the snow. He rose slowly, his shoulders sagging.

"Berold? It is Berold, is it not?"

Angrily Berold raised his head, swiping a hand across his face and under his nose. A fog of grief engulfed him enough that it took several beats of his sad heart to realize who had addressed him. Slowly, and with the history of his people on his shoulders, Berold knelt on one knee before Lilianna, extending his dagger toward her in a salute.

"Liannan lives on. Give good guidance to your kind, human, and the dwarves will remain allies."

He placed his hands on his thighs and stood slowly, nodding to Lilianna. His duty done, he tucked his dagger into its sheath and stepped away, already lost in memories of his son. Lilianna's hand on his arm stopped him.

"A moment. A gift for the return of my talisman." Lilianna pulled from her tunic the two feathers Cleo had given her. Making sure she had the old dwarf's attention, she bent and gently crossed them on Nero's chest, then stepped back. A soft glow began to emanate from the spot where the feathers lay, spreading slowly across his torso. Berold stifled a sob as the boy opened his eyes and slowly sat up. Radiant streams of light emanated from his whole body, a serene smile on his face, and both arms now wholly intact. Gently Lilianna grasped the old dwarf's hand, her long human fingers intertwining with his calloused grip. Then, in a swirl of snow, Nero was gone.

———

Berold's bones and his heart ached, but the child had given him closure. Ignoring his discomfort, he stomped his way across the trampled snow to the healer woman who was working on Dundar, her small pouch of herbs loosened and spread out before her.

"This one shall live," he thought. There was comfort in that.

Feeling Berold's eyes on her, Sarafina stopped her ministrations and acknowledged him with a nod, whispering the consoling sentiments that form when one has nothing else to give. "I am so very sorry. Your son died a hero."

Berold nodded and turned away, bumping into Thom, who had moved across the ledge with his mother. The old dwarf quickly wiped the back of his hand across his eyes and glared at the young human.

"I think this, um, belongs to you." Sheepishly Thom reached into his belt and pulled the dwarf's old club loose, extending it cautiously. Berold frowned at it and snorted.

"Keep it, boy," he coughed, his voice gravelly from unshed tears. "I'se made meself a new one." His lips puckered in irritation, briefly revisiting the work involved in creating the club. "A better one." Then his shoulders sagged again, and the anger that had momentarily fueled him drifted back into sorrow. "It would have gone to me," he choked, swallowing his grief, "me own son, but you've earned it."

The old warrior began to move off, then changed his mind and slowly shifted his weight on his heels. He sighed and slapped Thom on the back. "You dun a fine job, lad."

HEALING

Tilga set the steaming mugs on the table, careful not to get too close to her guests. The house seemed cramped with the tall humans in it. Their spindly legs extended halfway across the room, as they politely tried to sit in the small, dwarf chairs. Berold didn't seem to notice. Moments before, his laughter, which she hadn't heard in a long time, had filled the room. Life, and those still living it, had moved on, honoring the brave individuals who had fallen in battle. Brave, like her son. It lightened her heart just a bit to think on it.

"Well, we's done enough for the season, I think."

Slamming his now empty mug onto the side table, Berold creaked to standing, snapped his suspenders into place, and addressed Olitus and Argath, all serious again. "I suppose you be wantin' to see the boy now? He's quite on the mend."

Argath and Olitus unwound themselves awkwardly from the small furniture, ducking to avoid bumping their heads on the stone ceiling. Nervously, Tilga stood as far away from them as was polite, safely tucked in her kitchen, rubbing her hands this way and that into her tea towel. Berold saw her out of the corner of his eye and smiled at her.

"Thank you, missus. I'll be back in a bit."

Argath and Olitus nodded their thanks to Berold's wife and hunched their way out the door. As it closed behind them, Tilga let out a sigh of relief.

"Big lunkers," she mumbled, picking up the empty mugs. "Don't see as how I'll ever get used to them."

The men slowly walked through the village, pacing their stride to match the old dwarf's stumpy legs. Stoic nods greeted them as they passed each doorway.

"Give um no mind. They's never set eyes on such as you before. The biggest thing they've ever seen until now is," Berold glanced awkwardly at the men, "Dundar."

Berold's reputation had changed dramatically since his return. The Dwarves of the Glenn had had time to absorb the knowledge that their leader wasn't the crazy old dwarf they'd thought. The stories had flowed back to the village. Stories of courage and a strong leader. And stories of loss. He walked with his head a bit higher these days. And eyes a bit sadder.

"Here."

Without preamble, the dwarf stopped in front of a cottage at the edge of the village. He avoided touching the gate but stood there attentively, facing the front door. It opened slowly, and Dundalee stepped gracefully onto the porch. Berold, obviously uncomfortable, coughed and waved his hand in front of the humans as an introduction.

"Please," Dundalee said. "Come in."

Argath reached for the gate, but it swung open, on well-oiled hinges, of its own accord. He stepped into the yard, followed closely by Olitus, and stopped at the porch steps. With an almost shy nod, Dundalee acknowledged Olitus, then smiled at Argath and spoke softly.

"It has been a very long time, m'lord. You are welcome here."

She entered the house, motioning for the humans and Berold to follow.

Even though the afternoon was mild, Dundar sat buried under a blanket near the fire. He smiled as they entered, shifting in his seat and nodding his hello to them. Dundalee stood back and quietly waited. Berold enthusiastically moved forward.

"I told you I would bring ya company while ya healed," he said heartily, addressing the younger dwarf. "You're comin' along nicely, so I thought you was ready for some cheer."

Berold beamed at the men he had escorted to the house, flourishing his arm at Dundar and bumping the table next to the boy as he did so. Recovering, he puffed up his chest.

"Gentlemen, I give you Dundar. A hero on the mend."

The younger dwarf tried to rise to greet his guests, but Olitus quickly motioned him to sit again, stepping forward to clasp Dundar's hand in his own.

"Well met again, Dundar," he said.

Argath stood back, his face semi-hidden in the shadow of the room, watching the younger dwarf thoughtfully. Berold, still smiling, nodded at Olitus, both silently acknowledging those who had fallen in their brave support of the One. He could live with the hero's death of his biological son. But now was the time to focus on his tribe and his responsibility to lead the younger generation.

"That's my boy." Berold chin bobbed up and down, proudly.

Stepping forward, Argath placed a gentle hand on the older dwarf's shoulder and knelt next to Dundar, picking up the book that had fallen from the side table when Berold had bumped it. Slowly he opened the book to the first page and traced the letter A with his finger. Argath spoke for the first time, his eyes, their corners crinkled from a deep smile, shifting from the tattered pages to the lovely face of Dundalee and then to the boy resting in the hearth chair.

"No," he said softly, looking at Dundar. "He's my boy."

NEW BEGINNINGS

F altofar had settled down to a semblance of normalcy once again. Crops had begun to flourish in the last days of summer, and the poisoned tides off the coastline had dissipated. The rivers swarmed with an abundance of fish, and any signs of the plague had vanished. The people of Faltofar had been told of a change in their leadership. Argath, son of Liannan, now held high council. Word was spread that Liannan had gone the way of the sacred priestesses to a retreat where she could focus on the One. Only the few who had witnessed the succession of power between grandmother and grand-daughter knew of Lilianna's future role in the leadership of Faltofar. Until she was ready to formally assume the responsibilities, Lili would continue her studies and train to enhance her skills as a warrior.

The children had returned to their home, insulated as children will be from any questions from the community by the half-truths the adults closest to them told. The chores they had left behind greeted them as if nothing had changed. Their studies had begun the week before, and, as with every new learning season, the taxing schedule of studies rendered them exhausted by the end of the day.

Finishing their evening meal, they sleepily blinked at the embers in the dying fire. Sarafina moved from the kitchen to a chair by the hearth, her mending in hand, making sounds only mothers make at the bedtime hour. Her children, both staring into the flames, ignored her.

"Mother, Master Blisk said something today I don't understand."

Thom poked a stick into the fire. When he didn't continue, Sarafina, one eyebrow raised, set her mending down.

"Well?"

Thom glanced over at Lilianna, who was dangling a thread for Mosely to bat. Cat and girl had been inseparable since the children come back from the high country.

"Well, he talked about a new beginning for humans and dwarves. He said something about us 'meeting halfway, starting with halflings.'" Thom bit his lower lip and tried to express what was bothering him. "He winked at me when he said it. Like I knew something."

Sarafina thoughtfully studied her son before returning to mending the shirt in her hand. The needle rose and fell several times before she set it down. She hesitated a moment before speaking.

"Ah, Master Blisk. He speaks out of turn sometimes, I think. Surprising in a Rememberer."

Lilianna stopped scratching Mosely under his chin.

"I've never heard that word before, Mother. A Rememberer?" she questioned, frowning slightly.

Laughing, Sarafina stood, motioning for the children to head for bed.

"It is a dwarf word. Now, off you go. Your Uncle Argath arrives tomorrow with your father. Chores will need to be done early."

Lilianna followed Thom up the stairs. With a soft goodnight to her brother, she parted the curtain that separated her half of the upper floor from Thom's. As the material dropped back into place, she moved quickly across the small space she called her own to a shelf on the far wall. Liannan's talisman rested there, nestled in the center of the delicate gold chain that had borne its weight for years. Unconsciously Lili played with her own talisman, studying the intricate craftsmanship of the one on the shelf, so much like her own, yet somehow different. Impulsively, she pulled the leather thong over her head and placed her talisman on the shelf next to her departed grandmother's, studying them a moment longer. A plain wooden box sat atop her favorite stack of books at the center of the shelf. Rubbing her neck where the leather chafed her skin, she carried the box to the window, setting it on the sill in a softly distorted patch of moonlight that filtered through the rough pane. Opening the lid, she pulled the beautiful black dagger from its resting place, turning it this way and that. Gently she ran her finger along the dark glass, searching for, and finding, the one imperfection in the blade.

"It is dangerously beautiful." With the dagger in one hand and its box in the other, she slowly walked back to the shelf, feeling the weight of the dagger's handle rest lightly in her palm. She set the empty box back on the shelf and took a deep breath.

"Okay." A single word. A single exhale.

Raising the dagger to the level of the shelf, she thoughtfully traced a lazy figure eight, the sign of infinity, over the two coins. They began to move, sliding closer together, the glow from their metal faces illuminating the determined set of the young woman's face. Within moments, the two coins had merged into one. Reverently, Lilianna placed the dagger back inside its box and closed the lid. When she draped the golden chain around her neck, the sliver of obsidian embedded in the metal glinted softly in the dim light.

———

Blisk hummed to himself as he dipped the quill into the ink and signed his name to the entry. He blew on his signature and squinted out the window.

"Not much time left in this growing season," he mumbled sadly. "But, at least I can plant a fall crop."

Blowing one last time on the drying ink, he closed the book, groaning softly as he stood up from the table. "These old bones are starting to get achy."

Before he placed the thick volume on the shelf next to his figurines, his fingers traced the title, *The History of Faltofar,* almost reverently.

Picking up his hat, he settled it firmly on his head and moved to the doorway, cautiously scanning the path to the garden and the fields surrounding his land. With a relieved smile, he stepped onto the porch and grabbed the hoe leaning against the wall of the cabin. Almost skipping down the porch stairs, he hoisted the tool up to his shoulder and headed toward his garden, humming to himself and unconsciously scratching a mosquito bite on his bare bum.

CHARACTERS

Argath (AR-gahth): Eldest son of Liannan and twin brother to Arialla.

Arialla (AR-ee-AH-la): Eldest daughter of Liannan and twin sister to Argath.

Berold (BAIR-ohld): Leader of the Dwarves of the Glenn and married to Tilga.

Dideon (Di-DEE-un): Second in-command to Olitus

Dundalee (Dun-DAH-lee): Dwarf sorceress and mother to Dundar.

Dundar (DUN-dar): Half-breed son to Dundalee.

Liannan (LEE-ah-non): High chieftess to the Highlanders and foremost commander in Faltofar, mother to Argath, Arialla, Lionel, Theresea and Sarafina.

Lilianna (Lil-ee-AH-nah): Daughter of Olitus and Sarafina, sister to Thom.

Lionel (LEE-o-nel): Second son of Liannan.

Master Blisk (MAS-ter Blihsk): Educator and foremost Remember of Faltofar.

Morauth (Mor-AHTH): Sorceress banished in the final battle ending the Dark Days.

Olitus (O-LI-tuhs): Descendant of Rendar, Husband to Sarafina and father of Thom and Lilianna.

Rendar (REN-dar): Ancient hero who defeated Morauth in the final battle, ending the Dark Days.

Sarafina (Sair-AH-fee-NAH): Healer and one of the Dark children. Youngest daughter of Liannan, married to Olitus, and mother of Thom and Lilianna.

Sepherii (Su-FAIR-ee): Thought to be mythical creatures. Half-man, half-horse.

Thaddeus (THAD-ee-us): Head sentry to Liannan.

Theresea (THAIR-ee-see-ah): Second daughter to Liannan.

Thom (Tahm): Son of Olitus and Sarafina, brother to Lilianna.

Tilga (TIL-gah): Female dwarf, married to Berold.

Torr (Torr): Sepherii and the Watcher.

ACKNOWLEDGMENTS

The author could not have accomplished this creative work without the spectacular expertise of her editor, Linden Gross and the innovative eye of designer, Lieve Maas, Bright Light Graphics. Further gratitude to Jean and Brynna Gritter, Marci Sheehy, Bella Fassett, Dara Robertson, Debbie and Anndi Fruitman and Katrina Hays for their valuable insights.

I cannot dream up a more receptive environment to write than Dudley's Bookshop Cafe, where I spent hours, fingers hovering over the keyboard, pondering what my characters would do next.

And finally, Barney, I thank you for your endless optimism, sprinkled with constructive criticism, that took this story, first woven in firelight, to its resting place here.